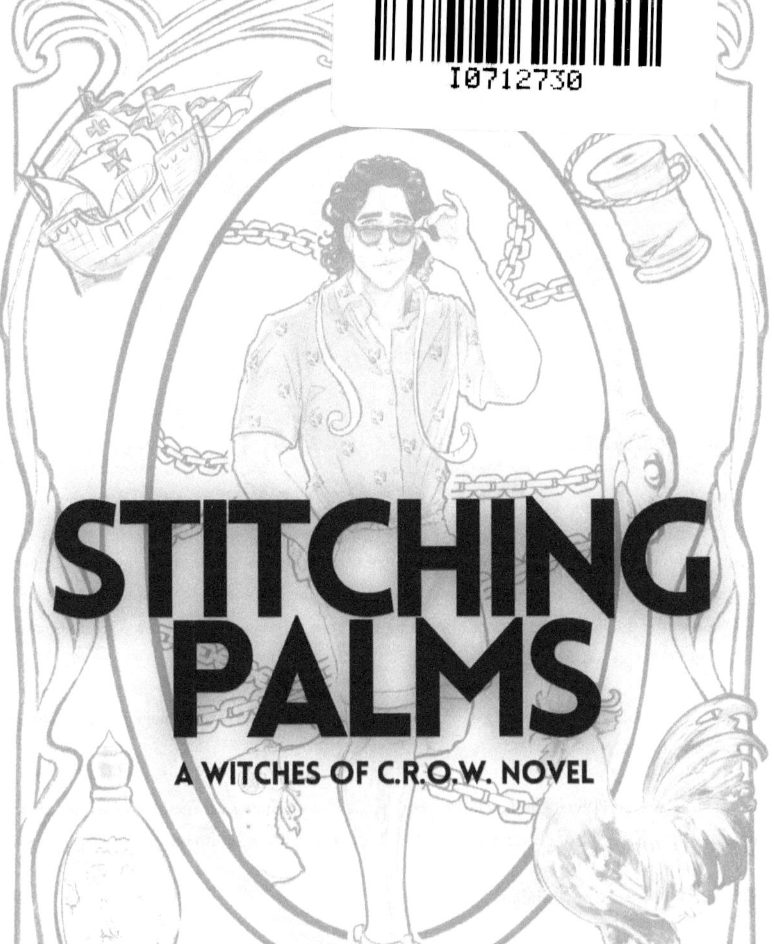

STITCHING PALMS

A WITCHES OF C.R.O.W. NOVEL

B.L. BROWN

GOOD INTENT PRESS

Book Cover by FantasySpriteStudios

Illustrations by FantasySpriteStudios

1st edition 2024

ISBN 979-8-9879716-7-3 (pbk)

ISBN 979-8-9879716-6-6 (ebook)

It's not a cult.

To Kind of a Whore and Chinball Wizard – for helping me find my true trail.
On on!

Mom – It means the *world* that you read my books, but please don't ask me questions about chapters 6, 13, 14, or 18.

Stitching Palms is book two in *The Witches of C.R.O.W.*, a series of stand-alone adventures within the broader Witchy World of C.R.O.W. featuring characters from *Witch of the Demesne.*

It is not necessary to read *Shady Depths* before enjoying Diego's story.

While this novel refers to events in *Ritual Income*, it can be read as a stand-alone (but I hope you're curious enough by the end to want to know more about Milla and St. Augustine).

Content and Trigger Warnings

Homophobia, grieving, self-harm (a reference to), on-page sexual acts (WILD-LY consensual), profanity, persecution, religious and sexual discrimination, religious trauma, the Spanish Inquisition, death, and drowning.

"A toothache, or a violent passion, is not necessarily diminished by our knowledge of its causes, its character, its importance or insignificance."

T.S. Eliot, Ink Witch

Ways
Fine and Faire

Aragon

sound
Audiomantic

Augurist *crystal witch*

fortune tellers
Chiromantic

Chronomantic *timey-wimey*

Hippocromantic *doctors/nurses*

Meteomantic *(Donny)*
weather witch

Obfuscari* *mind witches*

Obnubilari*

Technomantic

Vinefica* *poisons + potions (Rai)*

Corpomantic⁺

Český-Krumlov

good herb
Green Witch

Kitchen Witch

Light Witch *soul, truth*

animal handling (shepherds) Pastýř

Vestic *diviners*

Spalování *flame witch (Toby)*

Stitch Witch

Svítilna*
wee sparks

Ways
Forbidden and Foule

To be reported immediately to C.R.O.W.

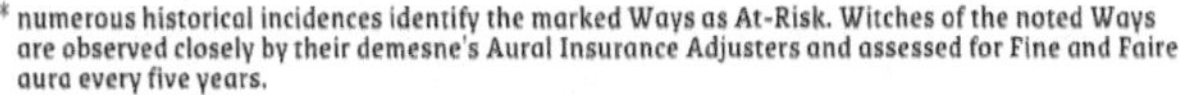

~~Corpomantic~~
Dark Witch *Master of shades*
Death Witch

* numerous historical incidences identify the marked Ways as At-Risk. Witches of the noted Ways are observed closely by their demesne's Aural Insurance Adjusters and assessed for Fine and Faire aura every five years.

LOS MÁRTIRES, 1513

"No puedo sacarlo," a voice mumbled in the dark. "Necesito ayuda, ¿entiendes?"

"No comprendo," Diego whimpered, too weak to raise his head. *I do not understand.* The ropes creaked under his weight, the hammock swaying with every roll of the ship. If he had the energy or strength to move, he would climb out of the hammock and claw out of the hold. He had come too far and survived too much to die in the dark covered in sweat, piss, and shit, and now there was someone in the hold who did not have the decency to let him die in peace.

"Necesito tiempo," the man murmured, more to himself than Diego. "Solo necesito tiempo."

The ship hit another swell, and the hammock tossed his fevered body side to side. His cheek pressed against the roughspun canvas, and he groaned, too tired and parched to scream at the pain. Goddess, the pain. It was more than anything he had known. A constant throb of fire in his jaw and sparks of white-hot agony. Sour spit rose on his tongue, his stomach churning on nothing as the hammock rolled with the ship only to come to an abrupt halt.

"Un mártir," the rambling voice said. *A martyr.* A blurry face rose into view; dark eyes scanned Diego's face. He pressed the back of a hand to his forehead. "Lo ha convertido un mártir."

He has made a martyr. Made it a martyr?

"¿Qué?" He made no sense. Why would anyone be made a martyr, and why would this madman need time?

"Bebe esto." *Drink this.* Before Diego could turn away, the man pressed a vial to his lips, tipping a thick, bitter beverage into his mouth. He coughed, and the man pressed a smooth hand over Diego's mouth. "Traga," he ordered. *Swallow.* "Es para el dolor. Necesito tu ayuda."

I need your help.

The pressure of his hand lit a fire along Diego's jaw. He bucked and jerked his shoulders, too weak to fight him off, too weak to rise from his hammock. The bitter potion trickled down his throat, and the man pulled his hand away, taking with it the harsh edge of Diego's pain. A fuzzy feeling bled out from his lips and into his head, sending him floating feet above the hammock.

"¿Por qué me ayudas?" Diego mumbled. *Why are you helping me?* His lips felt too large, and his tongue was a fat slab of immovable muscle, but the man understood. He leaned closer, features coming into soft focus. A close-trimmed beard, disheveled hair, clean but sunburnt skin, and those hands. Too smooth to be a sailor, absent the calluses of the enlisted and indentured gentlemen volunteers. Only one man in the fleet could have those hands and the opium to spare. Only one other man would care about a dying wretch like Diego.

Francisco Velazquez de Quesada: nobleman, doctor, witch.

"De Quesada?"

"No puedo sacarlo," de Quesada repeated his earlier ramblings. Words and sentences Diego only half understood. *I cannot pick it out.* "En mártir, necesito tu ayuda." *He has martyred it. I need your help.* He pressed the vial to Diego's lips again. "Traga."

The bitter sludge went down easier this time, and the warm, fuzzy feeling bled into Diego's fingers and toes, numbing the ache in his jaw. The ship pitched and rolled, his hammock caught in the swells, and Diego drifted in a haze with a hippocromantic's healing voice in his head.

"No puedo sacarlo. No puedo...no puedo..."

# ONE

DIEGO WAS NOT AN angry man. He had learned in his first life that there was too much to enjoy in this beautiful world to waste his days being angry.

But this Horned God-damned forsaken stretch of Florida State Road A1A was testing his resolve to enjoy every day of his second life.

All he had wanted was to text his roommate. All he had *wanted* was to pedal his borrowed bicycle to an area with reliable service and connect with the world outside of Key West. Instead, he was lying in the middle of the road, half-blind and tangled in the handlebars of his bicycle.

Nearby, the source of his current predicament clucked and pecked the road. Yes, he had been distracted by his phone, and *yes*, he should have been watching where he was going, but did Key West *need* to be populated by chickens with death wishes? No. And did they *have* to dart in front of bicycles, causing the distracted rider to slam on his brakes rather than prematurely flatten somebody's dinner?

Absolutely not.

"Maldito pollo."

The chicken ruffled its feathers and jabbed his ankle with its beak. He kicked out, groping the asphalt for his glasses and hissing as gravel dug into his torn palms. Bringing one hand in front of his face, he blew long strands of dark hair from his eyes and squinted to assess the damage. A car horn blared, the chicken clucked, and Diego lay where he was, tangled in a borrowed bicycle and seriously reconsidering the life choices that had led to this moment.

Not that he had had much in the way of choices. One minute, he had been navigating the torments of the Inferno as best he was able, and the next, he was naked in a graveyard, parched beyond belief and trying to understand the sobbing, bleeding little witch on the ground.

Not his best look, but then again, neither was this.

"Horned God dammit." He struggled with the strap of his beltbag, attempting to disentangle it from the handlebars. Horns blared, and cars swerved to avoid the witch on the ground. Spit slapped against asphalt, and he had just begun processing the fact that someone had *spat* at him when he heard the sharp clang of metal slamming against metal.

"The hell is your problem?"

Diego twisted, freeing himself from the handlebars in time to catch the blurry figure of a slender man swinging a baseball bat at a passing car. The bat connected with the rear fender, and the driver swerved down the road, tires squealing.

The man rushed toward Diego and crouched, backlit by the sun. He swept something from the ground and tucked it into a pocket. "Hey, are you alright?"

"Sí." He pressed a hand against the ground to rise and immediately jerked it away, hissing in pain. "Or maybe, no."

"Let me see that." The bat clattered to the road, and he gripped Diego's wrist, turning his palm face up. "Oh, wow, yikes." The man slipped behind Diego, hooking arms under his and helping him to his feet. "You good to walk?" Diego nodded, and the man gathered his bat and Diego's phone from the ground. "I'll get your bike; my shop is just there." He pointed a lean, tanned arm across the road, but Diego, nearsighted Stitch Witch that he was, focused on the cuffed sleeve of his shirt and the thin leather bracelets wound around a suntanned wrist. Beads in soft greens and blues were threaded through the leather, anchored by a singular white bead.

With a gentle press against the base of Diego's spine, he prompted him onward. "I have a first aid kit in the back."

Dazed by the tumble and the touch, Diego limped to the sidewalk while his savior wheeled his bike out of the road. He propped it against the wall of a store, and only then did Diego blink from his stupor, close enough now to read the words on the window.

Southernmost Pawn

"Head on back." The man held the door open for him. "I'll put your bike behind the register."

"Gracias." Diego nodded at the man as he entered the store, shivering at the hum of energy as he crossed the threshold. "Thank you, um ..."

"Travis," he said. "Trav. And you are?"

"Diego."

"Diego," he repeated. "Come on in, let's get you cleaned up."

True to his word, he wheeled the bicycle behind the register before hurrying back to the door and flipping the sign to 'closed.' "I have a lot of valuable items in here," he explained, turning the lock. "Don't like leaving the store open if I'm not up here to supervise."

"Makes sense," Diego said, squinting to see Travis—Trav better.

"Oh, right." A blurry look of surprise flitted over his face. He set Diego's phone on the counter and patted the front pocket of his shirt. "These fell off when you, well, fell. Here, let me." He stepped close and slid the glasses onto his face faster than Diego could react. They settled gently over the bridge of his nose, and Diego inhaled as Trav's features sharpened into stark clarity.

Tanned and fine-boned, his cheeks were lightly freckled, the barest dusting giving away that this was a man who spent hours in the sun, or at least, had lived in Key West long enough for the warm golden-bronze tan to no longer be a seasonal affair. A delicate mole beside his eye drew attention to the rich, hazel iris and thick eyelashes beneath his brows, a shade darker brown than his sun-bronzed hair.

When Diego had first risen, and his roommate had been released from the hospital, she tucked him onto the couch for a "movie night," thrusting a bowl of popped corn in his lap before scaring Diego to the Ninth Ring and back by pointing a rectangle at the blank frame on the wall and illuminating the room in colors he had never known to exist. The movie's name escaped him, but the love interest, a young man determined to pass a young woman off as a lost princess, sparked a minor obsession with what his roommate Milla described as "peak nineties boy crush."

Diego still had no idea what that meant, but the man standing in front of him had the floppy haircut and endearing, boyish good looks of every one of those cartoon crushes.

Trav blinked as if suddenly realizing he lingered too close. He pulled his hands away, albeit slowly, and the apples of his cheeks deepened in color. A shy smile spread as he stepped away, and Diego's gaze dropped to a plush lower lip.

"Gracias," he managed. "Again."

Trav dipped his head, a wave of hair flopping forward. It was all Diego could do not to reach out and brush the locks away. The twitch of his fingers and a flash of pain distracted him from the attractive man in front of him. Glasses on, he startled at the injury to his palm, hissing as he spied flecks of asphalt and Horned God knew what else. "Mierda."

"I've got you." He led Diego down an aisle of record players, radios, clocks, watches, and phones. The energetic hum was stronger here, a crackling buzz that he felt in his teeth and fingertips. "Bathroom's back here. Well, my apartment, which has a bathroom and a first aid kit."

"You live in the store?" Diego eyed a smartphone propped in a locked display, attempting to discern where the hum was coming from. A faint aura of desperation wafted from the device, blending with the muddled energy clouding the aisle.

"Above." Trav shouldered open a door. Warped wood protested against linoleum, revealing a narrow stairwell wallpapered in Victorian damask and lit by out-of-place gothic sconces.

"Qué?" Diego huffed at the contradiction, earning a smile from Trav.

"Great, isn't it? The owner of the shop has—*had*," he corrected with a tiny frown, "an eclectic taste."

"I can see that." Diego followed him up the stairs, carpeted in what, to his Way, felt like genuine Persian thread. A ghostly slither of silk threaded across his fingertips. He curled his hand into a loose fist to keep from stooping low to feel the fabric.

"This way." Trav spun at the top of the stairs, gesturing to the left.

The stairs climbed to a wide, surprisingly spacious studio. A decent kitchen took up one corner, and a wall that fell two feet short of meeting the ceiling portioned off space for a bedroom in the other. The edge of a door was just visible beyond the foot of the bed, a fire escape, or perhaps a closet. The only truly private space in the apartment was the enclosed corner opposite the bedroom that Diego assumed to be the bathroom.

Like the stairwell, the apartment had been outfitted by someone with an eclectic taste. A modern, white leather sectional and chromatic area rug portioned off the living area. Half a dozen throw pillows with woven images of celebrities and cheeky sayings pulled in the colors from the rug, and the end table hosted a lamp with a bronze base sculpted to resemble a muscular forearm. Exposed brick made up two of the four walls, and they were dappled with pastoral scenes someone with an artistic bent had taken a brush to. Diego spied ghosts hiding in the woods around a moonlit cottage, a sea serpent grappling a brigantine in stormy seas, and a massive, humanoid creature stalking a pine wood.

"Is that a skunk ape?" He stopped beside the last painting, admiring the clever addition.

"Hm?" Trav glanced at the painting and chuckled. "Oh, yeah. My, um, Martin added those a while back."

Something about his tone and the warmth that bloomed in those hazel eyes had Diego tucking away a tiny pang of disappointment. "He is very talented."

Trav sniffed, blinking as he trailed his gaze up to the ceiling. "Bathroom's through here."

Where he'd been expecting a simple room with the most basic of amenities—a sink, a toilet, a shower—he was treated to a spacious, modern luxury. Floor-to-ceiling glass panels enclosed a honeycomb tiled shower with not one but *two* rainfall showerheads. Plush cotton towels hung from multiple racks on the wall, and beside a broad vanity with professional make-up lighting was a toilet with an array of buttons he had no hope of figuring out on his own.

"Nice, right?" Trav crouched in front of the sink, opening the cupboard and withdrawing a rectangular teal plastic case with a pink latch. "Beyond being a pawn broker and sometimes artist, Martin fancied himself an interior decorator and designer."

"Well, whoever Martin is, he did a wonderful job."

"Yeah"—Trav gestured for Diego to sit on the toilet—"he did." He sat, resting his arm on the edge of the counter, palm up. Trav set the case down and bent at the waist to inspect the wound. "There's a lot of gravel in there." He raised his eyebrows, peering at Diego over the rim of his round frames. "What did you do to that chicken?"

"Nothing!" He straightened. "The pájaro idiota jumped in front of *me*."

"Maybe he was attracted to your cologne."

"I am not wearing any."

"Really?" Trav turned on the faucet, angling his face at Diego. "Well, whatever soap you use smells good. Sweet like sugar." He washed his hands, lathering thoroughly with soap before rinsing it away. "Martin always said you weren't a true citizen of the Conch Republic until you survived your first chicken attack. I suppose congratulations are in order.."

"I'm only here for a few weeks," Diego answered. Trav stilled, a thick towel clasped in his hands, and flitted his gaze over Diego, lingering a little too long on his face.

"That's a shame." He tossed the towel on the counter. "Let's see what we can do about these pretty hands."

"At least," Trav continued as he bent forward, "not with any sort of padding." The move brought his face in line with Diego's, and the lighting around the mirror made no mistake of the flirtatious glint in his eyes.

After half an hour kneeling on the tile or stooping over the sink, Trav stretched his arms overhead, groaning as he rocked his hips forward. "Getting too old to be on my knees for that long."

Diego pinched his lips, palms throbbing but now cleaned of debris.

"At least," Trav continued as he bent forward, "not with any sort of padding." The move brought his face in line with Diego's, and the lighting around the mirror made no mistake of the flirtatious glint in his eyes.

"A gentleman would never keep you on your knees for so long." The words were out before he could stop them, and it was this sort of recklessness that had gotten him in trouble in his first life. But caught by those hazel eyes and knowing the gentle touch of this man, Diego could not help himself.

"And are you a gentleman?" Trav asked with a smile, leaving Diego mesmerized by the contrast of white teeth against dusky lips.

"I—" He curled his fingers over his palm and winced, breaking the moment.

Trav lightly shook his head. "Mind if we move this to the kitchen?"

Diego nodded, keeping his mouth firmly shut as he was directed to a chair. Trav washed his hands again, then laid out an assortment of cotton swabs, ointments, and bandages. "My mom was a school nurse," he explained without prompting. "Had a whole routine for cleaning scrapes and bruises."

"Lucky for me."

Trav gave a noncommittal hum and set to work. His touch was soft and gentle, and he habitually ran his tongue over his lips when concentrating. Diego looked away to keep his imagination from running wild, attention landing on a sheaf of papers and a handful of photographs splayed across the table. The papers appeared to be intake forms, not too dissimilar from the acquisition forms he and Milla received with the antique purchases they made for her store. Serial numbers, descriptions, certificates of authenticity, history of ownership—all the legal records required to trade on occult boards legitimately.

Diego's attention drifted to the photographs, of which there were far more than the forms. The items depicted were standard mortal treasures: rings, a pearl necklace, a guitar signed by someone named Les. Diego almost averted his gaze, not wanting to pry, when the corner of a photograph sticking out from under the picture of a tin samovar caught his eye.

It was nothing at first glance, a medallion-sized ring hewn of marble or quartz, but the prickling at his fingertips told him otherwise. He nudged the samovar photograph aside with his free hand, gasping as the full image was revealed.

"Almost done." Trav's gentle grip tightened on his wrist. Diego blinked, tearing away from the horror in the photograph to find the pawnbroker's eyes on him. "Sorry, was that too hard?"

"Qué?"

"Did I hurt you?"

"No!" Diego blurted. "No, it was fine, thank you. I mean, I am fine, I only ... those papers ..."

Trav glanced at the forms, confusion pinching a tiny line between his brows. "The register?"

"Register?"

"For the sheriff." Trav swept the papers and pictures together, removing the offending image from sight. It did not help. The shape of that medallion was seared behind Diego's eyelids. It was ruin and destruction and it was in the hands of this shopkeeper. "I have to register everything I take in with the Monroe County Sheriff in case any of it has been reported as stolen."

"Those items came in today?"

"Oh, no." Trav dropped the stack on his kitchen counter and settled in the chair opposite Diego, reaching for his untended hand. He squeezed a decent amount of ointment on Diego's palm, spreading the goo with a clean cotton swab. "Most of them are at their default date."

"Default date?"

"They're due to go on sale in the next day or so."

"On sale," he repeated, too bewildered to think clearly. "That last piece, the-the medallion, where did you get it?"

"Same way we got everything else," Trav answered. "Either somebody pawned it, or Martin found it."

"Do you know who?" Though put away, across the room and out of sight, Diego could feel the weight of that medallion like an anchor around his neck. A sweat broke out across his shoulders, his heart rate rocketing.

"I'm not sure?" Trav cocked his head. "If it were pawned, it would be on the paperwork, if I can find it. Martin handled the intake, but he didn't get to finish that last batch before he … um, died."

"Oh." Diego straightened. "I am sorry."

"It's fine," Trav said. "Still an open wound; I don't like to talk about him much. Not yet, at least." An awkward silence stretched, creating a distance that had not been there before. Trav spread an ointment on Diego's right hand, numbing the lingering ache almost immediately. He laid gauze over the wound and wrapped the hand in a bandage, and only when he was done did he look up. "All finished." He brushed his fingers over Diego's knee and rose, gathering supplies from the table. "My mom would tell you to keep those covered for a day, avoid getting the wrappings wet, and then buck up and get over yourself."

"Noted." Diego forced his attention away from the stack of papers and back to Trav. "And what would you advise?"

"Keep them clean and come back here if you need them re-wrapped." Trav sent him a small smile as he dumped packaging and used cotton swabs in a trashcan.

Diego easily returned his smile, eyes lifting again to the counter and the papers, wanting to catch one last look at the medallion, just to be sure. "If it is not too bold to say, I believe I will."

TWO

"Pick up, Milla." Diego paced the kitchen in tight circles, chewing on a thumbnail and waiting for his niece to answer. Having been added to the tower in the middle of the century, the kitchen was the only room with decent service, and even then, it was spotty. The West Martello Tower and Key West Garden Club was a stone, mortar, and steel construct on the southern edge of the key. It had once housed Civil War Troops and now served as the seat of Morgen Tage's demesne. A fitting fortress for a witch raised in the fabled towers of the Black Forest. "Pick up, pick up, pick up."

The ringing stopped, he held his breath, and an atonal voice came over the line. "Whoever this is, text me like a normal, modern human being."

"Milla, pequeña bruja, I need you to answer the phone for once in your very short life." He ran a hand through his hair, the dark, shower-damp strands curling lightly at his shoulders. "I am having a *real* issue down here. I do not care that you have wandered off with tall, Darkly, and handsome; I need your *help*—"

"Have you tried sending her an SMS?" A cold, crisp voice jerked Diego from his panic, reminding him why he preferred to leave the tower to make his calls—for a fortress, the construction was terrible at maintaining privacy. He ended the call, thrusting his phone into a pocket before facing the Morgenhexe head-on.

Imposingly tall, austere, and ageless, Morgen Tage, the Morgenhexe, strode into the room, her wide-leg Herringbone pants swaying perfectly in a non-existent breeze. Pride bloomed in Diego at that. He had spent the better part of a week tailoring the pants to do *just that*, and to see the effects of his labor and his Way in action was a desperately needed win.

She stopped beside the counter, her blonde hair wound in an elegant chignon displaying her graceful neck, and poured coffee from the ever-ready French press. Diego settled back on his hips, taking in the ensemble, her hair, the subtle dusting of makeup, and clicked his tongue.

"What is it?" Morgen murmured.

"The blouse." He sidled close, eyeing the short-sleeved gentian blue button-down. "Are we married to the scalloped collar?"

"The cascade-collared blouse is at the dry cleaners, and you have held the notched-collared blouse hostage for a week." She raised a steaming cup of coffee to her lips and cocked an eyebrow, waiting.

"I will accept fault for that oversight"—Diego raised a singular finger—"just this once. Going forward, tuck that scalloped mess in the back of your closet. Save it for pleated skirt season and leave the Hepburn trousers for the mandarin collars."

"Noted." Morgen finally sipped her coffee, eyes fluttering closed with pleasure. When she opened them, cold, piercing blue fixed itself on Diego. "How are your hands?"

He held them up, showing Morgen the half-healed injury. Red lines scoured his palms, his olive-hued skin still stitching itself together. "They should be healed within the day."

"Wunderbar. So what else has happened to have you in a snit?"

He danced his fingers against a thigh and poured himself a cup of tea from the pot he had steeping. Firmly gripping the ceramic mug, he dropped his hip against the counter and met the Morgenhexe's gaze. "Do you know how I died?"

"Dental hygiene," she said. "Or lack thereof."

"I can hardly be blamed for dying of an abscessed tooth in the sixteenth century," Diego deadpanned. "You remember what it was like."

They shuddered in unison, sipping from their mugs side-by-side and watching the sunrise before Diego spoke again.

"It was greed."

"Greed?" Morgen watched him from the corner of her eye. "I did not take you for the sort."

"Not mine. De Leon's."

Morgen's stern mouth pulled tighter and, to his great surprise, she blinked. "As in Ponce?"

"Sí."

He crossed the kitchen to sit at the table shoved against the wall, and the witch joined him, settling straight-backed in her chair. Her poise held momentarily before she sighed and leaned forward, flatting her palms on the table. "I will need you to start from the beginning, but why are you focused on your death this morning?"

"It was a curse," Diego answered. "A cursed item in de Leon's possession. It led to my death and the deaths of over a hundred gentleman volunteers on his La Florida voyage."

"C.R.O.W. has no record of Ponce de Leon being cursed," she argued.

"They would not have known. The cursed item was given to de Leon by a Calusa chief we encountered before sailing for Bimini. We anchored in an-an estuario—"

"An estuary."

"—to take on water and hunt, our ships required repairs. The people of the estuary," he said the word carefully, picking apart the vowels and consonants with his tongue and tasting how the different threads wove together to create something new, something whole, from the disparate strands. *Aestus*, his Way whispered, *aestuarium*. The tide, the tidal part of the shore. The place where the river meets the sea. "We thought they wanted to trade. They approached with open hands, and de Leon thought them simple. Stupid."

"The common mistake of the colonizers," Morgen mused. She summoned the teapot from across the room and topped off Diego's cup.

"We fought for weeks," he continued, raising his drink in thanks. "They sailed their canoes to blockade our ships; they attacked in the hours before dawn. We captured their warriors, and they drowned our sailors. They used their Ways to keep the fish away and ensure no freshwater made it aboard, starving us out until de Leon finally begged for a meeting with their chief.

"He left in a war canoe dressed in his finest. We watched from the ships, tired, hungry, scared." He stared into his tea, eyeing the swirl of tiny bubbles in the dark brown liquid. "And he returned within the hour with a new piece of jewelry hanging around his neck." Setting his cup aside, Diego snapped his fingers, pinching a summoned pencil as he slapped a piece of paper on the table. His hand was sure, steady, and he drew the medallion as he remembered it, as it had appeared in the photograph.

Every scale and each jagged spine. The muscle-thick body and slitted eyes. When he finished, he turned the page so the image he had drawn was right-side-up for the Morgenhexe to review.

Her eyebrow kicked up, the slightest twitch of discomfort as she took in the detailed depiction of a snake eating its own tail. "An ouroboros?"

"The Calusa chief promised de Leon the medallion would lead him to a fountain of riches. We were taken by the lie, desperate to leave the Calusa and their brackish waters behind. It was easy to believe de Leon had traded knowledge for knowledge; why else would the chief give us the key to life everlasting?"

Morgen pulled the paper from the table, holding it up to review each spine and scale. "An ouroboros is a depiction of Infinity. Eternity. I can see how de Leon would believe it to represent the famed fountain, but to corrupt the meaning behind the symbol—"

"Is anathema," Diego finished. "Lo sé, but the Calusa were not held by the laws of C.R.O.W. I can only assume the chief had had contact with a Spaniard before our ships arrived, that he knew de Leon would be fool enough to accept the medallion as a gesture of peace. They filled our barrels and holds, they escorted us from the estuary, and none of us saw the trap they had laid."

"Greed?"

Diego nodded, swallowing a bitter mouthful of tea. It hit his stomach, hot and vile, and he closed his eyes to work through a momentary roll of nausea.

"The Calusa had un malvado sentido del humor." Morgen cocked her head, waiting, and Diego translated. "A wicked sense of humor. The chief corrupted the symbol, he, or his witches, laid a curse on the ouroboros. We did not know—how could we know?—until days into our journey with the heat of summer bearing down. De Leon was consumed." He ran his tongue against the back of his teeth, tonguing the divot and smooth gum where no tooth had re-grown. "We sailed into settlements along the southwestern coast, raiding their villages for handfuls of gold, but it was not enough. He began demanding payment from his sailors, his 'gentlemen volunteers', claiming we owed him for passage to La Florida, for the riches of Puerto Rico." The words turned bitter, tainted by an ancient anger. "Many of us joined his fleet with no money to our names. Witches, Jews, men like me, we volunteered to save our lives, seeking a new world, a better life, only to fall prey to the same trap: pay or die."

Morgen lowered the drawing on the table between them as she absorbed his words. "C.R.O.W. did not do right by our witches in those early days."

"No"—Diego shook his head—"no, you did not." He let the accusation sit between them, justified in the doing. Morgen had been there when the Inquisition rose from the ashes of the Hundred Years' War, helping her *jezibaba*, her mentor, Margarete von Leipzig, form C.R.O.W. alongside La Voisin and Catherine of Aragon. When Morgen shifted in her seat, Diego continued. "I could not pay. I fled Zaragoza for the coast and 'volunteered' on the first expedition that would take me. My sister had been burned, my contacts, my *friends* unwilling to help. To help was to be complicit in the crime of being a Jew or a witch or a-a man of my inclinaciones. I had nothing for de Leon to take, so he took my tooth.

"Six men held me down, men I trusted. Men who had shared my cot. De Leon ordered them to hold me down as he pried the one bit of gold I owned from my jaw." He exhaled a shaking breath, tongue again probing that barren space in his jaw. "I can only hope he died as swift and painful a death as I."

"De Leon died in 1521," Morgen stated. "Shot by a poisoned arrow."

"Eight years." Diego closed his eyes, centering himself on knowing he was *alive*. "Ese bastardo lived for *eight years* after I died?"

"If historical records are to be believed," Morgen said. "You would be the only first-hand account of those voyages, and your premature death keeps us from knowing the exact details of de Leon's passing." Her dismissiveness earned an incredulous stare from Diego. "What C.R.O.W. holds in its libraries was compiled by an Ink Witch some years later, his histories a collection of spoken word stories, and none of them mention a cursed item." She tipped her head to the side, eyes darting left to right as she thought. "I will have them sent over for you to study; perhaps there is a reference to the ouroboros our scholars missed."

"How could they miss something as dangerous as this?" Diego tapped the drawing of the ouroboros. "This is a dangerous curse. Whoever owns it or wears it, mi diosa, maybe it is only a touch that is needed; they are cursed to be consumed by their greed."

"De Leon famously lost a ship to the shoals of Key West."

Diego nodded. "Weighed down by gold, the caravels could not clear the hidden reefs. I was already taken by fever on the San Cristobal when we lost the Santa Maria. He demanded the crew to dive and retrieve the lost gold. That was the final straw before mutiny broke out. They restrained de Leon in the hold of the Santiago, and the remaining ships attempted to navigate to Puerto Rico.

"A hurricane separated our fleet, and the San Cristobal made landfall along the northeastern coast of La Florida. We sailed north for the small settlement de Leon left behind in St. Augustine."

"Where you died," Morgen said. She tapped the drawing. "And that has exactly what to do with the ouroboros?"

"I saw it." Diego dug his nails into his palms, shuddering at the sharp twinge from the injury to his hands. "Yesterday at a pawnbrokers on First Street. You did not return until so late, I had no chance to—" Morgen stared at him, her face expressionless, body unmoving. "It was the exact piece in a photograph. When I questioned the pawnbroker, he did not know where it had come from, only that it was due for sale in the next few days."

"This ouroboros," she paced out, "this cursed item is in my demesne." Diego nodded. "And whoever dons the ouroboros is driven to collect and horde treasures until their insatiable desires lead to their downfall?" Another nod. "When did it get here?"

He shook his head. "No sé."

"If this item is as powerful as you say, I would have felt its arrival in my demesne."

"I do not—"

"Did he touch it?"

"I—" Diego pouted, unable to answer beyond speculation. A shiver built in his spine at the thought of Trav handling the ouroboros. Of those hazel eyes clouded with the lust for treasure that had consumed Ponce de Leon, his gentle touch corrupted by greed. "He said the item was taken in by another man weeks ago."

She sat with that, sipping her coffee and studying the drawing. "This cannot fall into mortal hands."

"Estoy de acuerdo."

"And here I thought you had a real problem."

"Pardon?"

Morgen steepled her fingers. "If the item is with a pawnbroker, our path is clear."

"I do not follow."

"You were correct to want to involve my foster daughter, but she cannot help you from … wherever she is. On the other hand, I am a very old witch with a very old bank account." Morgen reached across the tiny table, setting her fingers on

Diego's wrist. Her touch was firm, solid like an immovable, everlasting stone. "The solution is clear: *I* will procure the ouroboros and ensure it is handled responsibly by C.R.O.W."

THREE

THOUGH NO BELLS JANGLED when Diego opened the door to Southernmost Pawn, Trav glanced up when he set foot in the store. His glasses had slid down his nose, and he peered at Diego over the tops of the rounded frames, brows obscured by a floppy fall of hair.

At the way his eyes flitted over Diego, he knew he had chosen his outfit well. Shoulder-length hair pulled into a low bun, he wore a fitted cream and burnt sienna striped button-down paired with off-white chinos, knowing full well his warm, olive-toned skin would glow against those colors. And perhaps he had left the top three buttons undone with the sole intent of drawing attention to his neck and chest, but Diego would never admit as much. Not out loud, at least.

Trav straightened, pressing the glasses back into place while smiling and saying something to the customer he was helping at the counter—a young man in boardshorts and a loose tank top. The man smiled and nodded, wandering down an aisle of vinyl records.

Diego's cheeks warmed, and he glanced around the store, trying to keep from smiling outright. As the day before, a wave of energy greeted him, thick in the air like a fog. He curled his fingers in an attempt to single out the threads of magick and only managed to crinkle the freshly applied bandages on his palms.

Trav sauntered closer, narrow hips swaying in trim tan pants cuffed at the ankles. His loose linen shirt, this one a sage green accentuating his tan and making those hazel eyes glow, was again cuffed at the elbows and buttoned low, revealing more tanned skin and fine collarbones. Diego pulled his lower lip between his teeth, dragging his gaze away from the suggestion of muscle and smooth, hairless skin, and Trav's smile widened.

"Already want me on my knees?"

Diego's eyes bugged, and he sputtered, the warmth in his cheeks exploding to a full-on blaze. "P-pardon?"

Impossibly, that smile grew larger. "Your hands. Did you want me to redo the bandages?"

"Oh! No, por la Diosa, no." He gestured at Morgen lingering by the door. "She re-wrapped them for me this morning."

Trav's smile dipped as he noticed Morgen, the color washing from his cheeks. "I'm sorry, I must have misunderstoo—"

"You did not." Diego corrected in a low voice. "Only, we are here on a business matter."

"Oh?"

"There was a photograph in your apartment of a particular item."

"You're going to have to narrow it down," Trav said. "That was a sizeable stack."

"The medallion," he clarified. "A snake, eating its own tail."

"Ah." Trav slid his hands into his pockets, rocking on his heels. "Unfortunately, that piece is not currently available."

"Sí, I know." Diego nodded. "You said it would be available tomorrow; however, I have someone interested—"

"I thought you said I shouldn't sell it." His expression blinked from interested to somber. Almost sullen.

"I said you could not sell it," said Diego. It would be easier if he could explain, and had the Morgenhexe not been breathing down his neck, he would have. It had never sat right with him how witches, even before C.R.O.W. formed, cut the mortals out of their world. Magick was pervasive and everlasting. It affected the day-to-day lives of every creature, mortal, magick, or otherwise, in the world. To reduce humans to little more than beasts of burden was to tread the same line witches often looked down on the mortals for crossing.

"I see." The last hints of good humor faded completely from Trav's face, his voice flat. "Because you had a buyer, I assume?"

"Because identifying valuable items is what he does," Morgen answered.

Trav tipped his head to the side, appraising Morgen and her outfit of the day—a tweed midi skirt and butter-yellow three-quarter-sleeve sweater belted at the waist. A brown silk scarf wound loosely at her throat, the tails dripping down her rigid spine, "And you are?"

"His client." She sniffed and plucked a bronzed device from the shelf that looked like an abstract sculpture of a single-masted ship affixed with dials, knobs, and a miniature telescope. "And Diego, or BiminiBikini1513 as he is known in your circles, represents my interests."

Trav stared at her.

"You have a Lunar Sextant on your shelves in the store that operates as SouthernmostOccultGoods on the boards, and you do not know who BiminiBikini1513 is?"

Trav's eyes trailed to Diego, the sullen and cold expression replaced by utter bewilderment. "Am I supposed to?"

He shrugged.

"Perhaps you are more familiar with his colleague," Morgen continued. "I believe she goes by the handle xBlackxParadexPrincess95."

Trav blinked rapidly, head tremoring slightly. "Alright, that one I do know, but only because I've seen it written on purchase orders."

"You sell these items on the occult boards?" Diego asked.

"Martin did," he explained. "I was never involved with that part of the business, but toward the end, his recordkeeping wasn't the best. I'm still trying to make sense of it all, to be honest. From what I've seen, this Black Parade Princess was a frequent buyer, but the shipping address was for an antique store in St. Augustine."

"Southern Gothic," Diego said. "Black Parade Princess is my ... niece. She opened the store a few years ago to trade in curios and antiques."

"And you work for her?"

"Somewhat." He wavered a hand in the air. "I run my bespoke tailoring from a room in the back and help her select items for purchase, refurbishing those that require the attention."

"Useful man to have around." Trav's cool demeanor further warmed. "Don't suppose you know what a—" he glanced at the sextant in Morgen's hands.

"A Lunar Sextant," she said. "A rare nautical tool used to navigate the seas on a night with no moon or stars. Sixteenth century, if I am not mistaken. How did you come to have it?"

"I think...I think Martin found it on a dive?"

Morgen nodded, setting the item down and, to Diego's shock, smiling. "I will be browsing while you discuss the acquisition of the item in question. And the sextant." With a quick nod to Trav, the Morgenhexe spun and headed down the nearest aisle, selecting a vinyl from a crate and reading the liner notes.

Self-conscious now that he was alone with the pawnbroker, Diego scanned the shelves, following what threads of magick he could discern from the fog to different items that had no business being in a mortal pawnshop. A compass beside the sextant exuded an air of determination, telling him it would always point to the object most desired by the wielder, a pocketwatch hexed with a confusion spell (likely intending the wearer to be five minutes late in all things), and a bronze bowl buffed to a shine that he immediately recognized as a scrying dish.

"So," Trav said after a moment, standing closer to Diego than before, "the Lunar Sextant?"

"It is a navigational tool." He picked up the scrying dish and turned it over in his hands, wondering what a pawnshop would ask for such a treasure. He ought to make an offer for all of these items. Despite his misgivings about the separation of magical from mortal, these items would only confuse and spread fear among those not indoctrinated into the Ways. That Diego knew all too well. "Meant to be used on a night when there are no celestial bodies in the sky." A warmth blanketed his back, and Diego suddenly became very aware of how close Trav was standing. Sandalwood and citrus filled the air, and he gave in to the temptation to inhale deeply before turning around.

As expected, Trav was close, less than a foot away, his eyes fixed on Diego and a soft smile on his lips. "How would that even work?" His voice dropped lower, and the sound set off a fizzle low in Diego's belly.

"Magick," he answered, slipping on a sly smile of his own.

Trav blinked and backed away with a chuckle. "And the bowl?"

Diego looked at the scrying dish in his hands, turning it over and thumbing the engraving on the rim as the magick in the bronze spoke to his Way. It was Eastern European in origin, the metal inlaid with several different threads of vesticism—a branch of divination magick. Running his fingers over the braided engraving, his Way hummed to life, identifying the illusion spells used to fill the water in the dish with an image of the seeker's desired knowledge. An augurist's allure had been tied to the crystal inlaid at the base of the bowl, meant to boost the vestic's Way when divining the future. He let his Way pick at the magick, pulling at the stitches to reveal the chronomantic hex hidden underneath, one intended to tear forward in time.

"A scrying dish," Diego answered, "used by fortune tellers to predict the outcomes of a specific circumstance. Hungarian in manufacture. See, here?" He turned the bowl over to reveal the engraved sigil on the bottom. "This is the signature of Balog, a well-known fortune teller from Budapest. His work was highly sought after at the turn of the century."

"Twentieth or twenty-first?" At Diego's silence, Trav added, "If it's only two decades old, I'm never going to be able to sell it for what Martin thought it was worth."

"Twentieth," he said. "Balog was killed in the Great War."

"World War One?"

Diego bit his tongue and nodded, making a mental note to review his history.

"Oh, thank God," Trav exhaled. "Makes sense it was used as a scrying dish. The woman who pawned it used to work in Mallory Square grifting tourists with her fortune telling." He scanned the shelf, eyes widening as he spied whatever it was he sought. "Ah, here we are." He reached past Diego, and the move wafted a cloud of intoxicating citrus and sandalwood right up his nose. It was all he could do not to bury his face in the source of that scent. "She pawned these as well. What do you think, worth anything?"

He held a pack of cards in one hand, looking at Diego with a bright-eyed hopefulness that raised the fizzing in his belly to an outright flutter. A part of him did not want to assess the cards for fear they were worthless, and the knowledge would wipe the charming look off of his face, while another part of him realized if he took the cards, he would have a reason for their fingertips to brush.

So he did, admiring the subtle pink that rose in Trav's cheeks. The cards were worthless, of course. He knew it the moment his fingers touched the deck. A modern tarot designed by a mortal artist. Beautiful, yes, but absent even the slightest whisper of the occult. Though the same could not be said for a large amount of the store's inventory.

"These are unique—"

"Never mind," Trav cut him off. He propped his elbow on the shelf, cupping his jaw in his hand. "If they're worthless, I don't want to know. Have dinner with me."

"¿Qué?"

"Dinner. Comida. You and me." He grinned, a broad, bright-toothed thing that crinkled both cheeks. "I have so many questions about your work." He leaned closer. "About you. I'd like to ask them in a more intimate setting."

The skin along his scalp prickled, and Diego cast a glance around the store. It was empty, save for Morgen browsing the aisles, but the old fear reared its ugly head. "Can we?"

"Why not?" Trav's smile faltered. "I know parts of Florida aren't exactly welcoming, but this is Key West. The Conch Republic. Changes in attitudes and latitudes, or whatever. So long as you aren't an asshole, no one cares what you do."

"I suppose..."

"There's a bistro off Duval, I know the sous chef. Best charcuterie and tapas in town, they have this cured pig leg on the counter and they shave off—"

"Jamon?" He perked up. "They have jamon?"

"Thought that might get your attention." Trav laughed, brushing his knuckles against Diego's shoulder. "So, is that a yes?"

"I ..."

Trav trailed a finger down Diego's arm, no more than a few inches, their skin separated by his floral button-down, but he felt the touch as though it were seared into his bones. "Unless you have other plans?"

The flurry in his belly erupted with the fury of a derecho, threatening to knock him off balance. "No."

"Then it's settled." His finger pulled away, and Diego caught himself leaning after the fleeting touch. "Dinner tonight, you and me."

FOUR

"Ten years now? Eleven?" Trav tipped his head to the side, a glass of wine dangling from his fingers. "Hard to believe I've been here that long."

"I understand." Diego gestured for his wine glass and topped it off. "Time has a way of slipping by when you are not paying attention. Some days it feels as though I fell asleep in one century and woke up in the next."

"Most people call that 1999." Trav winked.

The bistro he had chosen was intimate, their table tucked in a cozy corner beneath an Art Nouveau poster for Moet & Chandon. Fairy lights strung from the ceiling reflected in Trav's glasses, casting the pawnbroker in a warm, almost mysterious glow. It was the sort of table, and Trav the sort of companion, that begged you to lean in, come closer, and *Diosa* did Diego want to.

No one had batted an eye when two men walked in the front door, standing too closely to be confused as mere friends. The sommelier had not frowned when Trav ceded the choice of wine to "his date," and Diego's answering blush had only earned a warm smile, so why did that wink raise the desire to glance over his shoulder?

"Unless...did they not do Y2K in Spain?"

"¿Disculpa?"

"The millennial new year, Y2K...or is New Year's Eve not celebrated in Spain the way we do it here?"

"Oh, sí, we celebrate." Although how a twenty-first-century New Year was celebrated throughout Iberia, Diego had no idea. "We eat twelve grapes."

"Grapes."

"At midnight you must eat one with each chime of the bells. If you succeed, you will enjoy prosperidad and good fortune."

"Doesn't sound too hard."

"No, until you remember the grape of choice is the Valencian Vinalopó. The skin is tough and bitter, and the seeds ..." He made a face and feigned choking. "If you are lucky, you manage to procure and prepare your grapes before the chimes."

Trav settled back and sipped his wine. "Did you manage it?"

"¿Cuándo?"

"The last New Year's Eve you spent in Spain. Or ever."

"Not on my last New Year, no." Diego spun his glass slowly, watching the fairy lights dance in the scarlet liquid. "I was in Santiago de Compostela with a friend."

With Ruben.

Tired, hungry, scared. They had fled Zaragoza with the stench of his sister's pyre fresh on their clothes, begging to trail behind caravans, stealing horses and donkeys, doing what they must to escape. "The bells of Catedral de Santiago de Compostela are rung thirteen times on the New Year." He saw the question forming on Trav's lips and answered before it could be released. "So the devil may have an hour for his tricks."

Diego upended his wine glass, swallowing half a pour in one go. Setting it down, he gripped the stem to keep his fingers from trembling.

An hour for the devil. An hour for Ruben to summon cards and cups and juggling balls, entertaining the drunken crowd for a bit of coin to keep them from sleeping in yet another dung heap. An hour for a fanatic to bring the nearest Inquisitor to their corner of the plaza.

An hour for Diego to run before the crowd tore him apart.

"How did that become a tradition?"

He blinked, hauled from the smoky air and the angry yells of Plaza del Obradoiro. Trav watched him expectantly, attentive to Diego's every word.

"Eating the grapes at midnight." He propped his chin in his hand. "Haven't heard that one before."

As with pumpkins, holly boughs, and bunnies, magick was the root and the cause. Grapes and their vines represented abundance and fertility. Their skins and seeds were used in rituals appealing to the Triple Goddess, their juices the basis for prosperity potions only the most skilled vinefica could concoct. To peel, de-seed, and imbibe the grapes at the tolling of the new year, a ritual performed at the liminal edge of becoming, was magick in its most basic form. A desire, an intent, and a sacrifice—twelve tolls of a bell in exchange for a year of prosperity—all in one.

But how to explain centuries of cultivated witchcraft to this mortal?

"I am not sure," Diego lied. He darted his gaze around the bistro, desperate to move the topic off of himself, his past, and the still painful memories of his final days in Spain. To his relief, the waiter returned, notepad in hand.

"Are we ready to order?"

"Yes!" Trav swept the menu from the table, and Diego watched, mesmerized by the way excitement transformed him as he ordered. He smiled when he spoke, one eye crinkling more than the other, and his features became more boyish, more innocent. A particularly exuberant nod sent a wave of hair tumbling free from the swept-back style, and Diego was struck.

No witch he had known or knew ever smiled so innocently or gave themselves wholly over to enjoyment like this. Witches were intentional in all things, their restraint a necessary and crucial part of the responsibility of wielding magick, and here was this mortal, this *man* grinning wildly over the idea of pairing jamon with pan-seared scallops and matchstick pears.

Diego pointed blindly at the list of cured meats and murmured the suggestion of another bottle of wine, utterly bewitched.

Trav settled in his chair when the waiter had gone, twirling his wine glass by the stem. "It must be nice to come from a place so steeped in tradition."

"Does your family not have traditions?"

"They do." Trav's smile fled, and the wine glass stilled. "Christmas, Easter, and Pentecost were big in my house growing up. Sunrise service, wearing our best 'Sunday clothes,' moments of prayer, renewing baptismal promises made without our consent ..." Bitterness underscored his words, the glee completely wiped clean from his face. He crossed a hand over his front, absently plucking the fabric of his shirt away from his ribs. When he looked up, Trav's features were hard. Sharpened by an old anger ... or hurt.

Diego lay his hand on the table, fingertips an inch away from Trav's, wanting to show comfort but unable to close the distance. "I am sorry if I—"

Trav slid his palm forward and pressed the tips of his fingers against Diego's.

"You didn't," he said in a low voice. "But thank you. It's an old wound, but it's no secret." He straightened, pulling his hand away. "My parents are super conservative, so you can imagine how they handled my coming out when I was sixteen." Diego could not, but he did not think admitting as much would be any help. "They sent me to a camp outside of Gainesville, thinking it would 'fix' me." He huffed a bitter laugh. "All it did was teach me how to scale fences. I hitchhiked down to Key West with twenty-seven dollars in my pocket and a brand new driver's license."

"Was that not dangerous?"

"Hell yeah, it was." Trav grinned. "A twinky little kid like me, plucked out of Kentucky and dropped in the middle of the Sunshine State? Christ, looking back, I can't help but think how stupid that was. I could have been robbed, raped, beaten, and left for dead on the side of the freeway...I'm not religious by any means, but someone or something was looking out for me."

"Why Key West?" Diego asked. Their waiter returned with the new bottle of wine, standing beside their table with a practiced smile.

"The 2015 La Rioja Alta 'Viña Ardanza' Reserva." He set the cork on a tiny plate and poured a small measure into a clean glass. "Aged three years in

American oak and a further three in the bottle." Diego inhaled as he swirled the wine, a bit of theater he had easily adopted in his second life. Before, when he was a young man just finding his way in the world, sniffing and tasting wine was necessary. Anything could be bottled, any number of ingredients used to alter flavor or mimic aging, but now? Now, he liked to savor that first taste.

His Way flared into being at the first touch of wine on his tongue. Cherry and blackberry, exotic spices with just the barest hint of cacao. He discerned the blend of Garnacha and Tempranillo, the subtle suggestion of the oak barrels, and a low balsamic thread. Swallowing the meager mouthful, he closed his eyes and hummed quietly as the velvet liquid rolled over his tongue, tingling with the natural sugars of vine-ripened grapes.

"Sí"—he opened his eyes and nodded at the waiter—"this will open up nicely."

The waiter's practiced smile warmed, and he moved to fill Diego's glass, stopping at a gesture and redirecting the pour to Trav, who sat back in his chair, eyes fixed on Diego. Once the waiter left, he leaned forward.

"I could watch you enjoy wine like that all night."

"Keep complimenting me, and you might get your wish." Diego could blame the wine for his loose tongue, but he had not had enough to drink for the lie to stick. He liked this, the pawnbroker and his easy conversation, the way the fairy lights sparkled in the lenses of his glasses and gave his pretty eyes a simmering heat. The way Trav's focus was intent on *him*. "¿Por qué Key West?"

"Luck," Trav said, bashful for the first time. "Sheer luck, all of it. Sloppy Joe's hired me on as a barback almost immediately and that's where I met Martin."

"And you were with him until he passed?" Diego sipped his wine, tamping down an ugly rise of jealousy at whatever role this Martin had played in his life.

"Yes," Trav answered, then set his glass down just this side of too-hard, throwing his hand out, fingers splayed. "Not like that." Red bloomed on his cheeks. "Not at all; Martin was a regular at Sloppy Joe's. Always tipped well and made sure the bartender sent some of those tips my way. I didn't realize what he was doing until months later. No one else tipped the barbacks; we just got a cut at the end of the night, but he always set down an extra twenty."

"How did you not realize?"

"I was seventeen and sleeping outside, smoking whatever pot I could get my hands on." Trav shrugged, too easily for it not to be a performance. "He found me on my lunch break, plucked the joint from my fingers, and asked what the fuck I was doing." His eyes took on a distant gleam, as lost to the memory as Diego had been in his. "He was the first person to ask me what I was doing. Martin had this way about him, something that made you want to trust him, to open up and admit *everything*. One second I was convincing myself to get on my knees and blow the man who had been tipping me for months, and the next I was sitting on a crate and sobbing out my story to a complete stranger.

"Martin just put his arm around me and said, 'It's gonna be okay, kid.' That was it, 'It's gonna be okay.' He offered me a job in the pawnshop and said he would work around my schedule at Sloppy Joe's if I wanted to work up to bartender." Trav dipped his chin, a tiny laugh escaping as he slowly shook his head. "Said he was tired of finding me passed out in Mallory Square, and if he saw me using the public beach showers again, he'd drag me away by the ear."

"He sounds wonderful."

"He was." Trav's face fell, and he pressed his glasses up with a knuckle, wiping under an eye.

"I am sorry, I did not mean to press."

"No, it's fine. I—" He blinked and scanned the ceiling, taking a moment before finishing his thought. "I haven't been able to talk to anyone about him. There's not really anyone *to* talk to, and it ... it hurts, but it's nice. You know?" Diego nodded, some sixth sense telling him Trav was not done. His pain, his grief, was a pillow bursting at the seams, and he had just begun picking at the stitching. "He moved me into the apartment. It wasn't much at first. An inflatable mattress, a minifridge that stopped working whenever it was over eighty degrees, a sink, and a toilet. We trucked up an old a/c unit and cleared out the storage. Over the years, we built the kitchen and bathroom and partitioned off the bedroom.

"I'd never touched power tools before Martin, and now I feel like I could renovate a house. He enrolled me in Key West High to finish my Senior year, paid for me to attend college, even taught me how to free-dive..." Trav's gaze unfocused somewhere between himself and Diego. "He left everything to me." The wine glass slowly spun in his fingers, and a sheen of tears clouded his eyes. "I owe him *everything*, and he gave everything to me."

Before he could think better of it, Diego reached across the table, taking Trav's hand and squeezing gently. "I am truly sorry for your loss."

Trav's fingers twitched and squeezed back, his gaze finally sharpening in Diego. "He was more than an employer," he said. Diego nodded, urging him to continue, to lance the boil of grief. "More than a friend, or a role model he was—he was ..."

"He was a father."

"Yeah." Trav blinked, this time not wiping away the tears that fell. An embarrassed laugh escaped, and he pulled his hand free, sweeping his glasses away to dry his face. "Wow, you must think I'm a terrible date, crying over charcuterie after a few glasses of wine."

"On the contrary," said Diego, "we have yet to receive our food."

He blushed, ducking his head. "I promise not to weep on our second date."

Diego pinched his lips together in a smile, savoring the flurry the promise of a second date set off in his belly. "I look forward to it."

The conversation drifted away from Martin and second dates when their food arrived—the promised pan-seared scallops paired with jamon shaved tableside and carmelized matchstick pears, pan con tomate topped with sobrassada and manchego, escargot sauteed in garlic-parsley butter, and a ceviche with fresh caught Key West pinks—flitting from topic to topic with comforting ease. Trav spoke of the sunken galleons whose hulls were used to shore up Key West when it was little more than a bone reef and sandy shoals.

"We used to dive out by the mangroves. He believed there was treasure to be found tangled in the roots."

"Did he ever find any?"

"You've seen the store. It's an eclectic collection, to say the least."

Diego spoke carefully around growing up in Zaragoza, using the practiced replies centered on surviving architecture and the surrounding countryside, faltering when Trav asked why he left.

"I volunteered," Diego answered half truthfully, "in the Armada." At Trav's pursed lips, he clarified, "The Spanish Navy."

"How are they with Don't Ask, Don't Tell? Does Spain have a similar policy? They repealed it stateside, oh, over a decade ago now, but you can imagine how well that's going."

"Don't ask, don't tell?"

"Well, I get that Europe is more relaxed around homosexuality, but is it as ideal as it's made out to be?"

"Ah." Memories of pyres and hangings, friends vanished in the night, and Ruben's pained cries flooded Diego's mind. He frowned, unsure how to answer the question without having to explain his experiences as a Jewish witch who preferred the company of men in the sixteenth century. "It was many years ago now that I served," he settled on. "Things are different now, of course, and I certainly earned my sea legs, if you follow."

To his relief, Trav smiled and nudged Diego's ankle with a foot. "I think I do."

And there his foot remained through the rest of dinner, idly drifting up Diego's calf while Trav smiled and chatted, the caress safely hidden beneath a tablecloth. He reveled in the touch and the attention, cherishing the moments as something precious that was his and his alone.

Trav kept close on their meandering walk past the Hemingway House, their knuckles brushing when they turned east at the concrete buoy marking the Southernmost Point. Couples sat shoulder-to-shoulder on Higgs Pier jutting out into the Florida Strait, cast in romantic moonlight and lost in each other.

Seeing the couples on the pier, Trav tugged Diego toward a cluster of palms beside the volleyball court, abandoned this late at night.

Perhaps it was the safety on the empty beach, or the wine in his system, or the way starlight reflected in Trav's glasses. Perhaps it was a whim or a lapse in his better judgment, but Diego could no longer withhold the desires he had fought against for the duration of the evening.

He squeezed Trav's hand, tugged him closer, and kissed the man.

Trav tensed in surprise, a tiny little grunt lodged in the back of his throat, and then his hand was at Diego's face, thumb trailing his cheekbone as he returned the kiss. His tongue swept Diego's lips, warm and seeking entry, nibbling on his bottom lip until the witch relented. He tasted of wine and the cinnamon sugar dusting on the torrijas they had split for dessert, his tongue warm and probing. It was a hungry kiss, a devouring, greedy kiss that demanded Diego shut out the rest of the world, his fears, and his past and focus solely on Trav.

Fingertips pressed along Diego's scalp as he angled his head to kiss him deeper. The world spun lazily around them, or perhaps they spun in place because Diego's back was pressed against a palm tree, and him half risen on his tiptoes to level their heights. Trav worked a leg between his knees, pressing bodily against Diego as his hands wandered down his sides to grip him by the hips. Beyond their private embrace, someone whistled and it was enough to bring Diego crashing back to earth, his eyes flying open and only then taking in where they were, what they were doing.

He wormed a hand between them to rest over his racing heart, pushing lightly to break the kiss and look him in the eye. "I cannot—"

"I understand."

"It is not you, it is ... there are people on the beach and—"

Trav pressed a kiss beside Diego's eye and leaned back. Color rode high on his cheeks, visible even in the low light, his lips bee-stung and oh, so tempting. "I understand," he repeated.

"I do not mean to push you away."

"You aren't." They both glanced down at Diego's hand clutching the front of his shirt. Trav raised his head, gaze flitting from one of Diego's eyes to the other. "Did I come on too strong?"

"No! No, it is me; I am in my head about ..." Diego glanced helplessly at their surroundings, the wide open spaces, the *people*.

"Hey, *hey*." Trav crooked a finger under his chin, redirecting the focus onto him. "It's okay, I understand, only ... can we do this again?"

"The dinner," Diego asked, "or the kissing?"

Trav's answering smile was heart-achingly beautiful, and Diego's stomach flipped. "I was thinking both."

FIVE

THE TRICK TO A perfectly hemmed pair of pants was in the stitching. Too tight, and the leg would never fall correctly, pinching at the ankles or hitching to the side. Too loose, and you risked an unraveled hem. But done just right, with a steady slip stitch by hand of course, the hem would be invisible and the fall of the leg beyond compare.

Diego plucked the needle from his teeth and pinched the air above a spool of thread. A thin strand of black unraveled from the spool, rising like a charmed snake and threading itself through the eye of the needle, end knotting neatly together.

He unfolded the hem, inserting the needle into the fold and pulling it through until the knotted end caught. Pressing the hem back into place, he picked up a few threads of the orchid-dyed cotton weave and slipped the needle along the edge before gently pulling the thread taut and repeating the process. Losing himself to the monotony of a solid stitch to keep his mind from wandering to the beach just out the front door and the very fresh memory of being pressed up against a palm tree.

"I would like to involve the cultists." Morgen's voice shattered his focused calm.

"O, por la Diosa." He pricked the tip of his finger with the needle and cursed, glowering at the half-finished hem. Popping the finger into his mouth, he whirled around to glare at the Morgenhexe. "I am going to stitch bells into your collars if you cannot announce yourself."

"I did announce myself." She settled on a chaise lounge shoved beside a blown glass window reinforced with crosshatched iron. It overlooked the northern edge of the Key West Garden Club grounds and offered an unimpeded view of the Higgs Beach dog park.

After witnessing a fourth golden retriever make a solid deposit in the Fecal Bank of Key West within the first hour of his residency, Diego had re-arranged the furniture so that his makeshift sewing table faced away from the window, then quickly relented due to the lack of natural light. In a compromise, his sewing table now sat perpendicular to the wall and window, his main view that of the bed and an abundance of throw pillows of varying shape and softness, with the door to the room at his back.

"Rather loudly and quite clearly," Morgen continued. "I would like to in-volve the cultists in this ouroboros issue."

Diego tossed the pants on the table to press a non-bleeding hand to his chest. "*Why?*"

"Because your shopkeeper is drowning in occult items, and as long as they remain easily accessible, the Staid populace—"

"Human," Diego said. Morgen blinked at the interruption. "Call them what they are: human."

"What they are is incapable of traveling the Ways, and therefore Staid," Mor-gen replied. "And so long as those items are easily accessible, the *Staid* populace is not safe. You remember how they reacted when that augurist went rogue and allured a metric ton of gravel."

"I ... do not?"

"It took the American Oversight Committee years to collect all those 'pet rocks'. No matter." She waved her hand between them. "I would like to involve the local cultists to procure the occult items." At Diego's sputter, she raised a finger. "Short of summoning C.R.O.W. to attend to the matter, what would you have me do?"

"Have Milla buy the items through legitimate means and secure them ourselves." He crossed his arms, punctuating his point. It was the path of least resistance; his roommate had the Way, means, and clout on the occult boards to do so, and it kept Trav away from the cultists and C.R.O.W.

"Has she returned any of your calls?"

Diego opened his mouth, closed it, and frowned at the half-hemmed pant leg. "No. Yours?"

"Nein." Morgen picked at the upholstery, a furrow appearing between her brows. "I cannot gather that amount of occult inventory without C.R.O.W. growing suspicious, and my foster daughter has gone to ground after the events in St. Augustine. The cultists are prominent in my demesne; it is likely your pawnbroker knows and trusts a number of them. If not him, then certainly his predecessor was familiar."

"How can you make that assumption?"

"How could I not?" She fixed him with a glare that warned of a lecture. "Any mortal exposed to a large amount of magick, whether all at once or in dosages over time, is bound to become addicted. It is no coincidence my demesne is home to so many cultists, Diego. With Big Torch Key and my Enforcers so close at hand, the Conch Republic is a magnet for magick and those seeking a taste of what we wield with abandon. Honestly, I am surprised there are not more cultists flocking to the island. A credit to their leader, I suppose, for separating the wheat from the chaff."

The way Morgen spoke of mortals, as though they were a separate species altogether, prodded a tender bruise deep inside of Diego. Not too long ago, as far as his lived years were concerned, he had been separated from witches as Other. Less than. And the ease with which Morgen continued to tout these ancient ideals threatened to re-open a slow-healing wound. The last year and change of Diego's second life had taught him much about mortals and how far removed the world was from the one he'd died in.

"We have a fair amount of cultists in St. Augustine," he said, for lack of anything else to add. "Milla is not fond of them."

"Hardly surprising," she tutted. Having a flock of cultists leeching off of the magick she feeds into the territory puts her at great risk—not only with C.R.O.W. but with the cultists themselves."

"¿Cómo es eso?"

Morgen flitted a shrewd gaze over Diego. "Because the amount of magick Ludmilla wields in her little finger would be enough to melt their mortal brains."

"Vistoso," he muttered. *Colorful.* Morgen shrugged one shoulder, looking all too much like the witch they discussed. "But why the cultists? If they are so attracted to the magick, what is to keep them from collecting the occult items for themselves and misusing the power?"

Her cool gaze hardened to diamond sharp, and something ancient and wicked flashed in the depths of those crystalline blue eyes. "Me."

"Well, bruja, as terrifying as you may be, perhaps there is a more subtle way to approach this ordeal." Diego picked up his sewing, swallowing down the chill brought on by the power behind that singular word. He went to work on the hem, retreating behind a well-practiced mask of indifference. "One that does not call C.R.O.W.'s attention and keeps the items out of the cultists' hands."

He could feel her eyes tracking the needle's pick, pull, and drag; her piqued interest was as nerve-wracking as it was flattering. Morgen had been coming into her Way when the laws of C.R.O.W. were still being argued in the great halls of Europe. She had witnessed the rise and fall of empires and, if the rumors were true, survived a bargain with the devil himself before becoming an Enforcer, a member of the Tribunal, and lastly, the *jezibaba* of a Death Witch. To have her attention was to have scholars poised in the wing, quills at the ready to take note of whatever it was the Morgenhexe deemed worthy of her time.

"Go on."

"My Way has been building too long—"

"Then put down your needle."

"—and as I do not exist, in so far as C.R.O.W. is concerned, it would be good for me to have a means of practicing my Way without calling attention."

"And you are suggesting ..."

Diego glanced up as her words died away and found Morgen poised on the edge of the chaise, truly curious.

"I will do it." He pulled the thread taut and snipped it with a half-thought pinch of his fingers. "Trav trusts me"—he paused as Morgen cleared her throat, covering a tiny smile with her closed fist—"and picking apart the magick imbued in the occult items allows me to burn off the excess while being useful."

"Altering my wardrobe is not useful?"

"Altering your wardrobe is a dream." He swept a hand over the wide-legged trousers, pinching his fingers and reversing the motion to press, pleat, and fold the garment before presenting it to Morgen. "But I could do this in my sleep. Working in the pawnshop will allow me to stretch a little."

Morgen flicked her gaze from the hemmed pants to Diego, her expression shrewd and suspicious. He smiled, as innocent as the day he was reborn, and she nodded.

"Ulterior motives aside, and do not think your affection for the pawnbroker has gone unnoticed, de Bimini." Another stern glare was cast his way; this one tempered with amusement. "I agree it is better to have a witch I trust working with the occult inventory than a cultist with questionable loyalties."

"You—" The blood rushed from his face, and he blinked, not sure he had heard the witch correctly. "You trust me?"

"Of course I do." Morgen took the trousers and tucked them under an arm. "If you cannot trust a witch almost as old as you are, who can you trust?"

And with that pearl of wisdom, she left.

"You want to what, exactly?" Trav balanced a tray on one hip, nudging items aside on a shelf to make room for a set of crystal coupe glasses.

"I would like to review your inventory for any items that might sell well on the occult boards and help you navigate pricing and the certificados de autenticidad," Diego repeated. He reached for the tray, wanting to make himself useful to cover the lie, even if it were one of omission. Using his Way to pick apart the magick humming throughout the store and aiding Trav in navigating auctions and near-feral bidders, he could offset the guilt of attempting to locate and remove the ouroboros without raising suspicion.

"The certificates of authenticity?" Trav angled away, taking the tray out of reach. "That might be harder than you think; a decent amount of our inventory is salvage."

"Salvage?" Diego scanned their aisle, which would have been more at home in a thrift store than a pawnshop. Stacks of trivets, rolled table linens, mismatched silverware in trays, tea sets, coffee mugs, butcher's blocks, and knives. Salvage made sense; he could not imagine anyone assigning enough monetary value to cloth napkins and a butter knife to pawn the goods, much less for a pawnbroker to accept them.

Yet, for as much as the items on the shelves were junk, a thick fog of magick, too dense to be a web, permeated the store.

"From his dives." Trav set the tray down on an endcap. "Can we file for the certificates ourselves? Martin was pretty good about reporting what he found to the park staff, so anything he brought home was stuff they deemed worthless." He blinked, and the color blanched from his cheeks. "Unless"—Trav's eyes danced over each item—"unless he *didn't*. He was off near the end. Diving more and more, getting careless with the register and his intake forms, that's what I've been trying to clean up for the last few weeks, and he might have ..." He leaned heavily against the shelves, running a hand through his hair. "Oh, fuck."

"What is it?"

"There's a law, a treasure hunting law. If you excavate or bring up anything from a shipwreck, you have to submit it to the state. It's a felony to sell found treasure from anything deemed historically significant." He scanned the aisles, jaw hanging slack. "I have no idea what was pawned and what was salvaged. I've been trying to reconcile his paperwork, but it was a mess at the end, and he brought in so much, so fast. If he didn't report it ... oh *Christ*." Trav sank to the ground.

"How bad could it be?" Diego crouched low and set his hand on Trav's shoulder.

"Five hundred dollars a day," he stated, eyes pinned on some point between his feet. "The fine is five hundred dollars a day per salvaged item. There are at least two dozen items in the back room that I can't match to the register, and that's before I even consider what's in the boxes and on the shelves and his storage unit; oh *fuck*." Trav groaned and covered his face, grumbling into his palms, "God damn, this store is a curse."

"Then let me help you." Diego settled beside him. The shelf dug into his back, forcing him to sit overly straight. "We organize what we can, I cross reference the boards anything you believe might be salvage, and we submit it to the state as needed." He glanced down the aisle, listening for any footfall or suggestion of others in the store, and, hearing none, put his hand on Trav's knee. "If Martin was not well in the end, you can stay ahead of ... of ... el enjuiciamiento by organizing the salvaged items and presenting them to the state for review. There must be laws to protect the inheritor of an estate if you are acting in good faith."

Trav lifted his head and stared at Diego for a beat before saying, "Prosecution."

"¿Qué?"

"Enjuiciamiento," Trav said. The accent was wrong, broad, and nasally American, but his pronunciation was correct otherwise. "Prosecution.

"Sí ..." Diego cocked his head, and Trav sent him a shaky smile.

"Took Spanish in high school, had a fluent practice partner." He put his hand over Diego's, squeezed, and slipped his fingers under Diego's palm, toying with the edge of a bandage. "How are these pretty hands doing?"

Diego flexed his fingers, regretting the lie he was about to tell. "They are healing." *Healed.* "The woman I am staying with, she wrapped fresh bandages this morning." *So you would not see what I am. What I am capable of doing.* "I am hoping I will not need the bandages in another few days."

"And you came by to offer me help in the store." A little smile danced across his lips, and finally, his eyes lit with a glimmer of mischief as he leaned closer. "If you wanted to spend more time with me, you only needed to ask."

"I—" Diego jerked his head back, slamming his skull against the shelf. "Ay."

"Christ," Trav blurted, pulling entirely away. "I'm just making a fool of myself over and over again with you, aren't I?" He rose and busied himself rearranging coffee mugs and saucers. "Can't take a hint, can't tone it down. You'd think after last night I would have known better."

Diego rushed to his feet, allowing himself one reassuring glance down the aisle before pressing his hand to Trav's lower back. "Last night was lovely. I am sorry if I caused you to believe otherwise."

Trav hung his head, sliding a hand into his pocket and taking a breath before looking Diego in the eye. "I'm a mess when I'm nervous," he admitted, "and I—I'm terrible at asking for help, but if you could? And I'll try to tone it down."

"I never said I wanted you to tone it down." Diego wrinkled his brow, trying out the words. Though not certain what it meant, he understood the spirit of the phrase, and this flustered performance by Trav was so precious he needed to say something to put the man at ease. "Where I am from, I am not used to being so ... so ..."

"Open?"

"Sí," he sighed, shoulders dropping at the relief of being understood.

"I get that." Trav worried that plush lower lip between his teeth. "I'll follow your lead, alright? If you aren't comfortable touching in public, that's fine. I want you to be comfortable with *me*, regardless of where." He set his hand under Diego's so they were palm to palm, trailing fingers along the bandage and down to Diego's fingertips, pressing the pads together. "And if you need to get comfortable, my apartment is right upstairs."

Diego exhaled, only able to nod because if he spoke, he knew it would be to say, "Now."

"But first, let me show you the back room."

"How is that different than your apartment?" Diego managed, and Trav's answering smile was a prize all its own.

SIX

If there was one thing Diego excelled in, it was organizing chaos. Hand him a knotted ball of twine, and his Way would flare to life, traveling the strand and knowing in an instant how it looped, twisted, and tied together. Hand him an item imbued with a Shade of horror or enchanted with a fading allure, and Diego would untangle the magick and repair the threads, returning the item to its original terror or charm.

Southern Gothic, with its eclectic collection of antiques and curios, was the pinnacle of tempered chaos. Mannequins who moved when you were not looking, a mirror that only showed flattering reflections, a genuine Hyderabadi rug with a history of flight. The shop in St. Augustine was a witch's dream, thick with magick kept in line by Diego and his particular Way. It was a mapped chaos, a known chaos designed and controlled by him. Diego knew chaos; he thrived in chaos, and one look at the backroom of Southernmost Pawn threatened the very pillar upon which he made his living.

With an apologetic look, Trav pushed open the door, revealing a space that was, for lack of a better phrase in both English and Spanish, a fucking mess.

"O, por Diosa." A wave of magick crashed into Diego, and he staggered back, fighting the desire to flee. Tables lined the walls, and boxes and crates filled every flat surface, including the row of shelving halfway up the walls. The space beneath the tables was no better. Taken up by boxes packed to the brim, some sat open with flaps hanging like limp petals, while others strained against tape one strong breeze away from giving up.

The only saving grace was a window on the rear wall looking out onto a pleasant, palm and poinciana-shaded yard. A kettle-drum firepit and an Adirondack chair sat on the patchy grass, and bistro lights had been strung over a tidy path meandering across the yard and disappearing behind a thick veil of weeping willow. Squinting, Diego made out the shape of a structure tucked in the furthest corner of the yard. A pagoda, or shed.

This would be a refuge at night, under the moon and stars. A quiet haven away from the pawnshop and bustle of Highway A1A. In a way, the garden reminded him of Trav. It was in the easy nature of the path and the Adirondack in desperate need of a good sanding and stain.

"I probably should have warned you," Trav said, calling Diego's attention away from the yard. "This used to be an office, but I had to move all of *that* upstairs to use this for storage. It took me a week to clean out his condo, the landlord was pissed."

"¿Por qué?"

"He wanted to rent it out as soon as possible, threatened to sue me for obstructing his business, or something. I wasn't really paying attention." He frowned at the boxes. "I was too busy to be worried about his inability to show the property."

"Did you not have help?"

"A little." He fiddled with something in his pocket. "For a day or two. Martin didn't ... he didn't have many people left. A few acquaintances in the Keys, a handful of friends from New York, but they couldn't stay long, and ... I don't know, I felt like I owed this to him. He took such great care of me; he offered me help when I didn't know how to ask for it, much less know how to say 'thank you.'"

Diego nudged the door closed, listening for the soft *click* before taking Trav's hand and lifting on his toes to kiss his cheek.

His lips parted in surprise. "What was that for?"

"For letting me help." Diego laced their fingers together, squeezed, and slipped away. He let his Way lead him to a bin, cautiously hopeful. "Now, let me get to work."

Hours later, Trav threw his folder onto a table, loose leaf pages fluttering free. "We're done. I'm starting to see double, and your stomach has been growling for the last hour."

Diego blinked out of his Way, flexing the fingers of his right hand and massaging his wrist. The adhesive on the bandages chafed, and his arm ached as though he'd been doing wrist curls with a twenty-pound weight for the last four hours, which would be an achievement, considering he could barely manage two reps with a ten-pound weight.

While he frequently used his Way, he had never applied it at such an exhaustive scope. Milla and Southern Gothic usually brought in one to two items a week for him to pick apart, analyze, and stitch back together. It had been at least a year, plus the five hundred he was dead, since Diego had attempted to travel his Way to such extremes, and even then, never through such a dense cloud of indiscernible magick.

Eyes burning and muscles aching, he scanned the items strewn across the table. The first order of business had been to clear a workspace, which meant shoving more boxes under the tables or lugging them upstairs into Trav's apartment. From there, Diego had let his Way lead his hand, seeking out the most powerful threads of magick within the mass and attempting to follow them to their source.

He sorted the items he could into "Occult," "Not Occult," and "O, Por Diosa How in the Nine Rings Did This Get Into Mortal Hands?" and Trav flipped through a binder, reconciling the inventory against his records or, as had proven to be the more frequent case, filling out a blank form and doing the best he could.

But for all of their effort, Diego had barely begun when Trav called their halt.

"Acabamos de comenzar," he protested, reaching for the next item—a gold-plated fountain pen he was fairly certain would draw the bearer's blood as ink. Trav batted his hand away.

"You've spoken Spanish for the last hour, and my public education fluency is limited." He nudged Diego toward the door. "Come on, I'll make you dinner, and we can talk about literally *anything* other than pawned crap."

"Pero todavía hay mu—" Trav cut him off with a look. Diego cleared his throat, grasping for the thread of his Way that allowed him to think in English. "We have barely begun," he tried again, returning to the table. "I can clear that box while you cook and then take a break to—"

"No." Trav grabbed him by the shoulders, steering Diego from the backroom and the heavy, heady magick within. "We are taking a break. I will feed you, and then you and I will watch a movie or do something *normal*."

"You live above a pawnshop," Diego pointed out.

"And?"

"And that is hardly normal."

"Neither is identifying valuable items at a glance," he retorted. "Or is it at a touch?" Diego stiffened, ready to weave a lie to cover his Way, but Trav continued. "With those pretty hands of yours? I bet it's by touch." His hand slid down Diego's back, directing him to the stairs. He leaned close, the heat and the slightly dusty scent of him making Diego's parched mouth water. "Makes me wonder what else they can do." His breath crashed against Diego's ear, and he shivered, leaning into the press of Trav's palm. "Come upstairs? Let me cook for you. I'd make dumplings, but I think my flour has turned. Chicken and rice sound good?"

"It sounds delicious."

Herbs and ingredients filled the countertop, and half a dozen spice jars crowded around a bag of self-rising flour Trav claimed had turned. Diego sat at the table, a glass of Tempranillo in hand, watching Trav cook and sliding his bare feet over the rug beneath the dining set. He closed his eyes and let the history of countless evenings spent at this table wind around his ankles and stitch up his calves: laughter and tears, minor arguments, and the rare impassioned encounter. Year after year of scenes witnessed by the rug and now told to him. The laughter and the passion faded from the most recent threads, overwhelmed by sorrow, bitter despair, and loneliness.

Diego followed those final threads to the mortal, frowning as they wove themselves in and around Trav, as attached to the man as Diego was to his Way. The easy silence of his apartment became heavy, tainted by an unacknowledged grief. It would be easy to release the thread and leave it alone, but Trav's grief was an ugly knot wound around an otherwise lovely skein, and Diego was a Stitch Witch.

"How long did Martin own the shop?"

"Thirty years or so." Trav focused on chopping a pile of fresh, green herbs. "He moved down from New York after his partner died."

"I'm sorry."

"I never knew him." He removed the lid from the skillet on the stove, and a cloud of steam filled the air with the decadent scent of braised chicken thighs, smoked paprika, garlic, and cumin. He squeezed half a lemon over the dish, and saliva pooled on Diego's tongue.

"He died in the AIDS epidemic," Trav spoke lightly, as though reciting a memorized history. "Most of Martin's friends did, which is why there wasn't a lot of help to be had." He dug a serving spoon into their dinner, filling low-walled bowls with orange-colored rice and roasted chicken thighs, garnishing them with slices of lemon and sprinkling cilantro and parsley over each. "Said he wanted a fresh start after that. Couldn't stand the pity and the way people treated him when Jonathan died, so he quit his job, sold everything they owned, and moved to Key West. Bought the pawnshop off the previous owner a year later and made up the rest of his income with the salvage dives."

"And he never found another partner?"

Trav took up both bowls and headed for the table, hips swaying with each step. "He said he wasn't interested. Jonathan was his world, and while the world didn't end with him, Martin lost his desire to find a new one." He set a bowl in front of Diego, topped off his wine glass, and finally sat across from him, gesturing to their dinner. "Hope this is alright. I would've made a flatbread, but I think my flour's turned."

"This is lovely," Diego said, reaching for the wine bottle to fill Trav's glass. "And you?"

"Me?" He straightened, blinking back at Diego.

"You have lived down here for some time, long enough for Martin not to have left you alone."

"Oh." Trav looked down at the table, finger trailing the edge of his fork. "I have a few friends left over from high school." Peering over the top of his frames, he sent Diego a sheepish smile. "It was hard transferring in as a senior. I stuck with the other weirdos and outcasts. My closest friend was probably my Spanish practice partner, but she moved north for college like the rest."

"And no ... partners?" Diego pulled his napkin from the table and set it on his lap as an excuse to look away.

"Oh, I've had partners," Trav's voice held a smile. "Tourists in town for a week or two, a few boyfriends, but no one seems to stick around." He let that sit for a moment, and only when Diego looked up did he realize Trav had been waiting for him to do so. A sly grin curved his lips, hazel eyes gleaming from the candles he had lit on the table. "Worried about competition?"

"Competition? *I* am incomparable." He swept his glass from the table and tapped the rim against Trav's. "A treasure among men."

He pressed his wine glass to his lips, slipping out a reply before drinking. "I'd say you have me fairly convinced."

The conversation devolved to a place of everythings and nothings uttered between bites of food and sips of wine. Their dinner, braised chicken and Spanish rice that sent Diego reeling to a place long gone and far away, was delicious, and the man across from him even more so. In the privacy of his apartment, it was easier to breathe and be. Easier to get swept away in Trav's every tiny chuckle and how he focused on Diego and Diego alone.

As though he were the most important thing in the room.

The attention was a drug, lulling him into a limber, relaxed state. Never had he been the focus of such a direct, intentional gaze, never had he had the luxury of attention, and it was almost too much to bear. So much of his second life had been focused on Milla—ensuring she drank her tea, helping her manage the demesne and the occult boards, keeping her from scaring away the customers. And then there was all of the drama around the raw-head and whatever had happened in St. Augustine, the severity of which he still did not know, thanks to Milla refusing to answer her phone or return his messages. But this? Diego and a handsome man in a private space?

This was for Diego. Every quiet song hummed as Trav cooked their dinner, each suggestive glance and brush of fingers against his bare arm...this was just for him.

He could barely remember the last time something had been *his* in either of his lives. Bimini Bespoke, his custom tailoring, was run out of Milla's store, his business license attached to the visa she had secured with Morgen's help. It was no more his than it was a facade to hide behind.

In Zaragoza, he had assisted his hippocromantic sister, applying his Way on her home visits to heal broken women and injured men, returning home covered in blood only to be roused from his bed to start over again. He had been a tool deployed on the dying, his tailoring relegated to stitching wounds.

In de Leon's fleet, he had been one of the shortest, the slimmest, the most effeminate. His role on those voyages had been decided for him. Diego was not above a man's needs at sea for weeks at a time, but they had never asked about his desires or preferences. His lot had not been terrible, but neither had it been for him.

These coy glances and the way Trav tipped his head to the sofa, grabbing the bottle of wine and asking Diego if he cared for more … this was his.

"I can't thank you enough," Trav was saying, but all of Diego's attention was drawn to the finger trailing up the inside of his arm. Goosebumps raised as Trav circled the sensitive skin at the crook of his arm. "I'd be lost with all of the inventory. Was barely managing, to be honest."

"Dinner was enough," Diego managed. His throat was tight, and a deep hunger stirred even with a belly full of wine and arroz con pollo—one he had ignored for far too long.

"I doubt that." Trav pulled his hand away, sliding the glasses from his face and dropping them on a narrow table running along the back of the couch. With a smooth move, he swept the wine glass from Diego's hand and set it on the side table beside his own. "May I?"

The question lingered as Diego, distracted and starved, tried to parse the meaning in those two little words.

"The front door is locked, as is the door to my apartment. The curtains are drawn; it is just you" —he dropped his hand inside Diego's thigh, sighing happily when he widened his legs just enough for Trav to slide that hand higher— "and me."

He leaned closer, his chest pressing against Diego's arm and those hazel eyes boring into him. The lamplight's reflection drew attention to the multihued halo of green bleeding moss into the bronze.

"May I?"

He nodded, afraid to look away or speak for fear of spoiling the moment. A happy sigh left Trav as he swept his hand higher, cupping Diego and humming when he shivered. A thrill of pleasure shot into his groin, and he gripped the arm of the sofa to keep from rutting into his hand. Trav leaned closer, brushing his lips tentatively against Diego's cheekbone, his cheek, and finally, Diego turned toward his pawnbroker, connecting their lips in a soft, testing press.

Trav melted against him, sweeping his thumb over the modest length of Diego again and again until he thickened and groaned at the sensation.

"Trav ..."

"Is this alright?"

"Más que." He brought his hands to Trav's waist, pulling him into his lap and trapping his hand between them. "Do not stop," he panted, catching Trav's mouth and begging against his lips. "Por favor."

And there were no words after that. As on the beach, Trav kissed him deeply, denying Diego oxygen because to breathe would mean breaking away, and he refused to break away from this. He was safe, locked away with a man in his lap who kissed like Diego was his first meal in weeks.

His tongue swept deep, that hand working Diego's cock through his pants until he could no longer resist the urge rising in his hips. He rolled into Trav's measured grip, inhaling sharply through his nose when Trav swept his swollen head with a thumb.

He worked his other hand under the untucked placket of Diego's shirt, skimming up his torso and brushing a nipple. Pleasure shot straight into his center. He wrenched his mouth from Trav's, gasping and tightening his grip on the mortal's hips. Holding him in place as he rolled into his palm, groaning at the pressure and the tease. Trav nibbled on the lobe of his ear before lightly sucking at a spot on Diego's neck that had his eyes rolling back.

Trav relentlessly stroked, teasing that same spot with his lips, teeth, and tongue until Diego's strangled groans became outright moans. The rolling of his hips became hasty, seeking a release, needing skin against skin, touch, pressure, *anything* other than this maddening tease.

"I've got you," Trav whispered, breath hot against Diego's ear. The hand that had worked him into a state drifted to his belt, easily undoing the leather and his button.

He slid down Diego's front, sucking at his pulse point and flicking his tongue in the hollow of his throat, descending his body as that hand worked the zipper, easing the strain on his cock. Practiced fingers flicked the buttons on his shirt, and Trav spread the fabric aside, glancing briefly up at Diego before sweeping his tongue over one nipple, the other. Diego arched his back, seeking more of Trav's attention, and his kiss-swollen lips spread in a smile.

"Lift your hips," he whispered against Diego's navel. He was helpless but to obey. He raised his hips, gasping as Trav mouthed the head of his cock. Even through the cotton of his briefs, the warmth was mind-melting, and every desire Diego held in this life narrowed down to his cock in that mouth.

His hands sought purchase, grasping Trav's arms, his shirt, the couch, until finally, he curled his palm around the back of his neck. His fingers caught in a thin chain before knotting in all that glorious, floppy hair.

"Dulzora." Diego scaled his nails along Trav's scalp, thrusting into his mouth without intending to. Diosa, the man had worked him into a state, hazel eyes gleaming as he grinned around the head of Diego's cock, looking oh-so-pretty on his knees. "Por favor, dulzora, *please.*"

"Ciertamente." He hooked his fingers in the waistband of Diego's briefs, tugging to free his cock. The absence of fabric, moistened by Trav's mouth, was jarring enough to have Diego hissing—a hiss that eased into a gasp at the first brush of lips against his swollen, dripping head.

Hands at Diego's knees, Trav slid his palms up the inside of his thighs, spreading him wider to accommodate his shoulders. He teased Diego's shaft with his fingers, tonguing the rim of his head just this side of satisfying until Diego's legs trembled.

"You smell so good, Diego," he murmured, kissing up the length of his cock as he circled his fingers, spinning his wrist in a smooth stroke. "How do you always smell so fucking good?"

Without warning, Trav hitched high and took him down to the hilt. A groan erupted, stars bursting behind his eyes, and the witch tipped headlong into the sensation. Slick, wet heat, suction, and—"¡Diosa!"—Trav cupped his scrotum, kneading and tugging lightly, his tongue rolling against the underside of his cock.

The urgency Diego had felt at a stroke of the man's hand rose to dangerous heights. His breaths came in tiny, desperate pants, and he fought against the urge to thrust deeper, harder, wanting to draw out the beauty of this moment, of this man who was just his. Pleasuring him on his knees with color riding high on his cheeks. Trav's right hand disappeared from Diego's knee, falling out of sight while his left continued to tug and tickle, teasing the bridge of flesh behind his scrotum.

He was only half aware of the choked moans and equally urgent need in the man between his legs. Utterly lost to sensation and need until it was all at once too much.

His grip tightened in Trav's hair, hips thrusting of their own accord as a burbling heat rose, unable to be contained. Trav knew, he must have known, because that damned hand between Diego's legs slid back, his finger pressed into puckered flesh, and Diego unraveled with a shout.

Pulse after pulse, he released into Trav's mouth, who—Diosa bless the man—kept working Diego through his orgasm. Tongue rolling, cheeks hollowing, throat bobbing as he swallowed. Diego's head fell back, the room spinning as he shivered with the aftershocks. Only when Trav let his sated cock slip from his mouth did he recognize the sound of twinned pants and happy sighs. He raised his head, blinking down at Trav, grinning sheepishly at him from the floor.

"Can I..."

"No need." He reached for a box of tissues on a shelf beneath the table, cleaning release from his hand. "God damn, you're pretty when you come."

Diego blinked, jaw-dropping at the brazen language, at being called...pretty. Heat blossomed on his chest, climbing into his cheeks as he struggled for the words, the sentiment to share. He wanted to thank Trav, wanted to haul him up from the ground and into his lap to riddle his body with as much pleasure as the man had given Diego, and the thought of it made his face burn.

SEVEN

"—FOR NOW," MORGEN'S VOICE ribboned up from the kitchen, slowing Diego midway down the spiral staircase. "And the items are being cataloged by one of my own, we will know if anything goes missing."

"I'd be offended if the accusation wasn't warranted," a man replied. His tone was light but sharp, a jest hiding the seriousness of the topic. "We'll keep the pack in line."

"As best we can," a woman added. "But you know how they get—one of them catches scent of a trail and the rest follow. It's only a matter of time before—"

"My witch has assured me the process will be speedy, a week at most," Morgen said, the dismissal in her voice clear. "All you need do is keep your cultists at bay until we are ready to commence removal of the items in question."

"Why wait?" the woman pressed. "Wouldn't it be better to grab them one by one rather than en masse?"

"Tammy has a point," the man said. "Trav knows me, and I was close with his predecessor. It won't be weird if I pop in and grab a few items at a time."

Diego stilled at that, one hand against the stone and toes at the edge of a stair. Trav had not mentioned knowing any of the local cultists, but it stood to reason Martin had been familiar with them. Horned God, it would have been impossible not to be with the amount of occult items in the store.

Already, his palms were itching to get back to the store, his Way prickling with the need to unspool the magick choking every aisle. Though his Way was not entirely to blame—after last night, he was as anxious to get back to Trav as he was to clear the backroom.

Never in Diego's many years had he felt so safe or so free to act on his whims. His life in Zaragoza had been spent glancing over his shoulder and keeping an ear out for any passers-by whenever he was lucky enough to meet with a like-minded witch or man. While sailing in de Leon's fleet was better, the needs of men acknowledged and blithely ignored by witnesses, it had always felt as though he were performing a service or was merely a man of convenience in location, willingness, and size.

But the way Trav had gazed at Diego, how he had asked permission and slid to his knees ...

His body was still humming with pleasure when he left the pawnshop, his arms aching for the weight and comfort of Trav. He had fallen asleep half-hard, kicking himself for returning to the tower, and woken with a pressing need for relief.

Bendita la Diosa for ensuite bathrooms and modern plumbing.

He could not remember a time he had worked himself so desperately to the memory of a man's mouth around his cock. Whenever he closed his eyes, the image of Trav on his knees, hair tumbling over his brow, appeared as clearly as if painted by a master's hand. Trav's quiet moans of pleasure echoed in Diego's mind as the run of the shower drowned his stifled groan.

Emptied but nowhere near sated, he had dressed and headed down the stairs, eager for a quick cup of tea to warm his hand on the walk to Southernmost Pawn, only to be stopped by Morgen and the cultists in her kitchen.

"There are a handful of pack members we can trust with this," the woman, Tammy, said. "We'll keep a record of what they buy so you can compare it to your witch's notes."

The following silence stretched. Diego picked up the tapping of a nail against a teacup, the Morgenhexe deep in thought. It stopped abruptly, and she called up the stairs, "Are you going to join us or spend the morning lurking at the threshold?"

Diego flinched, feet slipping off the stairs. He scrabbled at the wall, grabbing the railing to keep from skidding down the remaining steps and tumbling into the kitchen. He gathered himself and descended the rest of the way, ready to greet the cultists and tell them to, in his roommate's words, kindly fuck off. The items were nowhere near cataloged enough, he and Trav still needed to determine what was salvage, and what was taken in through legal means. They needed to present the potentially historical items to the authorities, not hand them over to magick-hungry cultists under the direction of some backroom—or rather, kitchen—deal.

Diego had barely entered the room when a man with sun-bronzed, shaggy hair rushed forward. He grabbed Diego's hand in one of his, clamping down on his wrist with the other and shaking furiously.

"Hey, man. Nice to see you again. I'm Josh, and this is Tammy." He tossed his head at a woman near Diego's height. "We run the cultists down here in the Keys. You've been helping out at the pawnshop?" He closed his eyes, inhaling and starting up again before Diego could answer. "Oh, yeah. Yeah, you have. That's the good stuff right there."

Diego leaned away from the man who had just *smelled* him, attempting to wrench his hand free. "Qué estás—"

"Josh." Tammy wandered over, a stern, serious expression on her face. Somewhere in her mid-to-late twenties, she wore her dark brown hair in a ponytail secured with a bright teal scrunchi. Her apparel was casual but high-end: an off-the-shoulder cotton shirt in mauve with *But did you die?* printed in bold script, worn over a shimmery gray compression top and paired with yoga pants that must have set her back at least a hundred dollars. The material clung to strong legs and generous hips, and Diego's fingers twitched for want of measurements, needle, and thread. With her complexion and hair, a deep emerald a-line dress would do well. A boatneck to draw the eye outwards, chiffon for the underskirt. "Release the witch, dude."

Josh froze, one eye creaking open. He sent Diego an embarrassed half smile and released his hand and arm.

Like Tammy, he was dressed casually, as though they had wandered in from the gym, but where her attire announced means and taste, Josh's was more worn and relaxed. Board shorts hung low on his hips, and his muscle tank was frayed at the hem. Tiny holes pockmarked the fabric, though whether from moths or having been tumble-dried with jeans, Diego could not tell without a touch. He was lean, a rangy sort of thin one saw on runners or surfers, deeply tanned from living in the Keys, and vaguely familiar.

"Oh, dang, man." Josh ran a hand over his head and cupped the back of his neck. "My bad."

"It is alright." Diego waved him off. "Have we met?"

"Saw you in the store the other day," Josh said. "Pity she bought that Lunar Sextant before I could." He jerked his thumb at Morgen, who straightened in her seat—an accomplishment, considering her posture was rigid as a board at all times.

Diego scrutinized him, flitting his gaze from head to foot and coming up short. "You are a cultist?"

"Doesn't look like much, does he?" Tammy grinned, the corners too sharp and her eyes too serious. "He's the head of our pack, keeps everyone in line, though you'd never know he was capable at first glance." She stuck out her hand, and Diego accepted it, startled by the firm grip and singular jostle of his arm before she released. "Tammy, in this room, CicerHoe to the pack. And that one is Pubeus Virginus."

Diego sputtered, his brain struggling to catch up to the announcement. "P-Pubeus?"

"It's a pun." Josh hooked a thumb under the neck of his muscle tank, pulling free a cord necklace. Strung amid a colorful assembly of craft beads was the name

Pubeus Virginus spelled out in letterblocks. "Not their best, but arguing the name usually earns you a worse one."

"I do not..." Diego looked to Morgen for help. She waved him off.

"Es ist besser, wenn du nicht tust."

He cast a sidelong glance at the witch, reaching out with his Way and letting it pick at her words until the meaning formed in his mind.

It's better if you don't.

Diego snorted, turning away from the cultists to pour a cup of tea. When he had taken his first sip, Tammy cleared her throat and elbowed Josh, jerking her head in Diego's direction.

"Oh, right, yeah." He fiddled with the hem of his shirt. "As you probably overheard, Morgen wants our help removing some of the occult items from Southernmost Pawn."

"The lower-level stuff," Tammy added, "like the Lunar Sextant. Things he's already cataloged and registered with the Monroe County Sheriff."

"And you'll let us know what you find so we can keep ahead of innocent mortal buyers," Josh finished. "Wouldn't want anything falling into the wrong hands, right?"

"And you will give them to C.R.O.W.?"

"Not C.R.O.W.," Morgen cut in. "The items will be stored safely on Big Torch Key." She named the Enforcer Training Base on the northernmost of the Torch Keys, twenty miles east of Key West, and the only key not traversed by US Highway 1. Less than a mile wide at its broadest point, the narrow spit of land boasted barracks, multiple casting ranges, an arena, classrooms, and Morgen's office. For most of the year, Big Torch hosted all manner of witches undergoing training as Aural Insurance Investigators, or Enforcers, as they were colloquially known.

Witch hunters, brutes, and liars, as Diego thought of them.

The order had been borne out of a response to the Spanish Inquisition, hunting witches Forbidden and Foule and burning them alongside innocent men and women whose greatest crimes were worshipping a God or loving people the Catholic Church disapproved of.

"Why do we need cultist intervention?" Diego asked. "I thought the plan was for me to catalog and list the items on the occult boards for Southern Gothic to—"

"Has Milla returned your calls?" Morgen cut him off, blue eyes sapphire cold. "No? How many days has it been since you last spoke with her, Diego?" He pulled his lips between his teeth, counting the days but not quickly enough. "The store is overrun with magick, and my foster daughter is off doing Horned God knows what with her Aural Insurance Adjuster. Until we have heard from her, this is our only means of securing the items before C.R.O.W. takes notice."

"Ever get the feeling you're only getting half the story?" Josh muttered to his companion.

"Now you know what it's like talking to you," she replied, dry as a desert wind.

Diego set his cup down hard enough to send a wave of tea sloshing over the side. "Why involve the cultists? If they do not get to keep the items, then what do they get out of this?"

"We look out for our own," Tammy said with no little amount of pride.

Morgen's mouth turned down. "They continue to enjoy the benefits of operating in my demesne." Her words were measured and even, sending a warning trill up Diego's spine. He edged away from the table as she rose. "Ours is a symbiotic relationship that shores up my demesne's defenses. If my foster daughter is unwilling to recognize that within her territory, then at least I may rest assured one witch under her jurisdiction, a witch she *trusts*, is aware of the importance of the relationship between witches and the cult."

"What can cultists do for a demesne?" he scoffed, thinking better of it at the Morgenhexe's answering glare.

"I recognize that you were dead for the greater half of a millennium, Diego, but it would behoove you to pick up a history book now that you are a member of the twenty-first century."

"Whoa, alright, I'll take this one." Tammy slipped between them, putting her back to Morgen, which, Diego thought, was a bold move. But when Morgen neither protested nor turned the mortal into a frog, when she moved aside to let Tammy speak, he stepped back and reconsidered the mortal woman. The ease with which she diffused their argument and the boldness with which she stepped *in front* of the Morgenhexe told him much about the trust between them.

"We're mortal," she said. "We can slip into crowds where a witch would be noticed and can spread our numbers wide across a territory. We aren't disturbed by salt or running water and can act outside of C.R.O.W.'s rules."

"And how much have you told them about C.R.O.W.?" Diego asked, leaning around Tammy to address the elder witch in the room.

"Please, like your coven is a secret?" Josh slid beside Tammy. "We hunt magick and magickal items; it's what we *do*."

"Not like we have a choice," Tammy muttered. "Which brings us to the matter at hand: your pawnbroker is in trouble."

"I knew that."

"But do you understand to what extent?" Josh lowered his voice. "It wasn't a coincidence I was in there the other day. The damn store is a like a beacon. It's stuffed with magick, and it's only a matter of time before someone else in the cult or, God help us, a tourist, stumbles across the trove. We need to get all of that magick out of there."

"Immediately," Tammy added.

"As soon as possible," Josh agreed.

"Those mean the same thing." Diego danced around them, addressing Morgen. "You used to sit on the Tribunal, surely you can—"

"I am the Morgenhexe." The air around her began to gleam, a halo of light framing her head and shoulders. "I was here at the founding of C.R.O.W., and I will be here at its downfall."

Diego sent her a flat look. "That is upsettingly prophetic."

The witch waved him off, light dimming. "I can no more act outside of our laws and regulations than my foster daughter can."

"Considering she has run a demesne for the last two years as a Death Witch, which, last I checked, was número uno on the scale of All Things Wicked, I think you can find it within yourself to bend the laws a little."

She tipped her head in acknowledgment, and Josh tapped him on the shoulder.

"What do you have against cultists?"

"Nothing."

"Then what's the problem?"

"I—" Diego shut his mouth, not ready to discuss the discomfort he felt at the thought of the cultists anywhere near the pawnshop.

An ugly emotion burbled in his belly, the same he had felt when a horde of internet trolls threatened Milla and her store. In his first life, Diego was unable to spare his sister when the horde came; he had no hope of fleeing the crowd in Santiago de Compostela with Ruben when the Inquisitors swarmed. In his second life, he hoarded Milla like a treasure. Protecting the broken witch and stitching the pieces back together until she was able to tend her demesne and smile. His protectiveness of her was borne from two witches banding together against a world neither fully understood, whereas this was something else altogether. Something new and precious, and Diego was not ready for the witchy world to take notice.

"I do not see the need for you to intervene," he paced out. "Not yet."

"That decision is not yours to make." Morgen stubbed a finger against the table. "The cultists will visit the store and purchase the items you identify as ready for sale, leaving you free to focus on more pressing matters." Her decree straightened the backs of witch and mortal alike. "Joshua and Tamara will manage the purchases, supervising other members of the Key West Cult to ensure not a tickle of suspicion raises the head of your beau."

"I—"

"I am old, Diego, not blind." She leveled a look his way. "Your pawnbroker will remain none the wiser. You have trod carefully thus far; I do not see a reason to upset the apple cart."

"I thought they sold them in crates?" Josh whispered to Tammy, who nudged him with her elbow.

"We'll need a demonstration," she said to Diego. "You're new to the demesne; if we're familiar with your breed of magick, there's less chance we'll confuse you for the cursed item."

At *that*, Diego jerked his head around to glare at Morgen. "You told them?"

"You were not making any progress."

"It has only been *three days*!" he hollered. "Por la Diosa, what progress did you expect? That I would fashion a dousing rod to sniff it out?"

"I would not expect you to sniff out anything. Thus, the cultists."

"If the curse is as powerful as you described"—this came from Josh, whose easy manner had hardened enough that it was easy to imagine him leading a pack of magick-starved cultists—"we need to be able to single out its particular stink. If there is a magickal flare beyond the pawnshop, we need to be sure it's not you."

"Big Torch Key is riddled with Enforcers," said Diego. "Surely you have encountered a Stitch Witch or two."

"C.R.O.W. deemed your particular Way too weak to be of any use as an Aural Insurance Investigator," Morgen said. "We have not had a Stitch Witch train as an Enforcer on Big Torch for half a century."

Diego stared blankly at her, working through the flash of anger and caught in memories of opening flesh and picking through sinew and viscera, the long-forgotten feel of blood on his hands a sticky, sensory miasma. He clenched his fists against the rise of bile and the tremor in his fingers. Morgen tipped her head in deference, acknowledging the insult C.R.O.W. had paid toward his Way.

"As I said, Master de Bimini, I was here at the founding of C.R.O.W. I know much about the Ways that has been forgotten by its current leadership."

He eased his stance, filing the information away. He knew there was contention among witches regarding the laws and regulations of C.R.O.W. Knew there were covens of witches longing for a return to the wild, unregulated Ways. How could he not? His roommate had damned herself in a ritual intended to reintroduce wild magick to the world. The act had lost Milla her mentor and her anonymity, and she had retreated to St. Augustine, licking her wounds and restraining her Way until she was powerful enough for one last great act of magick.

Only instead of her mentor, she had gotten Diego.

Milla was one voice among the many witches considered Forbidden and Foule, and the cryptids, creepies, and crawlies C.R.O.W. lumped together as "Desecrants." The battle between the Fine and Faire witches versus the Forbidden and Foule had been waged alongside the warring powers of Europe. It had formed the foundation of C.R.O.W. in the sixteenth century, but to hear Morgen speak so openly against their governing coven, against the very laws she had helped usher into existence—that was information worth heeding.

"Something simple, maybe?" Josh fluttered fingers at Diego's elbow, calling his attention to the many holes in his shirt. "A minor casting so we can filter your magick out from the rest."

"You can trust us," Tammy added. "We know what we're doing."

Josh whipped off his muscle tank and held it out to Diego. "Just a little stitch."

"Just a little stitch." He glanced at Morgen before accepting the shirt, laying it on the kitchen table, and examining the holes in the cotton. He could not argue the sense of their plan; the items needed to be removed. Without Milla and knowing what he did of the laws requiring Trav's compliance, third-party buyers were the cleanest route. Better still, third-party buyers under the scrutiny of the Morgenhexe. Still... "Give me more time," he pleaded. "Give me a chance to find the ouroboros on my own. A day—*two.* I do not want to risk anyone else touching la cosa maldita."

"Agreed."

Diego exhaled, nodding his thanks to Morgen and facing the cultists. "If I cannot find it, you will only come when I am at the store. You do not bother the owner, you do not ask about the items in the backroom until instructed, and you never mention anything about a curse."

The pair exchanged a glance, some unspoken conversation happening between them in a split second, and then they nodded. "Deal."

Diego lay his hands over the shirt, calling on his Way to speak with the threads. The cultists inhaled and shivered as his magick tingled to life, an arrow-straight drive of heat to his fingertips. He pinched and smoothed, easing threads from the weave and tying them back together, ironing the creases and joining the burned, frayed ends until each pockmark in the shirt vanished, the garment renewed. "De acuerdo." He whipped it from the table and tossed the muscle tank at Josh. "We are agreed."

EIGHT

"Mornin'!" Trav's bright smile set off a flurry of butterflies in Diego's stomach. His wide v-neck shirt showed off the line of his throat, and Diego followed its fall, relishing the empty store and the chance to *look*.

Trav crossed his arms, leaning against the counter as Diego drank his fill. Broad-shouldered and tan, trim torso, narrow hips, and legs he knew were muscled and strong but as lean as the rest of the man.

He set a coffee on the counter, nudging it toward Trav with a finger. "I hope the order is correct; the woman at the cafe said it was your usual."

Trav took a sip, eyelids fluttering. "Oh yeah, that's the right order. What did I do to deserve this?" Diego's cheeks heated. He dropped his gaze to the counter, tracing the outline of a sticker advertising the security system used on the premises. "Never mind," Trav chuckled. "That was answer enough."

"I..." he picked at the sticker. "Last night was lovely, I wanted to say thank you."

"You already did," Trav said. Behind the round lenses, a heat simmered in his eyes. He set his hand over Diego's, gently trailing fingers over his knuckles. "I've been thinking about you all morning."

"Yo también," Diego murmured, glancing around the empty store. He ought to warn Trav of what was coming or remove him from the threat of the cultists and C.R.O.W.

He misunderstood, squeezing Diego's hand again before slipping away. "You probably want to get to work. The room's unlocked."

"There is something else I would like to do first." Diego grabbed his hand and led him to the crowded backroom, shouldering his paranoia long enough to cup Trav's cheeks and kiss the man properly. Those plush lips yielded to his mouth, parting to allow Diego to dip his tongue in if he desired. He pulled away instead to whisper, "Good morning."

"Good morning indeed." Trav nuzzled Diego's neck, dropping light kisses that pebbled his skin. "I was sorry when you left last night." His hands roamed Diego's back, one settling at the curve of his rear while the other cradled his head, nails scratching lightly and sending a shiver down his spine. He arched his back, gasping as Trav nipped his lobe. "My bed was lonely without you in it."

"Por la Diosa." Diego gripped his hips, seeking out Trav's mouth to silence him before his words carried them up the stairs.

As before, his kiss demanded all of Diego and more. He worked them deeper into the room until Diego's backside hit the table. The contents of the boxes rattled, cardboard dug into his back. He gripped Trav's shirt, struggling to keep his feet on solid ground. Every sweep of his tongue produced a sensory explosion of cherry chapstick and raspberry mocha, a sweet mixture he would forever acquaint with the mortal man.

Trav worked a leg between his knees, half laying over him on the table. He rocked his hips into Diego, and the friction had him dropping his head back with a gasp. Trav took it as an invitation, dragging his lips the length of Diego's throat and sucking the crook of his neck.

"Trav," he sighed and cradled the back of his head, pushing him lower. Horned God, he had come here ready to work, determined to identify as many occult items as he could, and at one kiss, he was reduced to a panting mess. His cock ached for want of touch, and Trav's hands wandered everywhere but where he needed them. "Por favor."

"I've got you." Those words sent more blood to Diego's cock, and his eyes rolled back as Trav finally—*finally*—cupped his erection, thumb pressing down the hardening length.

"Ay diosa mía, te necesito, dulzuro, necesito—"

"Dulzuro," Trav gazed up at Diego, halfway to his knees. "No, baby, you're the sweet one." He slid a hand up Diego's front, dragging his shirt away and planting a kiss on his navel. "Sweet like sugar and just as addicting."

"Trav." He worked his fingers into all that floppy hair, pulling it back to see his lover's face. "Mi dulzuro—"

"Bergstrom?" A man's voice called from the front of the store. "Hey, kid, you in?"

Diego froze, all heat and sensuality of the moment curdling into fear. Afraid to move, afraid to speak, he fought to breathe, but his lungs had seized at that voice, strong with the command of an Inquisitor.

"God dammit." Trav dropped his forehead against Diego's stomach. "Ward has the worst timing." He huffed, reaching down to readjust himself before lifting his head. "That's the county sheriff, I need to—Diego?"

Goddess, he could not breathe. Any moment, the Inquisitor was going to push the door open. He would see what they were doing, and there was nowhere to hide, no way to explain it away as anything but what it was.

"Hey, D." Trav stood over him, blocking Diego's view of the door. He cupped his cheek, and Diego jerked away, scrabbling off the table to distance them. "Diego, it's alright. It's just the sheriff here for the registry."

"Go," he croaked. "Ve, before he comes back here."

Trav pursed his lips, studying Diego for a beat before nodding. He brushed a hand against his shoulder in a gesture that was half forgiveness and half understanding and closed the door behind him.

Diego gripped the table's edge, head hung low as he worked to ground himself in the modern world. This was not Zaragoza. There were no more

Inquisitors, no need to fear being seen with a man in these new days. Diego knew this; he had seen it with his own eyes in films and read it in the books Milla kept on the shelf, but he had not experienced it in his very short time in modernity. The last year had been spent learning how to adapt, how to *live*, and teaching his roommate to embrace the same.

Milla would have told him he was being foolish, acknowledging his fears while drily observing only old men held on to old prejudices. She would have demanded to meet Trav, interrogating the mortal within an inch of his life before buying him a drink and leaving Diego to his own devices. Without her, he felt as though he had had a leg lopped off at the knee. For as much as she wished to remain unseen and ignored by the world, no witch lived louder or burned brighter than Milla, and Diego desperately needed her special brand of support at this moment.

He pulled his phone free and dialed, watching the screen as the call connected. Three rings and her voice chided him across the miles.

"Whoever this is, text me like a normal, modern human being."

"Where in the infierno are you?" he snapped and slammed his phone down. Trav's muffled voice came through the door, answered by the deeper voice of the sheriff, Ward. Diego tensed. The heat of their shared moment had passed; he had nothing to hide or fear alone in this room, but still, he exhaled as the voices carried up the stairs.

Shaking out his hands, Diego spun slowly, reviewing the room. He could not fix the fears of his past and could not will himself to accept this new world any faster than he was able to, but he could do something about this room.

He dove head first into his Way, picking and pulling at threads within the knot of magick, utterly absorbed in his task and increasingly frustrated by the hour. Trav checked on him after the sheriff left, asking questions Diego only half answered. He had no idea when Trav wandered off or how much time had passed. The moment he dropped into his Way, all else ceased to exist beyond the blinding mass of magick and Diego.

He could snag a thread with his pinky and half a thought in his first life, following the magick to the source. His sister had marveled at the ease with which he identified rot and infection in their patients, and she would follow his Way with her healing magick, removing the taint so Diego could stitch them back up again.

In this pawnshop, he was adrift in a sea of magick. It was noisy, a grating static that drowned out the world and made it impossible for Diego to concentrate on the thread he sought. A pulsing headache pinched the base of his skull, throbbing with every beat of his heart, but he ignored it through frustration and sheer willpower, working item by item and diving further into his Way to disentangle what he could. His piles grew, the Not Occult outweighing the Occult, with no ouroboros to be found. So he called on more and more of his Way, plucking strands and dragging them from the mass, working until the pounding in his skull became too loud, too sharp to ignore, and a voice shouted, "Diego!"

He dropped the record he had been handling and spun around, vision blurring. The backroom tilted, and he gripped the table's edge. "¿Qué?"

"Welcome back," Trav drawled. He leaned against the doorframe, waggling fingers in a tentative wave. "Don't suppose I can persuade you to take a break?"

"What time is it?" Diego croaked. He flexed prickling fingers that felt as though he had been sitting on his hands until he lost all feeling, and the blood was just now returning to his extremities. He knelt, clumsy fingers fumbling at the album. Trav tsked and strode into the room, sweeping the record from the floor.

Full of first pressings and thrift store finds, the last three crates on the table must have belonged to a dead or down-on-his-luck hipster. Most of the records were harmless, but a handful of hexed and allured albums were tucked among them, lying in wait like a snake in the grass.

Goddess knew how much time he spent de-sleeving and running his fingers over the grooves, cleaning each vinyl before re-sleeving those he deemed harmless. To his annoyance, they weren't organized in any discernible way, so he'd been alphabetizing the crates as he worked.

"Three, and I'm closing early today." He jerked his chin at the Occult pile. "You've gotten through a lot. These ready for me to match to the register?"

"Sí." Diego reached for the album in Trav's hand. "If they have a record, I can list them on the Occult Boards."

"Fantastic." He flipped the vinyl over, scanned the tracklist, and grinned. "Oh, shit, Annie Lennox. *Diva* is a classic!" Trav darted out the door. Piano chords filled the store a moment later, joined by strings and Trav's voice. Diego smiled to himself, flexing sore fingers as he left the backroom. Annie broke into the first verse, Trav grew louder, and a new thread of magick ribboned through the store.

He froze, startled by the clarity. After a day trudging through the thick haze, this was a slap to the face and a cold bucket of water, yanking the witch from his fatigue and setting off every internal alarm.

Hex, his Way whispered in warning. *Allure*, the magick teased across his cheek, turning his head.

He jerked his hand up, grabbing the thread before the dense, impermeable cloud absorbed it. It twitched in his fingers, prickling and sticky like uncarded wool. Tiny nettle-like splinters broke from the weave and bit into his fingertips. He blinked, too sluggish to parse out what his Way was trying to tell him, and deeper in the store, a glass shattered.

And another.

He dropped the thread and ran, skidding around a corner and gripping a shelf to keep from barrelling into a field of destruction.

Shattered mirrors, bell jars, and vases filled the aisle, their jagged edges glinting under fluorescent bulbs. Halfway down, Trav swung his baseball bat, sweeping items from the shelf and singing with abandon.

Prickling, sticky magick hung in the air like a humid summer morning. Diego's fingers twitched, recognizing the magick as a hex, but of which Way? Audiomantic was his best guess. Dancing Plagues had been common i,n the sixteenth century deployed by witches holding entire villages hostage until their demands were met. If that is what this was, all he needed to do was gain Trav's attention long enough to dismantle the magick.

Distraction was the key.

"Trav!" Diego clapped his hands together. The bandages on his palms muffled the sound, and he switched to snapping his fingers. "Trav, listen to me."

In response, Trav spun and swung his bat, knocking a glass ball off the shelf. Despite the mess, he wore a broad smile, eyes glazed with the tell-tale haze of a mortal deeply bewitched. Diego cursed, kicking glass away to clear a path as he edged into the aisle.

"Trav!" he tried again. "Travis, look at me."

"Dance with me, Diego!" He threw his arms out, knocking a porcelain ballerina off the shelf. "This is the best part!"

Annie Lennox wailed into the bridge, trilling in a loud soprano. Diego scanned the shelves for a stick, a broom, cymbals, anything to clear the glass or overpower the hex.

"If you won't dance, I will!" Trav shouted. He tossed the bat aside and kicked off a shoe. Diego cursed. Dancing plagues focused on the movement, exhausting the afflicted until they collapsed. Rarely did they come with the urge to dance *and* sing.

A different hex, then. Pied Piper?

The Pied Piper had been especially prevalent in the German states when Diego was first alive, but that was a "follow-the-leader" compulsion, not a "remove your shoes to walk barefoot on broken glass" compulsion.

Trav toed off his other shoe and stepped onto a shimmering pile of sharp edges. His voice hitched, dying out with the song's last line, and in the ensuing silence, he whimpered, "Diego?"

"Stay where you are." Diego kicked more glass aside, inching into the aisle. He could easily reach him from an adjacent aisle, which meant turning his back when he had Trav's attention. "Do not move, okay? Stay still, do not step on—"

The opening chords of "Walking On Broken Glass" cut in, the song replaying from the beginning. Trav blinked, his momentary confusion vanishing under a blissful smile, and he began to sing again, edging deeper into the aisle.

"Mierda." Diego plucked, pinched, and tweaked magick threads, seeking the hex's sticky prickle. Allures whisper free, calling to Diego. A vanity hex collapsed onto a pile of mirror shards, and Trav spun, bare feet stomping on glass. Tears leaked from the corners of his eyes, but still, he danced and sang, and Diego could not grab *hold*.

There were too many strands, too much magick in the store for one Stitch Witch to manage. The tendons in his fingers creaked as he fought against each thread, tugging, pulling, pinching. The song ended, Trav sobbed his name, and then that maldita canción began again.

Again.

It began *again*.

Diego whipped his head around, trying to remember where Trav stored the record players. Instruments and sporting equipment were near the front. Were radios one aisle over? Or two?

"It will be okay." Diego backed out of the aisle. "It will be okay, dulzuro. I can fix this." He hissed as a shard cut through the thin rubber sole of his shoe. With one last look at Trav, spinning, dancing, and sobbing, Diego ran.

The next aisle held clothing—suits and wedding dresses, shoes, and cuf-flinks—followed by power tools, a jukebox, clock radios, alarm clocks, and —*there*! At the front of the aisle sat a Thorens TD-125 MKII. Diego could have smacked himself for not attaching any magickal threads to the turntable. This model was one of the earliest turntables with electric speed control, designed by mid-century technomantics in Switzerland. Milla had its predecessor in her store and often used the latent magick in the machine to drive customers away.

"Gracias a la diosa por los pequeños favores." He hurried down the aisle and ran his hands along the sides of the turntable, grabbing the cord and following it to an outlet hidden by a row of speakers. One sharp tug. Cut off the source of the magick, spare the hexed mortal. Easy enough.

He yanked the plug from the wall, and the music kept playing.

"¿Qué?" Diego looked from the power cord in his hand to the empty outlet and back. "No. Nononono."

Across the shop, Trav sang in a shrill, pained voice. Diego threw the cord down and pulled the turntable to the edge of the shelf. He pushed the arm off the record, needle scraping over grooves, and Annie kept singing about her broken heart.

So he tore it free and threw it at the front window. Shards of *Diva* rained down on the front counter, and Trav kept singing.

"Oh, por Diosa, what *now*."

He hustled across the front of the store, working through the problem the way Milla would have: lay out what you know, connect the details to form a pattern and solve.

Removing power from the turntable and destroying the record would have dispelled any technomantic magick, and grabbing Trav's attention would have counteracted a hex. The moment before the song began, he had been able to gain Trav's attention again, but even without the music, he was still singing.

Although, Diego realized, *he was no longer dancing or clearing the shelves.*

So the technomantic magick in the record player had been effectively dispelled, which left him dealing with an audiomantic hex attached to the accursed rather than the item. A tandem hex, then, which would explain why he could not narrow it down to one particular thread amid the general noise of the pawnshop.

"I am here," Diego soothed. Trav looked over, wrapping his arms around himself as he sang, tears streaming down his face. "Do not move."

Eyes wide behind his glasses, Trav shook his head in tiny twitches as if he had water in his ears, beating the heel of his palm against a temple. "Get it out," he blubbered between verses, "please."

Diego pinched the air by his ear, his fingers cycling as he worked through the magick and finally felt the sticky prickle of that new magick. He followed it to

Trav, still beating the heel of his palm against his temple, and recognition flooded his senses.

An Ear Worm.

"Mierda." Diego scanned the store, spotting a pile of hockey sticks. He grabbed one, using the blade to sweep glass aside as he entered the aisle. Smaller shards prodded the soles of his shoes enough to have the witch swearing never to go without socks from this day onward. When Trav was within reach, he threw the hockey stick aside, gathering the trembling mortal in his arms. His skin was slick and sticky with a cold sweat, and his babbling had taken a feverish pace. Consonants and syllables fell off the words, the lyrics coming faster and faster as the Ear Worm sensed the threat of Diego.

"Shh, shh, dulzuro." Diego took as much of Trav's weight as possible, easing him off his feet and cradling him against his chest as he lowered to the ground. "I have got you; it is okay."

This close, the hex was an all-too-obvious spiral burrowing into Trav's mind like a weevil. He stroked his cheek, soothing him with nonsense words and a pacifying allure.

Ear Worms were slippery little cabrones. If Diego worked too quickly, or Trav jerked in his arms as he sought to remove the hex, it would double or triple its efforts, spiraling deep until even the most skilled Stitch Witch would struggle to remove it, driving the accursed victim mad in a matter of moments. Trav would be reduced to a murmuring, blubbering mass capable of little more than shitting himself and singing the same song over and over until it drove everyone around him mad.

It was a good thing, then, that Diego was a skilled Stitch Witch.

"Escúchame, cariño," he murmured, trailing the tips of his fingers around the shell of Trav's ear. He twitched, arching back against Diego, but the panicked cadence of the song eased. "Escúchame, do you trust me?"

Trav nodded, the faintest tremor of his head, and pressed his heels against the carpet, driving the shards of glass deeper.

"It is going to be okay; I have you." Diego kept his voice steady, working a soothing allure as he spoke and gauged the damage to Trav's feet. The hems of his pants were stained crimson, and from what Diego could tell, his feet were shredded and torn. He dropped his cheek against Trav's head, soothing the mortal until his trembling had eased and the song was a slur of consonants.

Only then did Diego address the Ear Worm. Closing his hand into a fist, he extended his little finger and pressed it into the canal, murmuring a dispellation into the weave of his allure.

"Ven a mí, amiguito."

Cool and calm, that was the trick. Remain calm, and never let the hex know how scared you are. Ear Worms fed off of fear and panic, increasing in power as they fed off the chaos of a frightened mind. He needed to keep Trav calm, needed to keep himself calm, and the hex would heed his summons.

"Ven a mí, amiguito." *Come to me, little friend.* "Ven a mí."

A tickle of thread swept over the pad of his finger. Diego exhaled, doubling down on his intent as he cajoled the hex closer, crooking his finger and catching hold of it outright. With an arm banded across Trav's chest, Diego held him tight, clenched his fist, and—"¡Cállate la boca!"—wrenched the hex free.

Trav tensed, his murmurs rising pitch until the song ended with a desperate scream. Diego held him tight, fighting against the thrashing in his hand. Magick bit at his fingers, seeking a new victim. He clenched his fist tighter, gritting his teeth against every pinch and poke until, with nowhere to go, the Ear Worm hex died a miserable, whimpering death.

Trav went limp against him, head lolling back and eyes unfocused. Panting, Diego eased his hold, patting his cheek and sweeping the hair away from his face. "Trav?" Every tendon in Diego's arm felt wrung out, his muscles bunching and cramping from overuse of his Way. "Trav, sweetness?"

"D?" He raised a shaking hand as if to cup Diego's cheek, only for the limb to drop heavily to the floor. "My feet," he whimpered.

"It will be alright," Diego promised, kissing his forehead. "I can help."

He nodded, and his eyes rolled back in his skull. The indiscernible fog of magick thickened, draping around the pair like a cloak, and Diego finally sobbed. Trav needed medical and magickal attention. Diego needed help.

But his phone was in the backroom, and Trav was too tall, too heavy to be carried out of the aisle, and dragging him would only cause more injury. Diego held him instead, whispering soothing words to keep him asleep and listening to his breathing to build his resolve. He needed Morgen and her cultists to clear the store. He needed Milla to answer her phone. He needed—

Sharp raps on the window jerked his head up. Diego blinked tears away, taking in the blurry figure of Josh, fist raised and ready to knock once more on the glass.

"Help me," Diego mouthed, clutching Trav tighter. "Help me, please."

NINE

"That was clumsy." Morgen glared at Diego from the door, her stern mien hewn from stone. "As a witch, you know better than to be seen."

"What was I supposed to do?" Diego threw down the diary he had been flitting through. Seeking a distraction from the hex and Trav, he had followed a weak thread of magick attached to a poem by a pre-teen witch just coming into her Way. Members of her family would have felt a connection to the diary, a sense of importance to the words of a girl witnessing the Civil War from her country home in Georgia, and determined its value generation after generation until it ended up in the back room of a pawnshop. "Leave him to samba on broken glass until his feet were ground to nubs?"

"You are so like Ludmilla," Morgen replied. "Sentimental to a fault. The proper response would have been to knock the mortal unconscious and call me." She tilted her head forward. "Immediately."

"I did," Diego protested. "The moment Josh and I had him free of the glass."

The cultist had been a Goddess-sent blessing. Together, they had gotten Trav upstairs, stretching his lank out on towels in the bathroom. Diego had begun working on his feet, cleaning the glass and stitching the wounds closed, stopping only when the cultist returned with Morgen and a chronomantic time witch.

"Yes, well." She twirled her hand in the air. "Regardless of *that*, it was still clumsy. A Stitch Witch your age ought to be able to determine one strand of magick from another. Is that not how your Way works?"

"Sí, but—"

"Then why are you wasting your time in a room packed to the gills with junk? Why have you not found this ouroboros?"

"Because I *cannot*." Slamming the diary down, Diego plunged his fingers into his hair. Exhausted, tired, *scared* of what else might lurk in this pawnshop. "It has all knotted together, and whenever I remove one strand, the rest pull tighter. I am afraid if I pull the wrong strand free, I will set off an-an avalancha of magick that is too big for me to contain." He let his arms drop to his sides and stared at the pile of occult items, their weight making it hard to breathe. "I held the album in my hands, Morgen. I should have felt the hex in the vinyl, and I should have sensed the hex in the turntable. I should have—"

"The Ear Worm was affixed to the grooves." Morgen stepped fully into the room, pushing the door half closed behind her. "And the Dancing Plague was worked into the turntable wiring, a piece of technomantic machinery invented far after your time. You would have never recognized the magick in the wires for what it was, nor would any witch worth their salt have expected you to do so."

"Trav was hurt," he stated. "A mortal was hurt in your demesne because of me."

"Mortals are hurt in Key West every day," she said. "I am caretaker of the demesne, not a babysitter of her citizens. If I worried myself over every stubbed toe or splinter, I would never get anything done." At that, Diego finally looked at her, finding concern and understanding where he was used to patient irritation. "It was quick thinking to unplug the record player and destroy the album, and you correctly diagnosed the Ear Worm. None but a Stitch Witch could have removed the hex with such skill. As clumsy as it was to miss the hex, you spared a life today. You ought to be proud."

He inhaled a shaking breath, centering himself on the unexpected compliment from the Morgenhexe. A bitter laugh escaped at the irony. Five hundred years ago, she sat on the Tribunal that ruled her foster daughter's brand of magick illegal. Five hundred years ago, that same Tribunal failed to protect the witches who had fallen out of favor with the ruling church of Europe. The wrong magick, the wrong religion, the wrong lovers.

The Tribunal's failure to act on behalf of their witches had sent Diego's sister to the pyre, had seen Ruben torn apart by an angry mob, and sent Diego fleeing to the ports of Lisbon where he signed his life away as a "Gentleman Volunteer" in de Leon's Armada.

And here she was, as tall and austere as ever and *proud* of him.

"Travis was hurt today," Diego stated. "He was hurt because we are not supposed to be seen."

"Diego—"

"He was hurt because we hide magick from mortals; we deprive the cultists access to the very thing that drives them out of their beds and onto the streets. He was hurt because we hold ourselves as separate and above the people who share this world with us. We let them get hexed and cursed, we allure them to do our bidding, and we *lie*, Morgen. We lie about what we are because C.R.O.W. thinks their little minds cannot handle the truth." A shadow flickered over the crack in the door, a tiny hum of magick seeping into the room. Diego stormed past Morgen and pulled the door open, coming face to face with a wide-eyed Josh. "He is proof mortals can handle the truth. Josh and Tammy and the rest of the cultists you bribe by pumping your magick into this demesne. This was not clumsy of *me*, Morgen. This was clumsy of C.R.O.W. for not evolving in the five hundred years I was dead."

"Whoa"—Josh put his hands up in surrender, eyes flitting over Diego—"lookin' good, man. Do you moisturize?"

"I —" Diego shook his head and wheeled around to glare at Morgen. "If we trained them what to look for, if we taught the mortals how to identify magick, how to protect themselves from hexes, then what happened today, what happened to de Leon"—*what happened to me*—"would never have happened.

Instead, we keep them in the dark and teach witches to be so afraid of their magick they can barely function!"

If Morgen was offended by Diego's criticism of how she had raised Milla, she did not show it. Stonefaced, she plucked the diary from the table, thumbing the frayed edge and contemplating the leather embossing. "My cultists will begin working with you tomorrow. Discover the ouroboros by the end of the week, or I *will* involve C.R.O.W."

Tossing the diary onto the table, she strode from the tiny room, nodding at Josh as she passed. Together, they watched the Morgenhexe leave the pawnshop, and only when the door closed behind her did Diego exhale and sag against the table.

"You got some balls for an old man." Josh sat beside him, nudging Diego with his shoulder. "Thought I was about to be first in line at the magickal buffet."

"I am either very brave or very stupid," Diego said. He dropped his head, pinching the bridge of his nose under his glasses. "Morgen could have me vanished with a snap of her fingers."

"You and me both, buddy." Josh rose and tapped his flip-flopped foot against Diego's shoe. "Best not to think about it and just get on with your life, you know?"

"No. I do not."

Josh shrugged, an inane little grin making him look even younger. "Even better. Less to worry about if you don't know what's happening." Diego had no reply to that, so Josh continued. "We've got you, Diego. You and Trav. The cult looks after their own."

"I do not even live here," he said. Josh shrugged and jerked his head toward the stairs.

"You should go up; the chronomantic she brought will run you through everything."

"Is he...?"

"He's alright, man, sleeping it off." The cultist dropped an arm around Diego's shoulders, guiding him from the room. "You did good. I once saw a cultist run himself into a heart attack while singing that Kate Bishop song at the top of his lungs."

"I am not sure I know it."

"I'm pretty sure he wishes he didn't."

The chronomantic sat at the kitchen table, surrounded by stacks of papers and folios and filing boxes from the backroom. He flipped through the register, scanning intake forms and the splayed photographs. Hesitating on a random form, he worried his lower lip between thumb and forefinger, then selected a photograph from the collection and clipped them together.

Diego stepped close enough to see the photograph: a red clay oil dispenser decorated with horizontal bands in a repeating pattern.

"Greek," the chronomantic said. His accent was thick, tripping off the tip of his tongue. "A family heirloom passed down through the generations." He turned in his chair and looked up at Diego. "A very large family, I would wager."

"What makes you say that?"

"Kitchen Witch allure." A stubby finger tapped the photograph. "Placed by the maker of the olive oil to enhance the taste, ensuring more is used than necessary. Harmless, really."

"Es eso así."

The chronomantic tipped his head to the side, studying Diego, so he took the opportunity to do the same. The man's face was utterly unremarkable. Two eyes, brown. A nose, neither hooked nor sloped, not too small, not too big. The jaw was a little weak, and his eyebrows a little too heavy, but not a singular feature stood out from the whole as memorable. It left Diego with the unsettling feeling that if this witch were to leave the room without him having taken a picture, it would be impossible to pick him out of a crowd.

"Your shopkeeper is sleeping," he stated. "Good work on his feet. I did what I could to reverse the age of the skin and avoid scars, but the older ones were beyond my capabilities."

"Older ones?"

"I suggested we call a hippocromantic, but Morgen advised against it. She said this was a delicate matter?"

"Somewhat," Diego said.

"Say no more." The chronomantic pushed back from the table and rose, coming eye-to-eye with Diego. "The team I work with specializes in delicate matters."

"It is lucky you were here then."

"Is it?" He smiled, the expression more practiced than genuine. "As I said, 'delicate matters'." He crooked his fingers as he spoke like Diego had seen Milla do a million times. "Morgen has been exceedingly helpful with our current assignment." Edging around Diego, the witch paused halfway to the stairs and twisted at the waist. "You are from St. Augustine, correct?"

"Sí."

He nodded and continued on his way. "Beautiful city."

Diego waited for his footsteps to fade, peering down the stairs to ensure himself the witch was gone. Josh stood sentry at the door, arms crossed, watching the chronomantic wander down the aisle and out the front door. After a moment, he nodded and glanced up the stairs at Diego.

"I'll lock up," he stated. "Go sit with Trav; they gave him some vinefica brewed thing to induce confusion; lucky dude won't remember a thing. He'll wake up thinking he took a mid-day nap and overslept."

"It feels too easy."

Josh's easy demeanor hardened, and for a split second, something ancient glinted in his eyes. "You and I both know magick is never the easy way." Whatever had peered back at Diego vanished, the cultist's shoulders relaxing. "He's in the bedroom; he should wake in an hour or so."

"Gracias."

"Think nothin' of it." He waved off Diego's thanks. "It's a rough world; we've got to look out for each other. Oh! On that note—are there any sweets up there?"

"I do not know, I can—"

"He'll wake up hungry. Anything sweet should work, but I find chocolate does the best."

And with that pearl of confusing wisdom, he left.

TEN

Unable to bear sitting still, Diego worked on the occult boards instead. Trav had made decent headway in matching items from the backroom to their intake forms and had organized his work in a way that was easy to understand. Stacks on the left were items past their 60-day holding period and ready for sale; those in the middle were still in holding; and to the right were the piles of unmatched photographs and forms.

He started on the left, building a spreadsheet using the application on his phone as Milla had shown him and entering the relevant data from the intake forms. Without a computer, the work was slow going, and he had just begun organizing a list of what was needed to create a trading account for Trav when shuffling footsteps from the bedroom raised his head.

Trav lingered by the partition, glasses dangling from a hand as he blearily squinted at Diego. The chronomantic, or maybe Josh, had changed him out of his bloodied pants and put him in a worn Key West High Swim Team shirt and a pair of flannel pajama bottoms. Had he not been recovering from a tandem hex, and had Diego not witnessed firsthand the state of his feet just hours prior, the sight of a sleepy, pajama-clad Trav with tousled bedhead would have clenched his heart.

Instead, Diego rose quickly, hands flat against the table to keep from running across the room and fretting over him.

"Hello," he forced out.

Trav slid his glasses on, and a sleepy grin spread across his face. "Hey, sorry about that, I must have—" a jaw-cracking yawn cut off his words. He stretched, raising his arms over his head. The hem of his shirt lifted, revealing skin and the faintest line of hair. "Drifted off. Wow."

"No problem."

Trav scratched his stomach idly as he neared the kitchen. His gait was steady; there was no limping or hint of injury. The t-shirt caught on his wrist, keeping that stretch of skin visible, and he paused at the edge of the kitchen, staring at the oven clock. "Eight? How long was I out?"

"You said you were going to lie down at three." The lie was bitter on his tongue, and he dropped his eyes to the forms on the table, unable to look at Trav as he spoke it.

"And you waited for me to wake up?"

"I—" Diosa, what did he say? The truth would only further enrage Morgen, but he did not want to lie to Trav. He could tell him he had hoped they could have dinner together or that he was worried about him, but would it make him sound too desperate? He danced his gaze over the forms, the photographs, his spreadsheet.

The occult boards.

"I wanted to list a few items on the auction sites," Diego managed. The omission felt wicked, like an outright lie, but he genuinely wanted to help Trav sell what they could through legal means. "Only, I do not have all the information I need to create an account for you."

Trav cocked his head, studying Diego before crossing the kitchen and settling behind him. His arms came around Diego's waist, hands clasping at his navel and pulling him back against a sturdy chest. The heat of him, the alarming comfort of his arms, was a welcome balm to the horrors of the day. Blood pulsed in Trav's arms, and his heartbeat was strong against Diego's back, the mortal hale and whole following his ordeal.

Trav nuzzled his neck and murmured into his skin, "Kind of you."

"It was nothing," he gasped. Trav nibbled his earlobe, hold tightening. Diego dropped his head back and eased some of his weight onto Trav. He hummed happily, the sound buzzing against Diego's neck and shooting low. "I think we have enough organized to set you up as a broker, and then we can—"

"Too much talking." A hand slipped under Diego's shirt, wandering up his front. Trav chuckled as Diego wriggled against him, sucking on the side of his neck and sealing it with a lick of his tongue and a gentle kiss. "You always smell so good."

He shivered at the praise and again when Trav blew lightly on the damp patch of skin. "Diosa, ten piedad."

"No mercy for you." Trav pulled his hand from under Diego's shirt, cupping his jaw and angling his head back. He kissed a line up Diego's throat, teasing below his navel with his other hand. "Not when you're so fucking sweet." His erection pressed against Diego's backside, a prodding tease driving him as insane as all of those tiny kisses, licks, and nibbles.

Horned God, when was the last time a lover had treated Diego like *this?* Treasuring his body and teasing him within an inch of sanity without fear of being discovered. Trav luxuriated in riling Diego up, growing harder by the second as he reveled in the pleasure of pleasuring. He worked the buckle of Diego's belt and undid the button of his pants, and his stomach violently growled.

"Uh." Trav froze, the tips of his fingers in Diego's pants. His stomach growled again. "Huh."

Diego angled his head, catching the mortal out of the corner of his eye. "I think we need to feed you," he said.

"Wow, yeah." Trav slid his hands away and stepped back, cold air rushing in where his heat had been. "Guess that's what happens when you skip lunch and sleep through dinner." He adjusted himself, cheeks flaming pink, and shot a bashful look at Diego. "Join me for dinner?"

"Of course," he said. "I am happy to cook if you do not mind me using your kitchen."

"I don't, but I want wine and something sweet and can only get one of those things here." Trav winked and spun toward the bedroom. "Happily, I know just the place to get both."

Diego stared at the menu, jaw hanging slack as he read the name of each item. Looking up, he took in the dining room for the third time, trying to find the words and only managing to force out the restaurant's name.

"Better Than Sex?"

"Great, right?" Trav beamed, swirling sparkling Moscato in a glass rimmed in white chocolate. Candlelight flickered in the lenses of his glasses, the dramatic lighting and deep red velvet ... everything casting the mortal in a mysterious, sensual shadow. It was all Diego could do to look him in the eye when every aspect of the restaurant was designed to put specific imagery in one's mind.

Specifically, the exact face he was making now as he sipped his wine—eyes closed, brow softened in pleasure, lips parted slightly as the pink tip of his tongue darted out to taste—on sheets made of the same crimson satin as the table cloth in a room draped in burgundy velvet.

"I am surprised they did not check our ages at the door." Diego turned the menu over, frantically searching for an item he could order with a straight face and failing.

"You'd be more surprised by how many people bring their kids in here."

"Children?" Diego squawked. "Why?"

"Hey, parents get to have fun, too." Trav pressed his fingers against the base of Diego's wine glass and pushed it closer. Raspberry sugar sparkled in the low light, adhered to the glass by a semi-sweet chocolate drizzle. "Speaking of..."

"You are a bad influence." He grabbed his glass and tipped it to Trav's.

He smiled and licked his lower lip, holding Diego's eyes with a heated stare. "I certainly hope so."

"Are we ready to order?" Their waitress sidled into view, tablet at the ready. She glanced expectantly from Diego to Trav and back. He cast a last, defeated glance at the menu, ready to pick the first item his eyes landed on.

"He'll take the Kinky-er Cream Pie," Trav ordered, sweeping the menu from the table, scanning it, and holding it out for the waitress to take. "And I would *love* the Double Stuffed."

Diego choked on a swallow of wine, slamming a hand over his mouth to keep from spitting it out. Not that anyone would notice red wine staining the wine-colored cloth, but still. Trav's attention flicked briefly to him, then back to the waitress, a smug little smile playing at his mouth.

"And two glasses of the Cab Franc."

"Be right back." She beamed at them both, tapping the screen on her tablet and wandering away.

"You had far too much fun with that."

"No." Trav settled back in his chair. His foot brushed Diego's ankle. "I have far too much fun with you."

He shrunk down, a blush crawling up his throat and cheeks. Trav drank that in, toying with the chain necklace he wore and refusing to release Diego from the suggestive weight of his gaze.

"Too much?"

"No," Diego answered. "I am only … I do not know how to respond."

"The truth would be nice." Trav swirled his glass, eyes flicking to Diego. His heart sank, and he quickly looked away, throat seizing. "You know what I think?"

Diego tried to respond, but the words would not form. What did Trav think? What did he *remember*? Did the vinefica's potion not work? Josh had promised he would be confused and would not remember, and now he was asking for the truth. Goddess, he wanted to tell Trav what he was, *who* he was, and how he'd been trying to help him, but Morgen's threat had been clear. Diego had been clumsy; he should have easily identified the magick in Southernmost Pawn, should have been able to recognize the various hexes, if not in the turntable, then the record. But he had not, and his clumsiness had put Trav at risk.

Trav, who tipped his glass at Diego. "I think you are enjoying this"—the glass waved from him to Trav and back—"as much as I am."

"Sí," Diego exhaled, relief a soothing balm. "I am." He sat up and hooked his foot around Trav's ankle. His eyes widened, and a hopeful smile parted his lips.

"I would like to continue seeing you for however long you're in town, Diego."

"That would be lovely," he agreed. "Very lovely."

The waitress gave a polite little cough, drawing their attention away from each other. "Two glasses of Cab Franc." She set her tray down on the table's edge, offloading their drinks and two of the most decadent desserts Diego had ever seen.

A slice of pale pie the size of his hand was placed before him, topped with a cloud of whipped cream so fluffy he half expected it to float away. Citrusy cookie crumbles had been sprinkled atop the whipped cream, and artistic sweeps of a light green gelee or sauce accented the plate.

Trav's plate was no less impressive: thick slices of bread drizzled in white chocolate and thick sugar crystals oozing a creamy custard and bits of chocolate wafer cookie. A scoop of ice cream butted against the decadent bread pudding, a thick, creamy drizzle melting down the curve from the warmth of the dish.

Diego had only just begun to comprehend the decadence of the desserts when a spoon dug into the tip of his pie. Trav shoved the bite into his mouth, eyelids fluttering in that way of his, and he fell back in his chair. "Oh, god, that's so good."

"I am glad you think so." Diego took up his spoon, reaching for Trav's bread pudding. He pulled the plate out of reach, then froze, realizing what he had done after digging into Diego's dessert.

"Shit, sorry." He grinned sheepishly and slid the plate closer to Diego. "Christ, that's embarrassing. I just ... I grew up with a lot of siblings. I have a thing about sharing food."

"But it is alright for you to share mine?"

"No, I ... I'm sorry. I should have asked." Trav's cheeks flushed, and he wrapped an arm around his front in a way that seemed protective. His fingers curled at his ribcage, plucking at the fabric, and he nudged the bread pudding closer. "Old habit, didn't have a lot that was mine with so many brothers and sisters around. Please, have some." When Diego did not move, he tapped the edge of the plate with his spoon. "Before it melts."

"If you insist." He kept one eye on Trav as he spooned a bit of the ice cream and bread pudding into his mouth, making full eye contact. Interest sparked behind his glasses, and Diego played into the hand he had been dealt, pursing his lips around the spoon and letting his eyes drift closed. He moaned quietly around the bite and opened his eyes to find Trav intent on his mouth.

"Well," he exhaled. "Now I am *truly* sorry I denied you the first bite."

They wandered Duval Street, dodging the crowds spilling out of restaurants and bars, partly to walk off the richness of their dessert and mostly because Diego mentioned he had not yet fully explored Key West.

"It was a bit of a rush decision to come down here," he said. "My roommate ... she got into some trouble, from what I understand, and it was in my best interest to make myself scarce."

"Is she alright?"

"No lo sé," Diego admitted. "She has not been answering my calls or texts. I am worried, but do not know what I can do from here."

"Do you need to go back?"

"At some point. My business is there, my life ..." He hesitated at a street corner, moving out of the way of an oncoming couple. The man on the left smiled in their direction, lingering an appreciative gaze on Diego. Trav grabbed his hand, tugging him close, and he tensed at the touch. There was a possessiveness to the grip, a declaration of ownership declaring him as Trav's and them as a pair.

"It's alright." Trav pulled Diego into the road. "Look, see?" He gestured to the crosswalk, painted in bold, bright rainbow colors. "I know Florida is a mess, but this is the Conch Republic." He declared it as though Diego would understand what he meant. The pride in his statement told Diego he should know, should understand, so he pasted a grin on his face, the same one that had served him well in St. Augustine as a reborn conquistador trying to comprehend this modern world.

To his credit, Trav saw the polite lie for what it was.

"You can be *you* down here, Brown Eyes." He cupped Diego's cheek, forcing him to look up into hazel eyes gleaming in the lamplight. His thumb traced Diego's cheekbone, his gaze intent and warm. "Why do you think I stayed so long?"

In his words was an earnestness, a belief, an *intent*, and Diego relaxed into his touch, grasping for Trav's hand and entwining their fingers. He did not know what that rainbow crosswalk meant beyond a vague understanding of Pride culture, the nuance of which he was hopeless to comprehend, but *this* he understood:

A beautiful man holding his hand in full public view without fear.

He exhaled, the freedom allowed to him in this second life finally finding a sort of home. Another couple passed them by, soft smiles and nods of acknowledgment rather than judgment, and a key piece of Diego unlocked, the pins easing into place. Trav must have seen the ease of his shoulders and the relief that relaxed his body because his grip on Diego's hand tightened. He dragged him onto a sidestreet, capturing Diego in the shadows with his body as a wall.

And for the first time in either of his lives, Diego allowed himself to enjoy it.

ELEVEN

IF THE SLUDGE IN his bowl was any indicator as to how Milla had been raised, then a significant amount of the witch's demeanor and attitude was now wholly explained. Diego scooped a spoonful of the gruel—because what else could it be?—and let it fall back into the bowl.

"And this is called...?"

"Griessbrei." Morgen sprinkled cinnamon over her bowl. "Considering how drunk you were returning last night, I thought it might do you well."

Diego squinted behind his sunglasses, his sluggish brain slow to work through her words. She set about eating her breakfast, having said all she intended to say. It was true; he had been drunk when he stumbled back to the Martello Tower—drunk on wine and margaritas and *life*.

Trav had made it his goal to show Diego all Duval Street had to offer, dragging him from bar to bar until well into the next day. He had lost count of the drinks, caring only for the mortal and his smiles, happily slurping whatever sugary cocktail was in his hand and following him like a lost puppy to the next venue. Hand in hand, just one pair of men in a bar full of the same.

He half-remembered stumbling to the tower and the feel of bricks against his back. Trav's hands on his waist, and the silken feel of his hair wound around his fingers.

It was almost worth the hangover he suffered now.

And the punishment.

He slid his sunglasses down, peering at Morgen over the rim. "Is this punishment for my behavior or your way of making amends?"

"I have nothing to apologize for." She sniffed and sipped her tea. "You were clumsy but acted quickly to resolve the matter. We must discuss the occult items left in Southernmost Pawn and our next steps. I have informed Joshua that—"

"I started organizing them for sale on the boards. Many of them have corresponding intake forms; once I have Trav set up as a broker—"

"Do you think that is wise?"

"Why would it not be?" Diego countered. "It is his store; the items with intake forms legally belong to him."

"Perhaps it would be best if he signed over brokerage to Southern Gothic," Morgen said. "If the relationship between his and my foster daughter's commercial pursuits is pre-existing, it will be easier to manage further occult inventory when you return to St. Augustine."

Diego dropped his eyes to the bowl of gruel on the table. He knew he would have to leave at some point. It was a fact he had happily ignored, throwing himself into Trav and the pawnshop, and after the events of the day before—the night before—the prospect of leaving sank like a hot coal in his stomach. As uneasy as the idea made him, it was something else Morgen said that raised an alarm. "What makes you so certain more items will move through Southernmost Pawn?"

"Occult attracts occult." She stated this as plainly as if it were painted on the wall. "It is likely his predecessor was a cultist. Joshua and Tamara are supposed to submit an active list of all members, if they neglected to inform me of the old man's involvement—"

"Martin," said Diego. "His name was Martin."

Morgen cocked her head, eyes narrowing. "If this Martin," she paced out, "was indeed a cultist, and they neglected to tell me, we have a larger issue on our hands."

"I am still not following; how would Martin being a cultist be a larger issue?"

"Occult attracts occult." She set her teacup down, regarding Diego before speaking again. "If he were initiated into their numbers as a cultist, that could explain the items in the store, but it does not explain why Joshua has not added his name to my registry."

"And?"

"And I am the witch of this demesne. It is my duty to ensure the safety of all those who dwell within its bounds and ensure those who are magickally afflicted or aligned adhere to the regulations of C.R.O.W."

Diego pushed back from the table, that hot coal churning his stomach. A wave of nausea rolled over him, paired with the prickling of an ancient fear. Mortals registered, witches pursued, and men and women burned. "Is C.R.O.W. registering mortals now?"

"No." Morgen cut him a sharp glare. "C.R.O.W. is not, but I am the witch of this demesne, and we attract all manner of magick and mortal. This Martin housed large quantities of the Forbidden and Foule for years, and occult attracts occult. You work for Ludmilla; you have first-hand experience. Southern Gothic exists as a magnet for the wicked and the weird."

"I had always assumed Milla was responsible for attracting occult attention rather than the items we housed."

"Did I say otherwise?" Morgen cocked a brow. "Regardless, the current lack of an ouroboros and abundance of other occult items may be the proof we require."

"Of what?" He pressed. She ate her porridge. "To do what?"

"What we must." She rose and set her cup beside the sink, leaving Diego with far more questions than he could answer.

Goddess, he needed Milla. She had grown up with Morgen; she would know how to address her riddles and moods and gain information instead of confusion. He pulled out his phone, ready to navigate to the contacts and try her number—*again*—and decided against it when a text from Trav filled the screen.

Am I seeing you today?

In the time it took for Diego to shower, re-wrap his palms, and dress, choosing a white v-neck and floral pastel button down that pulled out the gold under-tones in his olive complexion, and walk to Southernmost Pawn, the cultists had been busy. His first hint came in the form of a space where the Thorens TD-125 MKII turntable had sat, and the next was in the excitement humming from Trav.

"Twenty-two hundred, can you believe it?" He closed the register drawer with a hip, eyes bright and fixed on Diego. "First thing this morning, cash!" If the mortal were suffering from a hangover, either from magick, potions, or alcohol, it did not show. His outfit today consisted of pressed forest green slacks cuffed at the ankle, chestnut loafers, a white v-neck, and a tweed blazer with the sleeves cuffed. A gold chain was just visible over the neck of his shirt, and he looked for all the world like he was about to be whisked away to solve an ancient mystery about some long-forgotten continent.

"Then there was a woman waiting outside when I got back with your coffee." He gestured to the fresh coffee waiting on the counter for Diego beside a half-eaten chocolate croissant matching the crumbs on Trav's lips. "She bought up half the sports equipment. Said it was for an after-school program at the junior high."

"Eso es increíble." Diego slipped behind the counter and popped onto his tiptoes, kissing the corner of Trav's mouth. He flicked his tongue over his lips, tasting the buttery pastry flakes and remnants of chocolate, and whispered in his ear, "You deserve a turn of good luck."

He started to move away, and Trav hooked a finger in the belt loop on his pants, keeping Diego right where he was. "And what did I do to deserve that?" he asked. "In full daylight, no less."

"Just being you." Diego settled on his feet, tipping his head back to look up at Trav. "And I may or may not still be borracho from last night; my actions this morning cannot be held against me."

Trav's eyes widened, a spark of mischief flaring in his hazel eyes. He opened his mouth to respond, and Diego pressed a finger to his lips.

"No! Nono, haz silencio. I do not want to hear any terrible jokes about whatever it is you would like held against you." Gently prying his finger from the belt loop, Diego swept the coffee from the counter and pointed it at him. "I have work to do, and a man can only manage so much distraction." At that, Trav's smirk grew to an outright grin. Diego rolled his eyes. "And *yes*, you are a distraction. An encantadora distraction, and I have work to do."

Diego had decided on a new tactic after the Ear Worm and Morgen's ultimatum. Instead of following the strongest threads of magick box by box, he would take a leaf from the Inquisitor's manuscript and raze the backroom. No more intricate unravellings and tedious knots, no more setting aside items piece-by-piece for review and potential sale on the occult boards. He would enter that backroom and refuse to leave until the ouroboros was taken out of mortal hands.

"Fine, fine." Trav put his hands up in surrender, laughing. "Go get your work done, but when five hits, expect me to pester you for a dinner date." He waved him off. "And don't be surprised when you get back there. I didn't want to run up and down the stairs all day, so I moved a few things into the apartment to compare them with the registry."

The front door opened before Diego could respond, and Trav turned to greet his customer. The woman who entered hummed with faint energy, and she faltered at the threshold, nostrils flaring and eyes growing wide when she spotted Diego.

Cultist, Diego identified. Morgen had been busy, which meant Trav was in the safest hands possible. Or so he hoped.

"A few things" turned out to be the contents of an entire table. Diego wasted some unwanted time poking around what was left, ensuring Trav hadn't taken crates and boxes he had yet to work through. The last thing he needed was the mortal stumbling onto another hex when Diego was not around to help.

Satisfied he would not wander into the store the next day to find a petrified pawnbroker, he got to work. Stepping deeply into his Way had gotten easier over the last few days, and with less than a centering breath and flick of his fingers, threads of magick flared to life, wafting in a nonexistent breeze from the massive knot of magick clouding the store. He raised his casting hand and tangled the strands in his fingers, looping them around his wrist before diving into the nearest box.

Hours later, the ouroboros was still nowhere to be found. He had upended box after box, setting aside crystals humming with augury magick, a crystal decanter with a Shade of revelry blown into the glass, a necklace cast with an obnubilari allure to make the wearer more attractive, and a tennis bracelet imbued with a look-away hex. But no ouroboros.

Frustrated and hungry, he wandered to the front of the store in search of Trav. The aisles were empty, the shop's door was locked, and the sign switched to closed.

"Trav?" Diego's voice echoed through the shop, bouncing back at him from the angled mirrors running along the top of the walls. He walked the length of the instruments aisle, briefly noting the absence of the mandolin and a few brass horns. The echo of the magick they held lingered on the shelves, slowly dying out like the embers of a fire.

He stopped at the apartment door, not wanting to interrupt Trav if he were busy, but the strands of magick in the air were winding tighter and tighter around Diego, tugging him toward the stairs. With his hand on the doorknob, he called again, "Travis?"

Nothing.

"Lo juro por la Diosa," Diego swore, opening the door. "If you have gotten yourself cursed *again*, I am hiring a nanny." He jogged up the steps, stopping just shy of the top and sagging in relief at the sight of Trav hunched over his table, hard at work. He finished his climb, ready to call out again when the rest of the room came into focus.

Boxes from the back room were stacked against the wall, and he had removed choice items, laying them out along any available flat surface. The previously tidy kitchen counters were covered in the contents of the crates: costume jewelry, bowls full of rings and coins, leatherbound books, video game consoles, and stacks of game cartridges. Wedding dresses covered the sofa, and the coffee table hosted half a dozen Tiffany lamps.

The kitchen table fared no better. Stacks of paperwork and binders that had seen better days teetered in haphazard piles, and jewelry, baubles, and crystal ware filled any available space, leaving Trav precious little room to work. What space he had was shared with a half-eaten sleeve of Oreo cookies.

"Trav?" Diego rapped his knuckles on the stair rail, and when he showed no hearing, he crossed to the table, dropping a hand on his shoulder. "Travis."

He tensed, a tiny little flinch, and raised his head. Unfocused eyes gazed up at Diego; he blinked, and a groggy smile bloomed. "Hey, ready for lunch?"

"I am afraid we both missed the window for lunch." Diego cleared a stack of folders from the table, twisting at the waist as he searched for a place to put them down and settling for the floor. He pulled out a chair and frowned at the teetering pile of leatherbound books on the cushion. Abandoning the task, he plucked a cookie from the pack and held it out. "Or at least, one of us did. How many of these did you eat?"

"More than I probably should have." Trav's cheeks flushed. He frowned at the half-empty package and sighed. "That was full when I grabbed it."

Diego chuckled and popped the cookie into his mouth. The wafers were chocolatey without overpowering the sweet hit of the cream but nowhere near filling enough. Trav eyed the package, reaching for another Oreo, and Diego batted it away. "No more dessert," he stated. "Not until we feed you a proper dinner."

Twisting in his chair, Trav wrapped his arms around Diego's hips and tugged him close, propping his chin on the center of his chest. "I can think of something I'd like to eat."

Diego smiled softly at him, sweeping hair back off Trav's brow and meeting that heated gaze with a suggestive one of his own. He kissed his forehead, between his eyes, smiling as Trav gave a satisfied little hum and arched his neck, lips pursed.

"Needy," he chuckled, relishing the soft hair threaded between his fingers and the press of Trav's hands against his back.

"Greedy," he answered, rising in the chair to bring their mouths together and pulling away too soon. "But you're right," he said when Diego pouted. "I haven't eaten since my dive this morning."

"You went for a dive?" Diego tucked his chin, surprised. He had never considered what Trav did when they weren't together, but if the strength of his arms and firmness of the body hidden beneath those clothes was any tell, diving and swimming fit.

"Best cure for a hangover." Trav released Diego and rose, grinning down at him. "Actually, no. Second best."

"I cannot help but feel you are setting me up for a joke."

"Come on, you know you want to know." His grin widened, crinkling an eye, and Diego caved.

"Bien, okay," he laughed. "What is the first best cure for a hangover?"

Trav's grin turned wicked. He cupped Diego's cheek, trailing his thumb across his lower lip before leaning close. "Take me to dinner, and you'll find out."

TWELVE

MUSIC FLOWED FROM THE open windows of cars, filling the pleasant evening with Yacht Rock. With a belly full of ropa vieja and a head swimming from rum, Diego was hard-pressed to remember a better evening in either of his lives. It was amazing what a good meal and a beautiful man hanging on his arm and every word could do.

Following Trav's subtle directional tugs, he let himself be led on a meandering path through Key West, past cottages and beneath the sweeping branches of moonlit kapok trees. A group of twenty-somethings passed by, and when Diego gripped his hand tighter instead of pulling away, Trav leaned over and kissed his temple.

"This is nice." His tongue was thick from the many daiquiris they had enjoyed with their meal, but his tone, laced with desire and heat, was unmistakable. "Any idea how much longer you'll be in town?"

"I am not sure," Diego admitted. "I have not heard from my roommate, and there is still a decent amount of work to be done in your shop."

"Hm." He squeezed Diego's hand twice, leading him across a street. "I hope I'm not keeping you from anything."

"Not at all." Diego took his eyes off the road to look at Trav. "Nowhere else I would rather—"

"Whoa!" Trav jerked Diego out of the road, avoiding a runner swerving in their path. "Watch it!"

"Sorry!" She hollered back, digging in a canvas bag on her arm. Pink curls bobbed as she ran and threw a fistful of white powder. "Chicken!"

"Chicken?" Trav balked, and something hard and sharp stabbed Diego's foot.

"¡Maldito pollo!" He kicked out, catching whatever it was with the toe of his shoe. A chicken fluttered up, squawking at them both. "Si no estuviera lleno, ¡te comería!" He shook a fist at the rangy bird, ready to kick it again, when a bark of laughter halted him.

"Did you just threaten to eat that chicken?"

"It pecked me!"

"You are ridiculous." Trav pulled him close, gazing warmly down at him. "Utterly ridiculous."

"You think it is funny that I keep getting attacked by chickens?"

"Keep getting?" He shook his head. "How often has that happened?"

"The day we met, for one."

"That's right." He clasped both cheeks in his hands and kissed the tip of Diego's nose, sending heat roaring into his cheeks. "Then no, I don't think it's funny, but I can't really complain about it, can I?"

"Why not?" Diego pouted.

"Because every time you get attacked by a chicken, you end up in my arms."

"Pues..." A smile tugged at his mouth. "Then I suppose I cannot fault the chickens, even if they are pequeños bastardos desagradables."

A giggle bubbled out of Trav, and a hand curved around the back of Diego's head, pulling him in closer. "Utterly," he kissed his brow, "ridiculous." His lips graced Diego's, a soft promise of more to come. "Come on, let's get back to—"

Shrill whistles pierced the night, sharp and jarring. A woman rushed by, kicking the pile of powder and hollering an apology over her shoulder. Heat and sweat followed on the wind in her wake and something else. Something...mag-ick.

A low static tingling raised the hair along Diego's neck. Trav straightened, head swiveling after the runner. More whistles blew, heralding another runner and another. Two became four, became six, became an entire pack of sports enthusiasts, splitting around them like a river against a long-standing stone. Trav tried to pull Diego out of their path, only to be blinded by bright lights as a woman ran right into them.

"Whoa, look out!" She wrapped her arms around the pair, wrestling them against a white picket fence. She fiddled with her headlamp, and the light blinked out. Diego squinted, trying to readjust his eyes to the sudden darkness. "There's more coming; better keep aside."

"Yeah, no shit," Trav spat. It was the angriest Diego had heard him since he'd threatened a driver with his baseball bat. Just as he had then, he looked down at Diego, scanning his face, all anger gone in an instant. "You okay?"

"Sí, yes." He craned his neck to watch the runners stream by. Headlamps adorned every one of them, their whistles sounding in intermittent blasts until a voice rose over the din.

"Beer here!"

A cheer rippled through the crowd, and they increased their pace, the steady stream now an all-out sprint.

"Thank the gods," the woman keeping them against the fence grumbled. "I swear that dumbass lost the trail on the boardwalk through the mangroves. She's too damned cocky." Diego whipped his head around, recognizing Tammy's features now that his vision had adjusted. "Oh, shit, it's you two." She crowded them closer to the fence and watched the crowd, face pinched in worry. When the mass had thinned to a trickle, she dug into her sportsbra, retrieving a smartphone in a plastic baggy and firing off a message before looking at Diego. "Hey Diego, sorry about that. Good to see you again. Y'all want a drink?"

Diego shook his head, as stunned by the onslaught and sudden appearance of the cultist and the madness of the pack as he was by Trav's sudden mood swings. Even now, he inhaled deeply, his body tense and trembling with anger.

"Please say yes," Tammy hissed in Diego's ear, barely a breath above audible, but it was Trav who spoke.

"Yeah." The word left him like a sigh, taking with it all of his aggression. The tension bled from his body, his grip on Diego's hand lessened, and he exhaled with a sigh and a lopsided grin. "A drink sounds good. Where to?"

Tammy smiled, cuffing her fist against Diego's shoulder and jerking her head in the direction the runners had sprinted. "Shanna Key."

Tammy guided them to the pub, pointing out occult marks as they walked. Handfuls of flour, the white powder the first runner hand thrown, created a trail for the cultists to follow, and every few intersections, a symbol was scrawled on the ground—a circle with an X drawn through it. Smaller arrows, or in some instances the barest lines, stemmed off the circle and either pointed down a side street or straight ahead.

"Tells us which way to go, or if we need to stop and seek out the, um"—Tammy glanced at Trav, who had stooped to run his finger over one of the smaller lines—"trail."

Diego nodded, following what she was not saying. The runner with the white powder had caught the scent of magick, a thin, fraying thread that even now wound around Diego's fingers, and it was her job to lead the rest of the cultists on the trail, seeking the source of a power that, as mortals, they would never truly own.

"We use chalk to draw the symbols," Tammy explained. "It washes away in the rain, so the cops don't mind."

Trav rose, dusting his hand off on his trouser leg. "You aren't exactly quiet; don't the neighbors complain?"

Her nonchalant shrug matched her smug smile. "Most the locals know we're harmless, but now and then we get a snowbird from up north reporting a 'pack of wahoo runners flinging cocaine on the streets'. The fire department gets pissed whenever they're called to clean it up." She chuckled at a memory. "We finally got a fireman to join us, which helped, but the calls still happen occasionally."

"You are a ... running club?" Diego stared at her, trying to match how Tammy described the cult to Milla's spite-filled descriptions of the drunks in St. Augustine.

"A drinking club with a running problem," Trav spouted. Both Diego and Tammy gave him startled looks. "You used to come into Sloppy Joe's when I worked there. Wild crowd," he told Diego, "great tippers."

"We take care of our own," Tammy smiled at him. "Here we are." She stopped before a two-story, pale yellow building with deep green awnings. A white vinyl sign affixed to the side read *Shanna Key - Irish Pub & Grill* and both the Irish and American flags were hung over the wooden doors.

"The owner is one of us," Tammy explained as she opened the door. Vibrant fiddle and drum music spilled onto the street, paired with raucous, drunken yelling. "And the bartender reminds me a lot of you, Diego." The closest she could come to saying the bartender was a Mix Witch. "First drink is on me; just don't call me by my mortal name."

"And that is?" Trav asked.

"Wouldn't you like to know?" Tammy winked. "Call me CicerHoe."

She led them through the packed pub, shouting greetings and taunts at other members of the cult. Diego kept close behind her, with Trav hovering at his back. Cultists eyed him as they worked across the room, some leaning in and sniffing, others sharing surprised, interested looks. The skin prickled on his neck, and, as if sensing he was uncomfortable surrounded by this many cultists, Tammy reached back and grabbed his hand.

"Pubeus is at the bar," she shouted in his ear, pointing over the crowd to where Josh knelt on a stool, speaking with the bartender, a red-headed witch with a bright smile. Threads of magick wound around her arms, ending in frays at her wrists. Like sap from a tree, drops beaded off the strands and fell into every drink.

Josh—*Pubeus*—wore only a pair of black, split-seam running shorts and his beaded necklace, his tan skin glistening in a sheen of sweat. Every lean muscle was on display, along with two pierced nipples.

"That's the safest spot for you," Tammy said, leading him to the bar. "Ginger's drinks usually pacify the crowd, so you should be alright."

"Could I not have gone home?" he shouted back.

"Not a chance." Tammy shook her head vehemently. "The pack is too hungry. The last thing we need is one of them catching your scent out there."

"Scent?"

Her gaze drifted past Diego to Trav, who was observing the crowd with an interested smile. "Once they have it, they'll hound you around Key West. You want your boy a secret for now, right?" He nodded and tightened his grip on Trav's hand. "Then trust me, please? You're one of a handful in here." She ushered a pair of cultists away from the bar, gesturing for Diego and Trav to take their stools. "Stay for a round, let the pack get the jitters out of their system, and then leave out the back."

Diego nodded, unable to speak through his discomfort. The sweat of the crowd, the noise, and the heat had his skin itching. Whatever it was the cultists did; however it was they fed off the demesne, pulsed from their bodies, seeking out a source.

He knew little of the cultists or how they worked. They had developed after the Inquisition, during one of the centuries he was dead, and thus he had only had Milla's word to go by: they were loud, obnoxious drunks who hunted any witch they could find, inviting them to join in their rituals, and leeching off of their magick.

Her description brought old fears simmering to the surface: fears of being hunted in taverns and market squares and of being hounded down the narrow, cobbled alleys of Zaragoza, Bilbao, and Oviedo.

Even in this bar with a cultist he trusted, because Morgen trusted her, a jitteriness filled his limbs. There were too many eyes on him, too many witnesses to the witch and the man holding his hand. He scanned the crowd, all too aware of the attention levied his way, and met the eyes of a woman with short, wild curls dyed bright bubblegum pink. She stared at him from across the bar, blinking in disbelief before breaking away to whisper something to the cultist beside her.

"You alright?" Trav leaned close, his breath warm against Diego's ear. "We can leave if this is too much."

There was a note to his voice that Diego had never heard before—a quiet pleading belying Trav's desire. If Diego said he wanted to leave, Trav would not argue. He would sweep the witch from the room, and they would continue their night. But that wheedling note, the quiet hopefulness in his question…Diego squeezed his hand and hopped onto the barstool, tugging Trav beside him. "What would you like to drink?"

"A Snakebite, naturally." Josh spun around and gripped Diego's shoulder, giving him a little shake before twisting toward the bartender. "Four Snakebites, Ging, please, and thank you."

"Wine, por favor," Deigo corrected.

"*Three* Snakebites," the cultist threw up three fingers, "and a… red?" He cocked his head at Diego, who nodded. "And red wine."

"You got it." Ginger gave a salute, her eyes flicking briefly to Diego. There was a flash of recognition in that look, witch to witch, and, if Diego weren't mistaken, relief. Before he could ponder that, Josh's weight pressed down on his shoulder, and the cultist reached across his chest, hand extended toward Trav. "Travis, right? From the pawnshop?"

"That's right," he snapped, his tone as crisp and cold as it had been before Tammy invited them along. Instead of looking directly at Josh, Trav's attention was fixed on Diego's shoulder and the hand resting there. A muscle twitched in his jaw, and he dragged his gaze to Josh, shaking his offered hand once before letting go and none-to-subtly wiping his palm off on his thigh. "You were in the other day asking about the Pentax Spotmatic."

"Any chance you've lowered the price?" Josh waggled his eyebrows. "My Minolta shat the bed a few weeks back, and it's putting a cramp in my business."

"What do you do?" Diego asked.

"Freelance photography." Josh tipped his attention away from the pawnbroker, letting go of Diego's shoulder to lean close so he could speak without needing to shout. "Weddings, private boat tours, bar mitzvahs. My regular gig is with a local kayak company, photographing the tourists they take through the mangroves. That's where I met Martin."

"Of course it is," Trav muttered. He slung an arm around Diego's shoulders, and the bartender returned with their drinks, handing each cultist a pint glass. The bottom half of the drink was a pale yellow liquid, while a darker alcohol floated on the top.

"A Snakebite." Tammy raised her glass for Diego to see. "Cider on the bottom, Guinness on top, with a few dashes of cherry cordial."

"Like an alcoholic Kool-aid," Josh added with a wink. "Only, you know, for adults. Down in one!" He raised his glass. Half the bar followed suit and flushed, smiling faces hollered in unison, "One and done!"

In a flash, three-quarters of the bar had empty glasses. A voice in the rear of the room belted out, "S-H-I-"

"-T-T-Y!" the rest of the crowd shouted, breaking into song.

"Oh, gods, here we go," Tammy groused, grabbing her empty glass and disappearing into the singing crowd. Their lyrics were filthy, peppered with curse words and enough innuendo to ease Trav's glower and have Diego blushing.

The weight of Trav's arm was a steadying anchor, and Diego leaned into his warmth. Cultists eyed him as they approached the bar for drinks, and Tammy reappeared two songs later, her glass refreshed by a simple raise of her eyebrows at the Mix Witch behind the bar. On the stool beside Diego, Josh held court over his pack. He nodded and shouted soft insults at cultists, drank the shots bought for him, and led the crowd in song when the mood faltered, single-handedly keeping the party atmosphere of Shanna Key vivid and bright while Tammy wandered through the crowd.

As hard as they worked to keep the pack distracted from the witch at the bar, they could do nothing about the sidelong glances, and drunken, borderline lecherous smiles sent Diego's way.

It was too close to being seen, too close to the suspicious looks and whispers he suffered in Zaragoza.

He drank his wine and tucked closer to Trav, ignoring the looks as best he could, relying on the cheap vintage to muddle his nerves. With his second glass, Trav pressed a testing kiss to the top of his head, watching Diego with a similar sharp eye. He toyed with the fine gold chain around his neck, leaning closer. "Alright?"

Diego nodded, though his shoulders were tight. The itching of his skin had become a sunburn slap between his shoulder blades, the tension leaking from the magick-hungry cultists near intolerable. Half his wine was gone with a swallow, his fingertips blanching white from how tightly they pinched the stem.

"D." Trav stepped before him, using his taller body to close the witch off from the rest of the room. Josh said something, his fingers brushing Diego's arm, and at a glare from Trav, he slipped from his barstool and wandered away. "Let's get you home."

"I do not want to go home." The truth. He was too keyed up to go to the tower, too anxious to sleep. He would spend the night staring at the ceiling and twitching at every tiny sound. Every gaze in his direction was ravenous, and the crowd had edged closer and closer, their numbers too many for Tammy and Josh to corral.

No wonder Milla hated the cultists in St. Augustine. If this was how they reacted to a singular Stitch Witch, he imagined a witch of her power would be ready to crawl out of her skin to avoid feeling like she was a buffet laid out for a starving crew.

"Well, I don't want to stay here." Trav slid his hand around Diego's hip, tugging him close. "I don't like how these people look at you." Behind his glasses, those hazel eyes were so intent on Diego, he wondered if Trav sensed what the cultists could:

He was a witch with an aura of magick surrounded by mortals addicted to the power.

"I should be the only one looking at you like that," Trav murmured. His palm moved to Diego's lower back, easing him from the barstool. "Preferably alone and in my bed."

"Diosa,"—he knocked back the rest of his wine, pulse fluttering now for an entirely different reason—"ten piedad."

"What did I say, Diego?" Trav took the glass from his hand and handed it to the bartender, who pointed down a narrow hallway beside the bar. Trav nodded and maneuvered Diego in front of him, hands at his hips and lips near his ear as he guided the witch away. "No mercy for you."

THIRTEEN

"I shouldn't have asked you to go." Trav tugged him across the street and up a curb, his grip relentless. "Diego, I'm so sorry."

"Sorry?" Diego jerked to a halt, heels skidding on the sidewalk as Trav tried to keep moving. "¿Por qué?"

"I was selfish; they looked like they were having so much fun, and I-I don't know why I wanted to—you don't like crowds." He dropped his head back. Pale light painted his face from a nearby streetlamp, drawing attention to the high cheekbones and cut of his jaw. Defined yet delicate, his cheeks held onto the last softness of youth.

"You did not ask me to go," Diego pointed out. "You wanted to go, so we went."

"I didn't *ask*, even knowing that you—" He raised his head, gazing down at Diego with wide eyes. "I've been an ass."

"No."

"Yes," Trav doubled down. "I've been trying to show you it's *safe* down here. That whatever bullshit you've dealt with in the past doesn't happen here, but I've been forcing the issue, and the way they were looking at you—like you were a piece of meat, it was di—"

Diego popped onto his toes and silenced the rambling mortal the only way he knew how— by kissing those impossibly soft lips. Trav tensed, startled, before wrapping his arms around Diego. "It is alright, lo prometo."

"You promise?" Trav pulled back to search his face. "I'm so sorry."

"No more of that." Sliding his hands into Trav's hair, Diego pulled him in, kissing that apologetic mouth and taking his plush lower lip between his teeth. A gentle tug had Trav's hands splaying against his back, and what had begun as a soft kiss to reassure him he was fine, to show him there was no need to apologize because he had done nothing wrong, quickly turned into something else.

Something more.

As ever, Trav's kiss was a greedy, hungry thing. He slid a palm up Diego's spine as he cupped his rear, hitching him closer. Holding him tighter. That nip of his lower lip had ignited something in Trav, and he peppered near-frantic kisses against Diego's lips, his chin, his throat. A needy little moan escaped, and Trav returned to his mouth, claiming Diego with each sweep and slide of his tongue. Blood rushed from his head, pooling in deeper, more visceral places until he was no longer able to think of anything but this, of *him*.

Cherry cordial lingered on Trav's tongue, muddling with his chapstick and driving Diego insane. He forgot his worries, forgot the stares of the cultists, and poured himself into Trav.

The frenzy of the kiss, that all-consuming hunger, abated, easing into a deeper, more intimate space. Vaguely, he was aware of Trav turning him, of being eased against a wall. The hand that had so intently been kneading Diego's ass wandered to his front, knuckles grazing his rock-hard cock.

"Diosa," he groaned against Trav's lips, hips jerking at the touch.

"No mercy, Diego." Trav smiled against his mouth, breath wet and warm and coming in short bursts. "I still need to show you the first best cure."

"For what?"

At his whimpered reply, Trav slanted his mouth over Diego's, resuming the lazy, near-drunken kiss. Instead of teasing his cock again, his hand disappeared altogether. The jangle of keys snapped a tiny piece of Diego to the present.

"How far are we?"

"We're here." Trav glanced down and to the left, passive concentration raising his brows enough to distract Diego. He dropped his head against the wall—no, the glass—at his back.

"This is your store."

"Even better," Trav said, "this is my apartment."

"I did not realize we were so close."

"Right across the street." The lock clicked, and Trav tugged the keys free. "Come in?"

"Absolutamente."

He held the door for Diego, gently pressing at the base of his spine to usher him inside. The cloud of magick pressed down on him from all sides, a heady, disorienting pressure. He wobbled where he stood, reaching out for something to steady himself. Trav grabbed his hand with a grin, guiding Diego down the dark aisle and up the stairs. The magick was no less thick in the stairwell, and head swimming, he stumbled over his feet, gripping the banister to keep from falling.

"Easy there." Trav laughed, stepping down and turning Diego to face him. He took advantage of the half-formed question that split his lips, and if the magick clogging the pawnshop had not made it impossible to think straight, this kiss would have succeeded outright.

On the step above, Diego was taller than Trav, a treat he reveled in. His hands flew to the mortal's face, cupping his cheeks and angling his head to deepen the kiss. A sound lodged in Trav's throat, and he melted into Diego, snaking lean arms around his waist and clasping his hands at the base of Diego's spine to hold him close and precious. Whatever bauble or charm hung from the necklace he wore dug into Diego's sternum, a grounding discomfort in a kiss he was like to float away in.

He trailed fingers along Trav's jaw and down the sweep of tendons in his neck, savoring each goosebump raised by his feather-soft caress, every hitched breath and tiny hum his touch earned. Trailing the neckline of his shirt, Diego swept his thumb over Trav's nipple, hard beneath the cotton, and grinned against his mouth when Trav shivered.

"Diego." His name was an exhale and a plea in one, shivering into his ear and shooting straight to his core. He wormed his fingers into Diego's hair, tugging on the strands. "Up the stairs, D, please."

Diego's grin widened. He dropped his hand low, grasping Trav's cock through his pants. A gentle squeeze and the sweep of his thumb had him cursing. A curse that melted into a groan as Diego worked him. Cupping and caressing, applying enough friction to have Trav panting from the tease.

"Please, Diego—" He dropped his head against Diego's shoulder, holding onto him as if letting go would have him crumpling on the stairs. The need in his voice, the outright begging, overrode the wine and the heady magick muddling Diego's mind.

How long since he had last brought a man to this frantic of an edge?

How long since a man had spoken his name like a prayer?

Never in those last days fleeing Zaragoza. They had been too frightened of being discovered. Too exhausted from the road. Sex and desire taking a backseat to survival and secrecy.

Then Ruben was gone, and Diego boarded a caravel in Cádiz, never to set foot in Spain again.

On the ships then, in those brief meetings to relieve stress, though he could not recall a single instance of this deep privacy or delicate intimacy. Those meetings had been rushed and frantic, full of splinters against his belly or driving into his knees and his palms. Two men lost in the fervor of chasing mutual relief.

Never this sweet, mutual need, this mounting desire that drained every bit of blood from Diego's brain to engorge his cock.

He tugged on Trav's belt, leaning into his Way to pull the leather aside and undo his pants, the zipper peeling apart. Trav dragged in a rasping breath that stilled his hand. "¿Está bien?"

"Sí," Trav panted, rolling his hips to grind into Diego's palm. He nuzzled into the crook of his neck, kissing and grazing the sensitive skin with his teeth. "Yes, please, D, I need you."

"Te tengo, dulzura," he crooned, molding his hand to the shape of Trav, hot and hard in his palm. He worked him from root to tip, easing up the stairs and all but leading the mortal by his cock. A patch of damp spread where the tip pressed against his briefs, and Trav let out a low keening when Diego focused his attention there, pressing his thumb into the moisture and teasing his head only to scale his nails lightly down the length.

Slowly, painstakingly, they reached the apartment floor, their heights shifting and, with it, Trav's submissiveness. A sound halfway between a snarl and a growl left the man the moment he was taller. He caught Diego's head in his hands, him into a fervent, frantic kiss. Teeth butted against teeth, the earlier languorous sweeps of his tongue now feverish. He backed Diego across the room, skirting around boxes and past the couch.

Diego ceased his teasing, holding on as best he could. Trav was driven by a need, a hunger, that had him fumbling over buttons and all but tearing Diego's shirt away. It caught at the crook of his arms, unable to fall further, and Trav halted, glasses fogged and lips swollen.

Chest heaving, he gazed down at Diego, raising a hand to slip his glasses away and reveal pupils blown wide. Wanton heat gleamed, caught in the coral-amber light blooming like a Key West sunset from a salt lamp on his bedside table.

Trav's free hand rose to cup Diego's face, thumb dusting across his lower lip. He took it into his mouth, holding that heated gaze as he sucked on the pad. Trav's throat bobbed, and he worked his jaw before grinding out, "Near or far?"

"¿Qué?"

"Your glasses." A finger slipped under the arm, brushing the corner of Diego's eye. "I want to know that you can see me."

"Near." Diego pressed a kiss to the pad of his thumb.

"Wonderful."

His glasses were swept away, tossed onto the bedside table along with Trav's, and Diego's back hit the bed. His arms were still caught in the fall of his shirt, their movement restricted by the fabric slung across his back. Trav crawled over his legs, straddling his thighs. He swept his hands down Diego's front, pinching his nipples until he moaned and rolled his hips. It was too much, banking a fire he had never allowed to burn.

This aching slowness, the enjoyment Trav took in every featherlight touch and flick of his tongue over sensitive flesh, drove him wild. He rutted like a dog in heat, seeking more friction, more of Trav, only to be denied time and time again by his still buttoned pants, the arms of his shirt refusing free movement, and the mortal who pulled away from where Diego needed him most.

"I could play with you for hours." He sighed, pulling his cock free and giving it one lazy stroke before dropping his arm away. His erection stood proud between them, just out of reach, and *oh*, did Diego try to reach for it.

"Please," he begged, and Trav acquiesced, pulling his pants and briefs off before knee-walking closer. Diego awkwardly propped himself on his elbows, taking the head of Trav's cock into his mouth without prelude. Slick and salty, he swirled his tongue around the rim, flicking the slit and groaning at the sight of Trav dropping his head back. He grasped the back of Diego's head, holding him in place as his hips rocked, lightly fucking his mouth.

Trav was not a muscular man, lean and lithe, a slip of a mortal, and every sinuous roll of his hips hypnotized Diego, lulling him into a space he had never visited. A safe space where he could enjoy the slide of a cock in his mouth, the heat and the weight of it pressing down on his tongue as he pleasured the man above him.

"More," Diego managed, straining to take more of the man into his mouth. His cock strangled in his pants and throbbing from need.

"I can't," Trav panted. "Oh, fuck, baby, I can't give you more, I want so much more out of you."

His words, slurred on a tongue thick with lust, were the sweetest music Diego had ever heard. He hollowed his cheeks, sucking what he could of Trav's cock until the mortal jerked away. Panting heavily, he dropped onto his elbows, fisting the comforter on either side of Diego's head.

"You're a fucking tease," he growled, tossing his head back to glare at Diego. "A slippery little tease, aren't you?"

"Quizás," Diego simpered. *Maybe.* He thrust his hips, restrained cock grinding against Trav's. He shuddered, hissing through his teeth, and the fire in his eyes banked higher.

"Let's get these off of you." He slipped away before Diego could protest, nimble fingers making short work of the button and fly. He barely had the time to process what was happening before Trav took him in his mouth, briefs and all.

His hips left the bed, sensation roaring up his spine and setting every synapse in his brain on fire. Goddess, the damned man had kept him waiting, winding him tighter than sheetlines at full sail. Trav grinned at him, beautifully nestled between Diego's thighs. He whimpered, rocking his hips in place of outright begging.

"Do you need something, Diego?"

"Sí." He nodded, wriggling arms free from his shirt to grab Trav's shoulders. Longing to drag him up, needing his weight, his heat, his tongue. "Sí, dulzura, I need you."

"I've got you." He swept his tongue along Diego's waistband, circling his navel, and two fingers hooked in the elastic. A gentle tug was all it took to have his cock springing free. A smile curled Trav's mouth, that plush lower lip disappearing between his teeth. "I could watch that all day."

Each word crashed against his shaft, teasing him until he knew, without a doubt, that the moment Trav set his mind to it, he would have Diego tipping over the edge.

It was too soon. Too soon for the bliss of release. There was no need to rush, no need to hasten through this exhilarating torture. They had all night and each other, and Diego was dangerously at risk of wanting more.

"You know, I've thought about this."

"About what?" he managed, though the words stuck in his throat.

Trav licked up his palm, locking eyes with Diego. "A fist around your cock." And he did just that, gripping the witch and stroking to the tip. The cry that left Diego was neither in Spanish nor English, strangled half-words growing more desperate with every firm slide of Trav's palm.

Eyes intent on his work, he milked Diego's cock. Rolling his wrist in slick, sure movements and altering his grip, though never in a way Diego could predict. His arms gave out, his hips rolling into Trav's fist, seeking more, harder, faster, *more.*

The mortal denied him, slowing the pace whenever his cries grew too sharp, speeding up again when his breathing steadied. He was only half aware of Trav moving on the bed, only half aware of him again straddling his thighs.

A quiet snap was followed by the jarring dribble of something cold meeting Trav's grip. He jerked his head up from the bed as the cool warmed and slickened, heightening the sensation and easing the slide of Trav's palm. With his free hand, Trav stroked himself, grunting quietly before angling his hips to take them both in hand. Slick heat pressed against his cock, and every iota of awareness in Diego snapped into place.

"God damn," Trav groaned, pumping his hips to slide his cock against Diego's. "God fucking dammit, you feel so fucking good."

"Trav—"

"Beg for it, baby, por favor," Trav grunted, pumping harder. Diosa, it was too much. This pleasure, the heat of his palm, the slide of his cock. Diego's hips rolled, his nails dug into Trav's thighs, and he kept going, a wildness in his eyes as he looked down at Diego, splayed and moaning on the bed. "You're so fucking pretty when you say please."

"Por favor, dulzura, please." He shook his head from side to side, frantic with the need to come while not wanting this to be over. He hung on for dear life, gritting his teeth as the heat coiled tighter and tighter, the tips of his fingers and toes beginning to tingle. "Por favor, diosa, por favor, es tan bueno que no puedo..."

"No." Trav's grip loosened, all of that delicious friction slipping away like a dream upon waking. He dropped over Diego, kissing his chest, his throat, his jaw. "Not yet, tesoro, not yet. Breathe, Diego."

He tried. Goddess, he tried, but his lungs had given up somewhere around the time Trav had begun stroking him, the pleasure too much to manage. Instead, he panted like a winded beast, each tiny breath puffing against Trav's ear as he whispered soothing words that were as much a promise as they were a threat.

"I'm going to treat you so good, baby, so fucking good, okay? Just breathe, tesoro, breathe with me, baby. Walk back from the edge so we can keep going, alright? I want so much more out of you. I want you gasping my name, Diego. I want to see that pretty face when you finally come."

"Travis," he hissed when he finally had the air. Arching into him and clamping hands on the firm globes of his ass, keeping him still for one Horned God-damned second. Trav groaned at the touch, subtly pressing back into Diego's hold. "How can you call me a tease?"

"You good, baby?"

Diego nodded, catching Trav's lips with a kiss. "More," he demanded, kneading and spreading his cheeks to crawl his fingers toward the seam.

Trav gasped into Diego's mouth, such a tiny little sound, and all of the work he had done calming himself tipped overboard.

"I cannot wait, dulzura," he murmured. Releasing that glorious rear, Diego wriggled beneath him, working onto his front. Trav pushed onto his knees, giving Diego the space to do the same. "I need to come, dulzura, I need you to—" He glanced back and froze at the sight of Trav, kneeling on the bed, fully erect and for lack of a better description in any language, looking utterly horrified.

FOURTEEN

"I don't—" Trav swept a hand through his hair, flitting his gaze around the room. "I'm not—fuck, I mean…"

The mood had shifted so quickly, the heat in the room dissipating to an outright chill. Had he misread him? Diego could not see *how* when they had both been strokes away from groaning and messing the sheets. Not when Trav had whispered such filthy, lovely promises.

He twisted on his knees, ass in the air, to look back at Trav. "Do you not want to…?"

"No, I do." His gaze snapped back to Diego. "It's just, I don't…I'm not a switch."

Diego blinked, mentally glancing at his Way with an appeal to pick apart the words. His magick gave the equivalent of a shrug. "I do not understand."

"A switch, I don't…I don't fuck, Diego."

"Then what are we—"

"I *get* fucked," Trav blurted. "I'm a bottom. Jesus." He exhaled swiftly, brow wrinkling. "I usually clarify these things; I just thought that—"

Understanding dawned, and with it came even more possibilities, opportunities Diego had never imagined would come his way. Not after Ruben, who, while sweet and kind and caring, had never truly been his. Not after those years at sea as the slightest, the shortest, the most effeminate, but *now* ... deep in his chest, locked behind his Way and his broken history, a scrap of Diego unfurled. A side of himself the dictates of medieval society had never let him truly explore.

"No, no." Diego scrambled around, reaching for Trav. "I would love to!" he said, too loud, but the mortal did not seem to mind. His brow eased, a hopeful expression smoothing away the embarrassment. "Only I have not ... it is not something I am ..."

"You've never topped?"

Diego shook his head, again relying on his Way to define the word. Trav had acquainted "getting fucked" with "bottom," so it was simple enough to work out the context of "top." "Ha sido un tiempo."

It has been some time.

Trav sighed, easing onto the bed and stretching out alongside Diego. "If it is too much for tonight, I understand." Gone was all the filth and promise, replaced instantly by the care he had grown so used to in the man. He trailed a finger up Diego's arm as he spoke. "We can do other things, and when you're comfortable, if you're comfortable, we can come back to this."

That care, the quiet concern for Diego's well-being and comfort, and the ease with which Trav placed his desires aside to ensure Diego felt safe decided for him.

"I want to," he affirmed. Pushing upright, Diego settled over Trav's hips, mirroring their previous position. Interest parted his lips, and Diego traced the lower one with a finger, slipping it inside to wet the tip. Trav's eyes fluttered closed, his cock twitching. Diego took that as consent and added a second finger, sliding them deeper into Trav's mouth. "And I know you want to, so why should we stop?"

"Mm," was the only response Trav could give, tongue undulating against Diego's fingers, covering them in his saliva and drawing ancient memories to the forefront.

Spit and oil, hasty work in half-lit alleyways. A flash of pain followed by hard thrusts and a version of release that never quite sated the need.

This was nothing like those fearful nights in Zaragoza and the rushed instances belowdecks. Here, he had time; he had modern tools and Horned God be damned, did he have an all-too-willing partner.

"It has been some time." A lifetime since Ruben, enough time to become acquainted with a new role, enough time to forget. Diego bent at the waist, easing his fingers from Trav's mouth to whisper his explanation and seal it with a kiss. "Guide me?"

"Happily."

Pants were tossed aside, their briefs following, and Trav's instructions were given in a soft voice, guiding Diego to the bottle of lube. He started slow, watching Trav's face closely as his fingers tested the tight ring, massaging the muscle and slowly stroking his cock. Sweet whispers of "more" and "yes, like that" prompted his every move.

Trav kept his eyes open at first, nodding and assuring Diego, "It's good, baby. So good," and sighing when he finally pressed a finger in. Goosebumps climbed up his arms, his nipples pebbled beneath his v-neck. The intense look of concentration that had wrinkled his brow eased away when Diego turned his wrist, brushing against a place that had Trav's breath catching in his throat.

"Diego." He arched into the touch, dropping his head back. "Oh, fuck, baby, more."

Goddess, his voice alone had Diego hard as a mast, and that was nothing compared to the look of exquisite bliss on Trav's face. His lips parted, every panted breath joined with praise for Diego, for his fingers, his touch. Unable to resist, Diego bent forward, swallowing Trav's gasp with a kiss and sucking lightly on his throat.

The mortal shivered and groaned, hips rising to take more. Gently, Diego inserted a second finger, easing those inner walls until he felt confident of adding a third. Trav writhed on the bed, every groan dropping lower in his throat until he finally begged, "Please."

"On your knees." He hardly recognized his voice, the confidence with which he stated the demand. Trav's eyes flew open at the sound of it, a look of challenge sharpening the bliss.

"No." He hooked his legs around Diego, heels pressing at the base of his spine. "I want to see your face when you come."

Never.

Never.

Never in either of his lives.

A shiver ran through Diego, and he slid his fingers free. "What do I do?"

"The end of the bed," Trav said, wriggling lower on the mattress. Together, they got him situated on the edge, and he raised his legs to angle his hips better. "Hold me?"

"Sí." Diego hooked an arm around one lean thigh, tugging Trav closer to himself. He added more lube, tossing the bottle aside before taking himself in hand. "May I?"

"Fuck yes." Trav canted his hips, nudging Diego's cock and lazily stroking his own. "God, I'm so ready."

The sight of this man spread and wanton, his eyelids fluttering ... Horned God, it would be a miracle if he made it through this. Gripping himself, Diego notched against Trav, pressing in and cursing as the loosened muscle gripped him. The pressure, fuck, the heat, it was too much. More than anything Diego had ever known, and here they were, without a care, without a worry, with nothing but *time*.

"Dulzura," he prayed, easing in further. He reached for Trav, hand fluttering at the side of his face, wanting to feel the magick of this moment. But this was beyond the Ways; this was mortal magick. Connection, trust, and care bound up in a moment too precious to taint with spells and rituals.

Trav gasped, his hips twitching to accommodate Diego. "More," he pleaded, "I need more of you, baby."

"Sí. Sí, cualquier cosa por ti." Diego eased back only to press in deeper. *Anything for you*. And again, flesh meeting flesh in a sinful cadence. Trav's moans filled the room, underscored by Diego's restrained groans as he held onto the mortal and his release.

"Harder, baby," Trav demanded, ringing the base of his cock and drawing up in strokes timed to Diego's thrusts. His shirt hitched up, revealing a tanned stretch of skin, the muscles in his torso bunching tight. "Fuck...me...Diego...*fuck*."

Every filthy word, every demand, every pant and moan and half-formed thought that flew from those lips had Diego running toward the edge of his restraint. He angled his hips differently, seeking a new angle to stave off the inevitable, only to earn Trav's wild, ragged cry.

His curses became incoherent babbles, the flush in his cheeks bled down his throat, and that impossible vice gripped Diego tighter.

"Dulzura, I need to—"

"Yes, sweetness, yes." Hazy eyes gazed up at him reverent and drunk with pleasure. "Come, D, God fucking dammit, baby, I'm so close." He stroked himself faster, urging Diego on with his words. "I'm so-so..."

A cry left Trav unlike any Diego had ever heard. This was a man given over entirely to pleasure, riding the crest of his orgasm and floating in the bliss. His body tightened around Diego, drawing him impossibly deeper before release spilled on his belly, spurts landing on his shirt. The sight of it, of this man, brought to the absolute pinnacle by Diego's touch, Diego's cock, unleashed something feral in the witch. He knocked Trav's leg from his shoulder, bearing down and thrusting against him, chasing his release.

Bending over the beauty splayed beneath him, Diego sucked a come-spattered nipple through Trav's shirt, moaning at the salty sweetness. Trav cupped the back of his head, and the tenderness of the motion, the tingle his nails drew over his scalp, had his balls tightening, release just out of reach.

"Tesoro," Trav murmured in a thick, pleasure-heavy voice, and the whispered word became a command.

"Dulzura," Diego cried out. Heat shot from his groin, an explosion of bliss down to his toes. Every muscle in his body tightened, his breaths coming in shorter and shorter pants until it was too much.

Until *finally*, he tipped over the edge, groaning deeply as he emptied into Trav.

He stroked his arms as he came, peppering kisses on the top of Diego's head and guiding him back down to earth with whispered adulations.

Diego collapsed onto him, legs turned to jelly and head spinning madly.

"Oh, por la Diosa," he managed after a panting minute.

Trav chuckled, gently clasping his hands around Diego's head. The kiss they managed was awkward and sweet, the wax seal on a missive Diego would treasure in the coming days. "Stay," Trav whispered, wincing slightly as Diego slipped from him. "Stay with me."

He settled beside Trav, brushing strands of hair away from his face and toying with the thin chain that had crawled up his throat as they fucked. "Of course."

Diego twitched awake at the sound of a door closing, bolting upright in an empty bed. Dawn painted Trav's room in a soft, pink light, revealing the remnants of the previous night. His clothes lay in a hastily discarded pile beside the bed, his shoes and Trav nowhere to be found. He squinted across the blurry room, groping the bedside table for his glasses and sliding them on. The room sharpened into focus, and he made out the bleed of light under the bathroom door across the apartment.

Safe.

Diego fell back with a relieved sigh. The clicking of the door had been his lover going to the bathroom. Not a raid, not Inquisitors. Just Trav, who had slept the night in Diego's arms.

Blood rushed to his groin at the memory of what they had shared. Each pant and moan and the helpless little whimpers Diego had wrung from him. Half awake, he let his mind fall back on those sensations, the heat and mind-shattering grip of Trav's body, the weight of his arms as they fell into a deep, sated slumber.

The bathroom door opened, and a moment later, Trav was there, standing at the foot of the bed in briefs and a loose tanktop, his floppy hair rumpled and a cocky smile on his face.

"You're up," he said, whispering, though Diego could not tell for what reason.

"I am," he answered. The smile spread, and only then did Diego realize his hand had drifted to his groin, idly tracing the length of an erection he was only half aware had grown. "Apparently."

"Don't move." Trav knelt on the edge of the bed, pulling the comforter down before crawling in beside Diego and covering them both. "Wouldn't want such stellar morning wood to go to waste, would we?" Propping his head on a hand, he brushed Diego's fingers away, resuming the lazy, absentminded stroking.

Diego hissed, muscles clenching at the feel of Trav's hand, the sensation still so new.

"Shh, tesoro." He kissed Diego's bare shoulder. "Let me take care of you."

"Tesoro," he repeated, hips wriggling as wave after wave of pleasure lapped up his body. "I like it when you call me that."

"I can tell." Trav pressed his long body against Diego's, hooking a leg over his thigh and pulling him closer. Tightening his grip, Trav ducked his head, taking a nipple into his mouth and sucking. A tight moan squeezed out of his throat, and Trav did it again, whispering into his skin, "Each sound you make for me is a treasure, Diego."

"Dulzura," he pleaded, though he had no idea why. What could Diego want in this moment? There was a man beside him, worshipping his body, and Diego's mind was a million miles away, floating on a cloud of bliss.

Trav worked his way up to Diego's shoulder, nibbling his skin and sucking on his pulse. He nuzzled closer, hips rolling and rubbing his hardness against Diego as he worked his cock in tortuously slow strokes. "So sweet," Trav murmured. He drew a deep breath, exhaling with a flick of his tongue behind Diego's ear. "How can you call *me* 'sweetness' when you smell like sugar?"

"No lo sé, dulzura, por favor." A hand came up of its own volition, cupping the back of Trav's head to keep his mouth just *there*.

"What do you need, baby?"

"I need you," Diego panted, thrusting into Trav's grip, willing him to stroke him faster.

"Then take me."

The words buzzed against his skin, igniting the same impassioned fire in Diego as the night before. He twisted out of Trav's hold, rising on his knees and instantly missing the feel of his hands and mouth. So he swept up those teasing hands, pinning them to the pillows over Trav's head.

"I may not be using the word correctly"—Diego stole a kiss, tugging that plush lower lip until Trav arched into him with a groan— "but I believe you are a bit of a brat."

"What makes you say that?" Trav grinned at him, and the sight of it was world-ending. Hazel eyes bright with lust, a flush riding high on his cheeks. His rapid pulse fluttered, heart pounding so hard Diego could feel it in the wrists he held captive. It was a wonder to have this man in a bed with him for a night, even more so to have an unhurried morning.

He took his time with this follow-up kiss, wanting to savor these moments and sear every detail into his skin, so he leaned into his Way, sending strands of magick to coil around the mortal and sew every detail of this shared pleasure into himself.

Trav's body went tight, a modest flinch, and then he went boneless beneath Diego, moaning into the kiss. His hips sought him out, erection growing impossibly harder against Diego's thigh. His pliancy and submissiveness were a summons of its own, and Diego released his wrists, trailing fingers down Trav's arms, his torso.

He lingered at the hem of the tank top, glancing up as he tugged gently. "Take this off?"

Trav blinked like a drunk trying to sober up. His lips formed soundless words, and he brushed Diego's hands away with a heavy limb, the slightest twitch of his head all he could manage as a "no."

Undeterred, Diego nodded and kissed the center of Trav's chest, the outline of the pendant he wore hard against his mouth. "On your side."

He glanced up in time to see a slow grin crawling across Trav's face. He rolled onto his side, and Diego settled behind him, the position familiar and half-forgotten. "Yes, Daddy."

Diego snorted into the crook of his neck, snaking an arm around his front and tweaking a nipple. "Guard your words." Trav's answering whine shot straight to his cock. He ground eagerly against Diego, lifting his hips enough for him to pull the briefs away. "Are you sore?"

"No."

"Mentiroso." Diego nipped his ear. *Liar.*

"Quizás." His smile was audible. *Maybe.*

It was easier, this time, to recall the old motions, and though he fumbled with the tiny bottle, slippery from the night before, he remembered to crook his knee. Remembered to guide Trav's hand to his thigh, to press in slowly until he was seated entirely. Their breaths came slow and even as they started. Less the frantic fucking from the night before and more a lazy combining of selves. A cozy intimacy, unlike anything Diego had ever known.

Over time, his pace quickened, need building at the base of his spine. He slid his hand down Trav's side, gripping his hip for more leverage, a slight adjustment, before fisting his cock and stroking him thrust for thrust. Trav's body heated, his fingers dimpling Diego's thigh, pumping into Diego's fist as the witch pounded into him.

This time, Diego felt the oncoming climax. It was in the tightening roll of Trav's hips and the pinch of his nails. He heard in it the desperate pants and higher-pitched whines, felt it in the palm of his hand and the flex of muscles gripping his cock.

"Good," Diego praised, dragging his teeth along Trav's shoulder, biting down and kissing the pain away. "Eres tan bueno."

"D," Trav whined. "D, I'm gonna—"

"Do it." He rolled his grip at the end of Trav's cock, nursing the head and urging him to tip over the edge. "For me, dulzura."

More of his Way slipped free, magick winding around the pair and binding them together until the rush of blood in Trav's veins matched the torrent in Diego's.

Trav jerked against him, burying his face in the pillows to muffle his groan. As much as Diego wanted to hear him undone, as much as he wanted the memory of his ecstasy ringing in his ears, the sensation of Trav's pleasure stitched itself to his bones. It rumbled against his chest and drew his balls up tight, leaving him balanced on the edge.

Trav's cock pulsed in his hand, and sticky warmth flooded his palm. Diego's thrusts turned erratic, chasing that inevitable tipping point, and with one mind-blowing clench of muscle around his cock, he cried out, "Travis!"

"I'm here, tesoro," Trav panted, reaching back to hold Diego's hips flush to his rear. "I've got you."

FIFTEEN

"I WONDERED IF I would see you today." Morgen shuffled her newspaper, an icy glare stabbing Diego from across the kitchen. "When you did not return last night, I assumed otherwise."

He set the kettle to boil and selected his tea, side-eyeing Morgen as he filled the stainless steel mesh ball. Replacing his bandages and wanting to shower and change clothes were the only reasons he left the pawnshop. Even then, he had had to argue his way free from a surprisingly clingy Trav, who would have been happy to keep Diego in his bed, dozing and waking, only to exhaust each other once more. "Are you a seer now?"

"Do not be rude."

He chuckled and faced her, leaning against the counter with arms crossed. "Worried I have forgotten about your wardrobe?"

"Worried you have forgotten your purpose with the pawnbroker," Morgen shot back. "You were out with the cultists last night. Do you think that is wise?"

"Tammy suggested it would keep them off of my...scent?" The feel of the cultists' lecherous stares, the hunger in their eyes as they leered at him in Shanna Key, came roaring back, leaving him with a sticky sense of unease.

"Of course she did." Morgen set down her paper and folded her hands on top of it. "As a Stitch Witch, you would feel magick as threads and strands. A vinefica Potion Witch feels it as liquid lapping at their arms, a Vestic seer suffers from headaches and migraines. Ours is a sensory perception of magick and the Ways. Mortals are not so advanced." Diego snorted, dipping his mesh ball into a cup of boiling water. She kept on, pretending not to have heard. "To those mortals unlucky, or lucky enough, I suppose, to have been affected by large amounts of magick, whether by hex, curse, allure, or proximity to mass ritual, they are forever changed."

"Sí, lo sé." He carried his teacup and a small plate to the table, settling across from Morgen. "Every witchling knows this. A mortal affected by magick becomes a cultist." He wrinkled his nose. "It does not explain why Tammy referred to my scent."

"They are changed, their unadvanced mortal physiognomy forced to evolve instantly to accommodate the knowledge and presence of magick."

"You speak of them as if they are a different species."

"Are they not?" Morgen snapped. "They have no magick; they scrounge over resources like truffling pigs, fighting their petty squabbles while remaining blind to the truth of the universe around them. They burn our numbers rather than seek to understand, and those not cursed with a smooth brain can barely conceive the magnitude of our powers." Her voice grew deeper, more resonant, and despite his disagreement with Morgen's perception of humanity, Diego sat straighter, attentive to her every word. "They become addicted to the magick they can neither possess nor understand. They seek it out, and Horned God be damned if they ever find it."

"If they do?"

"They become obsessed." Morgen glared down at him, haloed by the rise of her Way. "They glut themselves on the magick, rolling in the Ways like pigs in shit."

He swallowed, staring into his tea as he remembered a conversation from days prior when he had been preoccupied with the memory of Trav's kiss. "You stated before that this demesne is home to so many cultists due to yourself and the Enforcer training grounds on Big Torch Key." She nodded, her silence prompting him to continue. "You assumed Trav knew the cultists, or if not him, then Martin."

"Which has been confirmed by Joshua."

"He met him in the mangroves," Diego said. "Trav said he used to dive, hunting salvage."

"And the magick in the items he pawned led him to hunt more. How much more of the inventory has proven to be occult?"

Diego thought about the backroom and all of its boxes. The treasures Trav had moved upstairs to match them to the register. The fear in his voice when he admitted he had no idea how much was legal for sale and how much he could be held liable for by the state. "Too much." Morgen nodded as though she expected the answer and something else she had said clicked into place. "When was Josh here?"

"He came to me after the completion of his duties to the cult." Morgen lifted her chin as though she found the acts of the magick-addicted distasteful. It was hypocrisy to wield magick as second nature and to find those desiring the same ability to be less than, an antiquated way of thinking, and Diego did not know why he had ever expected more from the witch. "He felt it prudent to report you had not only been fraternizing with his pack but that you left with the pawnbroker."

"We left the bar before the pack realized what I am."

"He took you to his home and kept you to himself," said Morgen. "And so I wonder, Master de Bimini, have you forgotten your purpose?"

When he had no reply, Morgen shuffled the pages of her newspaper and returned to whatever mortal story had captured her interest. Diego turned to leave, halting at the door as she leveled her parting words. "Following our initial discussion around the ouroboros you claim to be seeking, I took it upon myself to order reading materials from the C.R.O.W. library in Cesky-Krumlov. Perhaps you might find the writings of Señor Valdés to be illuminative."

It was late afternoon before Diego dragged himself away from the tower, his head spinning from the ramblings of a half-mad Ink Witch. The manuscripts were written in his native tongue, and it had been easy to lose himself in the dialect of his first life, even if Señor Valdés had been vastly misinformed.

Still, for all his supposition that de Leon was hunting the Fountain of Youth, his writings supplied crucial details regarding the conquistador's final days.

As Morgen had said, de Leon died eight years after Diego, which meant he had survived the curse for just as long. But what struck Diego was that Ponce de Leon had returned to the Calusa lands with two-hundred men and the aim to colonize. As before, when the Calusa had held them hostage before planting the curse on de Leon, they attacked, and the conquistador was shot with a poisoned arrow, eventually dying of his wounds.

Even stranger, Diego recognized a name in the history: Francisco Velazquez de Quesada. Ponce de Leon's doctor and a witch.

Being a lowly gentleman volunteer on a different ship, he had nothing to do with de Quesada, but he recalled the witch's somber mien and haughty demeanor from the few instances where they crossed paths. He kept close to de Leon after they fled the Calusa, especially in those final days before fever sent Diego to the hold, but at reading his name, a memory prickled, thick like a fever dream.

The memory of a hippocromantic and opium, the memory of a martyr.

Valdés' history mentioned de Quesada having a home on de Leon's Hispaniola estate. If his ramblings could be trusted, the witch had journeyed with de Leon to Spain when dealing with the Colombo brat's lawsuit and accompanied the conquistador on his return voyage to the Calusa.

Eight years.

For eight years, Juan Ponce de Leon kept Francisco Velazquez de Quesada by his side, visible to the degree that the historian Valdés had not only noted but commented upon. It was not unheard of for two men to remain companions, even when married to women and doing their duty by fathering heirs for Spain. It was common practice, especially in the Armada, so why did Valdés bring it up in recounting de Leon's final years?

And why had de Quesada returned to the brackish waters of the Calusa?

Head full of a history he could not hope to comprehend fully, Diego passed Morgen in the garden, wandering her stone labyrinth in the afternoon sun, and felt the weight of her piercing glare for the duration of his walk. She did not ask where he was going; she did not need to.

There was only one place on the island that Diego wanted to be.

Trav did not look up when Diego entered Southernmost Pawn. Hunched over a folder, he was absorbed in the register, referencing his inventory against a list on a notepad, scribbling notes, and toying absentmindedly with the gold chain he wore. His hair had flopped forward, making him look younger than he was, and a comforting warmth spread across Diego's chest.

He watched him for a moment, content to let Trav work. As when he had wrapped Diego's hands, his tongue darted out to moisten his lower lip. His button-down shirt was rolled to the elbows, the fabric lightly wrinkled, and the arms were smudged with grime as though Trav had been cleaning and moved directly to balancing his books.

Not wanting to distract him, he headed down an aisle for the back room and stumbled to a halt.

The door was open, and the tables were empty. Every box, every bauble and trinket, every thread of magick that had crowded the tiny space was gone.

Diego entered the room, fingers dancing at his sides as he grasped for any strand, any echo of the occult. All that remained were the frayed ends of threads wafting in a breeze. He followed what he could feel, relying on his Way to guide his steps across the back of the pawnshop, up the stairs, and into Trav's apartment.

Again, he stumbled over his steps, less out of shock and more out of sudden, overwhelming dread.

"Por la Diosa."

Magick filled the apartment, settling around Diego like a water-logged cloak. He edged into the space, spinning in a tight circle out of necessity. The couch, the coffee table, the counters, every available space was filled with the contents of the backroom and more. What had been tidy stacks against the walls now filled the floor. Piles of clothing he did not recognize, handfuls of jewelry, and cases holding coins, gems, and cufflinks. Plastic crates, cardboard boxes, trash bags, and stack after stack of books, albums, folios, and more.

Where had it all come from? He had spent days in the backroom, in the pawnshop, and so much of this he had never seen. So where?

Diego twisted, squeezing through a row of boxes to reach the kitchen table. He dug through boxes and folders in search of what he knew had to be there.

Because where else could it be? What else could have done this?

"Por la Diosa, no. Por favor no."

Abandoning the table, Diego waded through the clutter to the kitchen, yanking open drawer after drawer. Trav had shoved the stack of photographs in a drawer, safe and out of sight.

It was here, somewhere. The cursed ouroboros was in this pawnshop. With each passing day, he hoped he was mistaken. He had begun to believe that what he thought he saw was not real, that there was no threat.

Faced with Trav's apartment, he could no longer continue lying to himself.

It was here; it had to be, but *where*?

He yanked open a drawer, crying out in relief when the photograph of the tin samovar stared back at him. Gathering the photographs, Diego swept clutter from the counter, not even flinching as silver trays and cutlery clattered to the ground. He fanned them out, fingers trembling as he sorted through the collection. The guitar, the samovar, a set of pearls, a Dresden Shepherdess, oil paintings, gilded shoes, and a medallion hewn from stone.

The blood rushed from his face, and he swayed, gripping the counter's edge to keep from crumpling to the ground. Goddess, how he had hoped he was mistaken. There was so much of the occult in the store; he could have been wrong, could have made an assumption, and would have happily admitted fault, but there it was in the photograph—the Calusa Ouroboros.

Every delicate scale and intricate detail, just as Diego recalled. A phantom pain throbbed in his jaw, the long-lost memory of the gold being torn from his body.

Trav cleared his throat, startling Diego. His heart leaped, and he spun around to find the pawnbroker at the top of the stairs, his expression a mixture of guilt and anger. His pants were as rumpled and stained as his shirt, and a smudge of grime darkened his cheek and the bridge of his nose. "Where have you been?"

"At the tower." Diego blinked, thrown by the accusation in his voice. "What happened to you?"

"Went for a dive this morning, been working ever since." Trav picked through the mess, nearing Diego with a laser-focused intent. "After last night, I hoped you'd come by earlier."

"I was here this morning."

"You didn't have to leave." He stopped beside the kitchen table, fingers drafting over a pile of gold watches. "I wish you hadn't left."

"Yo también," Diego managed. He groped the countertop for the photograph, pinching it in his fingers and holding it up for Trav to see. "Where is this, dulzuro?"

He slid a hand into his pocket and squinted at the photograph, an absent expression washing away the anger. "What is that?"

"It was on the table the day we met. Where is it? The medallion."

"It's not for sale." Trav's voice sounded vacant as if he were repeating a phrase in a foreign language, reciting words without connecting knowing the meaning. "It's unavailable."

"Where is it, Travis?" He reached out with his Way, plucking at the knot of magick in the apartment. Sleeping hexes and nostalgia allures, chronomancy imbued to the clocks and watches, and reams of stitch witchery in the garments draped across the couch. All of it too loud and distracting, shrouding the ouroboros from view.

Trav shuddered, closing his eyes and inhaling deeply. His lovely mouth curled in a drunken smile, and he tipped his head back, humming softly before meeting Diego's stare. "You said I shouldn't sell it."

"I said you could not sell it," he corrected, pressing back against the counter when Trav took a step.

And another.

"You want it for yourself," he said in a guttural voice, crowding into Diego's space. Without breaking eye contact, he plucked the photo from Diego's fingers and set it aside, gripping the counter on either side of his hips. "And I want you for myself. Seems we both have something the other wants."

Diego exhaled a shaking breath, at once scared for the mortal and thrilled by his presence, his tone. "Sí."

Trav hummed, gaze flitting over Diego's face. He leaned forward and brushed a kiss against his cheek. "I'm glad you're here." A hand grazed Diego's hip, squeezing before moving away. "Sorry, it's such a mess."

"What is all of this?"

Trav scanned the room, chewing his lower lip. "It's Martin's." His shoulders dropped, and he sighed. "I had to clean out his storage unit and didn't have anywhere else to put things." Straightening, he ran a hand through his hair, leaving a smudge along his brow. "Some of it I can process through downstairs, but the rest of it, I don't know."

"This is more salvage?"

"Salvage, garage sales, junk, you name it."

The pit in Diego's stomach dropped further. He had already thought the task daunting, but this was unbelievable. "How much more is there?"

"This is the last of it." Trav pushed back from the counter, heading for the bathroom. Diego followed him through the narrow path between piles. "Bit more than you signed up for, huh?"

"Un poco."

"I understand," he said with a sigh. "I did warn you it was a lot; guess I should have clarified." Flicking on the light, he cast a sad glance at his apartment. "That medallion was one of the last pieces he brought it. He was weird about the intakes toward the end. Wouldn't let me help with the more valuable items, and then not at all. It was like he woke up one day and didn't trust me."

"I am sure that was not the case."

"The doctors said it was dementia." Trav waved him off, stepping into the bathroom. "Erratic behavior, forgetfulness, the hoarding, seemed like something they'd seen before. It just happened so fast. One day, he was *fine*, and then two weeks later, he—" Trav's hands faltered at the buttons on his shirt. He dropped his head and set his hands on the bathroom sink, shoulders trembling.

Diego wanted to hold him, wanted to stroke Trav's back while he let out the pain he held onto. Goddess, this was a still raw wound months from healing. His Way surged into his hands, threading around his fingers and begging him to stitch the man together, but he could not.

How could he?

Grief could not be erased; it could not be foregone. Grief had to be lived, and no amount of magick could erase the pain. The best he could do was what he had done for Milla—stitch the pain into the person until it became one more thread in the tapestry of their life.

"He didn't come in," Trav continued in a whisper. "I ran the store, and after closing, I went to his condo. I could barely get in the front door because of all of this—"

"Junk," Diego said.

"His treasures," Trav nodded.

"Treasures?" Diego gripped the doorway, alarm prickling his scalp.

"The condo was packed full, and he was ... gone."

"You found him?"

"No." He raised his head, eyes red behind his glasses. "No, he was gone. Ward found him."

"Ward?"

"The sheriff," he said. "Got called out to the mangroves and found Martin. He must have gone out diving and got stuck beneath the roots. It took two weeks for his body to-to—"

A choked sob escaped, and Diego rushed forward, wrapping arms around him. Trav heaved and trembled, finally letting go of the pain he had avoided. He grabbed Diego's arms, holding onto him for dear life, and Diego was all too happy to let him, cradling his lover as best he could.

In time, the tears subsided, the sobs lessening to sniffles. Diego pressed a kiss between his shoulder blades, and Trav relaxed against him, leaning into Diego's comfort.

"I need to take a shower," he finally said. Diego nodded into his back. From the stink of stale sweat and the grime on his shirt, it was evident that Trav had worked hard to move all the junk into his apartment.

Diego raised his head to meet Trav's reflection in the mirror. Though not exceedingly tall, only the top half of Diego's face was visible over his shoulder. He slid his hands low, untucking the plackets of his shirt as they held each other's gaze. Trav finally broke away when Diego slipped a hand under the shirt, feeling muscle tensing beneath his palms.

In that flinch, he remembered the night before. The brush of Trav's arm and his head shake when Diego attempted to remove his shirt.

"I will give you some privacy," he whispered, kissing his shoulder and slipping away. Trav slammed his palm down over Diego's hand, his shirt the only barrier between them.

"No, I—" He swallowed and shook his head. "You'll see eventually. I'd rather get the surprise over with."

Again, that prickle of alarm, this one coupled with an icy finger drawing down his spine. "See what?"

"It's hard to explain." Trav undid the topmost button, dropping his head to watch his hands work. "I was young, and when you're raised like I was, you tend to have ideas shoved down your throat. Of how you're supposed to be. I thought I was broken, that something was wrong with me."

"Nothing is *wrong* with you," Diego said, putting force behind the words. He stepped back as Trav twisted, a soft smile paired with those sad eyes.

"I know that now, but fourteen-year-old me didn't understand. I thought I was being punished for something, that being gay was a sin." He slipped his arm from the shirt, and Diego's eyes dropped to his rib cage. A myriad of short, pale lines stood out against his tan: tight slashes and hash marks, each an angry reminder of an ancient pain. Diego's hands flew to his mouth, his mind struggling to comprehend the horror of what he was seeing. "I tried to cut it out."

He pulled his shirt the rest of the way off, bunching it in his hands over his heart, and faced Diego head-on, light glinting off the thin gold chain around his neck. Diego searched his body, finding more evidence of the wrong that had been done to Trav. Both sides of his ribcage, in places no one would see unless they were lucky enough to know his intimacy.

His eyes burned, his Way raging at the unstitched wounds. He reached for Trav, needing to hold him in his arms and tell him he was perfect, he was beautiful, he was loved.

Trav must have seen the need in Diego's face and understood the shared pain of a haunted past. The need to connect with another soul who could understand. He tossed his shirt onto the sink, reaching for Diego, and hanging from that thin gold chain was the ouroboros.

SIXTEEN

"Morgen!" Diego burst into the kitchen, slamming the door against the counter. "Morgen, ¿dónde estás, vieja murciélago?"

He could still feel the shape of the ouroboros pressing against his skin, every ridge and scale, the coldness of the marble even though Trav had been wearing it for Horned God knew how long.

The mortal did not know. That much, at least, Diego had learned.

Every time he asked, his questions were deflected, and Diego distracted until it was easier to give in. Easier to soothe Trav and give him the pleasure and the connection he so desperately needed until he was sated and sleeping. And only when he fell into a deep sleep was Diego able to leave.

He had tried throughout the evening, offering to fetch dinner, to go to the corner market and grab drinks, to take Trav out of the clutter and the mess, hoping to get him away from the junk and the noise of magick filling the store. Each time he tried to leave, Trav either grabbed and held him or pulled him into the bedroom.

The knowledge of the ouroboros, of the curse, tainted their time together. It called into question every moment Diego had spent with Trav and shone a bitter light on the junk—the *treasures*—crammed into his apartment. That was how he had described the mess—Martin's treasures, and now his.

Diego fought back tears when Trav cupped his cheek, kissed him sweetly, and held him close to whisper, "Mi tesoro."

He had no idea how long he lay wrapped in Trav's arms. All he knew was that his body was weary, his mind running along the edge of panic when Trav's arms finally went boneless around him, his breaths leveling into a deep sleep. Diego had slipped from the bed and dressed, leaving with the quiet, hard-earned skill of a homosexual man in the sixteenth century. Once safely on the street, he ran to the tower.

"Morgen!" He paced the kitchen, picking at the bandage on his right hand. "Maldita sea la Diosa. Morgen!" A door slammed somewhere overhead. He tossed the used bandage on the table, flexing his fingers and curling his lip at the tacky feel of dried ointment on his skin. "We have a problem, Morgen!"

"I gathered as much." She rushed into the kitchen, tying off her robe and glaring at Diego. Even jarred from sleep, the Morgenhexe managed an air of propriety and grace. Hair the golden hue of dawn tumbled to her shoulders, and if Diego did not know better, he would have thought she had taken the pains to brush it before rushing to the kitchen. "What on earth could be so dire you felt the need to wake the entire tower?"

"I found the ouroboros."

"And?"

"And he is *wearing it*."

She blinked, and a hand drifted from her side to grab the chair back before the witch lowered herself to sit. It was the most emotion Diego had ever seen her display.

"Your...your pawnbroker is wearing it? For how long?"

"I do not know how I missed it." He continued pacing the kitchen, words pouring out of him now that Morgen was here. She was ancient, she was wise, and she would be able to help him because if she could not, who could? "His apartment is a mess; there is all of this junk left over from Martin, and I do not understand how I missed it; it was *right there* the whole time. It has been loose for five hundred years; how did C.R.O.W. miss this?"

"Ich weiß es nicht," she frowned. "I do not know, but they did. I have had my students on Big Torch reviewing our registries, and there are no records of this ouroboros—"

"It is real!"

"Sí, Diego, no dudo de ti"—*I do not doubt you*—"but there is no record, not even in the writings of Señor Valdés. As far as C.R.O.W. is concerned, the ouroboros and its curse do not exist."

"Death Witches, Dark Witches, cursed items." He glared at Morgen. "It seems there are many things C.R.O.W. does not believe exist."

She ignored the barb. "Which leads me to believe the ouroboros sank along with de Leon's ship here in the Keys."

"Eso es imposible," said Diego. "De Leon lived for years after the ship sank and was never without the ouroboros."

"After, then, once the poison on the Calusa arrow had run its course. How it got here is not important. Can you handle the matter, or would you prefer I handle things myself?"

A footstep creaked overhead. Diego glanced up, tracking the sound of some-one moving down the hallway toward the stairs. When he looked back at Mor-gen, her face was an unreadable mask.

"We cannot allow the curse to run its course," she said, "only to latch onto the next person to pluck the verdammt thing from the ground. If you are unable to handle the matter, it becomes an issue for C.R.O.W."

Diego peeled the edge of the bandage away from his left palm. "If you involve C.R.O.W..."

"They will have questions about you and your unique knowledge," Morgen finished.

"Could we not ask the cult?" he tried, though the idea was poor. What would he have them do? Stage a robbery and relieve Trav of the junk he called treasure?

"And risk one of their number becoming cursed?" She pursed her lips, fluttering them in distaste. "Horned God forbid one of them gains a taste of that magick. No, you will have to retrieve the item yourself. Can you do it?"

"You want me to-to *steal* from my..."

"I warned you not to get attached."

"I—"

"He is mortal, Diego. A mortal who is unlikely to survive the mess he has found himself in."

"De Leon was mortal, and he survived," he argued. "For eight years, he survived."

"And how many men died in his place?" Morgen countered. "How many men suffered the curse he survived?" Her voice rang through the kitchen, and the following silence was deafening.

Diego dropped against the counter, a numbness crawling into his limbs. How many men had de Leon sacrificed to survive? A ship had sunk on the shoals of what became Key West; Diego himself had been a victim of the curse. How many more paid the price for de Leon to live?

"Either you secure the ouroboros, or I *will* involve C.R.O.W." Again, the ceiling over their heads creaked, and footsteps started down the stairs. "If you care for the mortal, you will do what you know is best."

"Lo sé," he told the floor. "I know."

"Morning." Josh padded into the room. "What're you two hollerin' about?"

Diego's head whipped up, eyes bugging at the cultist in boxers and his beaded necklace, drinking directly from a carton of orange juice. He slowly craned his face toward Morgen, who did not even have the courtesy to look embarrassed. "Morgen."

"It is hardly your place to comment on how I tend my demesne, Master Bimini."

"*Morgen.*"

She raised one shoulder in a shrug and addressed Josh, now peeling a banana. "Diego and I were discussing the matter of the pawnbroker."

"You mean how he's cursed?" Josh asked around a mouthful of fruit. Morgen stiffened, glancing at Diego, who pushed away from the counter.

"How do you know he is cursed?"

Josh tapped his nose. "Reeks of it."

"It could be the number of occult items in his store," Morgen said, "or the remnants of the Earworm."

"Nah." He took a bite, chewing as he spoke. "We've been aware of the pawnshop since I picked up the scent on Martin at the mangroves. And the Ear Worm kinda smelled like a fog machine, with a hint of, like, when one of the tiny hairs in your ear screams before dying."

"Vivid," said Morgen. Josh winked at her.

"When did you notice the curse on Trav?" Diego asked, then held up a hand, stopping his response. "Better, why did you not think to say anything?"

"Wait, did you not know?" He looked from Morgen to Diego. "I thought you knew."

"How could I have possibly known he was *cursed*."

"I thought he was hunting a curse, right?" Josh cocked his head at Morgen, looking like a confused labrador. "We grab the occult items"—he pointed the remainder of his banana at Diego—"witch handles the big bad curse. Isn't that why you've been spending time together?"

"Sí," Diego's cheeks heated, "somewhat."

"I require coffee for this." Morgen crossed the kitchen, filling her electric kettle.

"What do you mean somewhat? Don't you have a deal with Travis, like I have with Morgen?" His voice rose, going sharper around the edges, and the banana wobbled from Diego to Morgen. "He brought you to Shanna Key." Morgen poured beans into a burr grinder, twisting the knob and causing Josh to raise his voice further. "You've been staying at the store with him, isn't that what's happening? Oh, holy crap, please tell me that's what's happening."

"What happens if I say 'no'?" Diego asked.

"Oh, fuck." Josh's face fell, the color leeching from his cheeks. "You really didn't know he was cursed?"

"I still do not understand how you knew."

"Because we can smell it on him!" He threw his arms wide. "Can't you?" Morgen and Diego shook their heads. "You must have, like, felt it, then." He appealed to the elder witch, who frowned.

"I have worked this demesne for thirty years," she said. "In that time, I have tracked every new piece of magick to enter the Keys, and none of them have been the cursed ouroboros."

"So it's been here the whole time, then." Josh nodded.

"But how can the ouroboros have been here the entire time?" Diego asked. "I swear de Leon was never without it."

"You were with fever," Morgen said, "and then you were dead."

"I—"

"What the hell is everyone yelling about?" Tammy stepped into the room, dressed in an oversized, off-the-shoulder shirt. Her hair was pulled into a messy bun, and last night's makeup was smeared around her eyes.

"Oh, por la Diosa, Morgen." Diego threw a hand in Tammy's direction. "Both of them?"

Morgen sent a smirk over her shoulder.

"They didn't know Travis was cursed," Josh explained.

"How could they not know?" Tammy startled.

"How could you fail to mention it?" Diego asked, his voice rising an octave.

"Because you made us agree not to!" She wheeled around to face him. "And don't you two have a deal? You brought him to Shanna Key."

"You invited us!" he shouted.

"Because we take care of our own!" she hollered back, then dropped her head, pinching the bridge of her nose. "Jesus Christ, you've been sleeping with him; how did you not know?" At Diego's baffled lack of reply, Tammy exhaled. "Okay, walk me through it."

"Morgen is old—" Josh started.

"Mind your words," the elder witch snapped.

"—but she hasn't been here long, so she never isolated the magick of the curse from the rest of Key West."

"Neither did you," Tammy pointed out.

"Which means it predates both Morgen and myself."

"Espera." Diego blinked rapidly as the implication of Josh's statement took root. He stared at the cultist, who barely looked a day over twenty-five. "Wait. ¿Qué?"

Josh raised his hands, waggling his fingers in the air. "Maaagick."

"So it predates you both," Tammy pressed on, "but we have a Stitch Witch new to the demesne. Didn't you notice the strands or whatever?"

Diego flexed his hands, the remaining bandage pinching his skin. He picked at the edge, seeking the words to explain the noise of the pawnshop and the overwhelming cluttering of his senses with all the magick it held. "I can feel them," he said. "I can feel the heavy magick, the weight of the curse, but I could not ... um, aislarlo from the rest."

"Aislarlo?"

"I could not take it out." He ripped the bandage free. "Could not identify its particular strand."

"Isolate," Morgen translated. "Do you think the heavy magick behind the curse kept you from identifying the Ear Worm hex when you handled the record?"

Diego shook his head, mouthing, "No lo sé."

"So we now believe the ouroboros has always been here." Summoning a spoon to hand, she stirred the hot water and coffee grinds in the French Press.

"I did not say that."

"You were also dead," she stated, "your history of the events can hardly be trusted. Joshua, when did you first notice the curse?"

"Ran into Martin at the mangroves earlier this year. He was diving for salvage."

"What were you doing there?"

"Dawn tour," he shrugged. "Martin surfaced as we took the group out, and I noticed he smelled different. The magic stink was stronger than before, but it still smelled like the Keys. I didn't think much of it until he died, and the stink started clinging to Travis."

Diego's stomach twisted, and that terrible numbness shot into his legs. He set a hand on the counter, crushing the bandage as he made a fist. "You were in the store..."

"Caught the scent on my way home from the mangroves that morning. It died down a bit when Martin passed, so I popped in to see what was happening."

"And you did not think to mention Travis was cursed?" Morgen rubbed her temple with a thumb.

"What's the big deal? I've been cursed, like, thirteen times."

"Ooh!" Tammy snapped her fingers and pointed at Josh. "Remember when that Kitchen Witch cursed you only to eat orange food?"

"Oh, God," he gagged.

Diego tossed his bandage into the trashcan and pulled open a drawer, taking out the BandAid box. "What is orange food?"

"Food that is orange." Josh pressed the back of a hand to his mouth. "Obviously."

"Cheetos still make him heave." Tammy sat at the kitchen table as Morgen set down the French press and two mugs. The cultist poured coffee for them both and added a dash of cream to hers. "And a week later, he was hexed by a Stitch Witch in San Diego."

"Never got rid of that one." Josh scratched his flat stomach, eyes going hazy with memory. "Whenever I see a red dress, I must put it on."

Diego turned on the faucet a little harder than he intended to but Horned God dammit, they were talking in circles, and he was still no closer to figuring out how to help Trav. Under near-boiling water, he washed his hands, aggressively scrubbing off the old ointment. His mind tripped over everything he knew as Morgen and the cultists recounted The Many Curses of Josh.

Ponce de Leon had been cursed, and his greed had demanded Diego's only gold be ripped from his jaw. The wound had festered. Diego had taken a fever and was sent to his bunk on the San Cristobal, damned to die, when the Santa Maria ran aground on the bone shoals and mangrove islands of what was then Los Martires.

The Martyrs.

Named by Ponce de Leon for their resemblance to suffering men.

How poetic.

But the sinking of the Santa Maria in Key West did not explain the curse's survival. Curses lived in items, patiently biding their time until an unlucky soul fell under their spell. Then, as with the Ear Worm, it ran until the host, or the item, was destroyed.

If the ouroboros had been on the Santa Maria, the saltwater would have been enough to destroy the curse. White salts, like sea salt, held a latent ability to disrupt magick. It was why white salt was used in scourings and banishments. Witches could not tolerate anything but iodized salt for that very reason. If the ouroboros had sunk with the ship, the curse would not have been able to survive Ponce de Leon's death; it would have had nowhere to go, which meant it was either returned to the Keys at some point or had survived here unnoticed.

So how did neither Morgen nor Josh, who looked twenty-five and was apparently much older, recognize the curse among the latent magick of the Keys?

And how did Ponce de Leon survive the curse for eight years when it killed Martin in a matter of weeks?

Diego dried his hands, feeling each thread of the cotton weave. He could see the pattern in his mind's eye and identify every strand of the gingham as clearly as one could see the sunrise. Tossing the towel aside, he flexed and shook his hands, relishing the catch of magick in his fingers before pulling two fresh bandages from the box.

He had one unwrapped and was ready to apply it to his palm when Josh crowded into his space, the heat of his bare chest warming Diego's arm. "What are you doing?"

"Putting on a fresh bandage." Diego showed him his palm. "Trav still thinks my hands are injured; I have been reapplying these to keep him from suspecting what we are."

"You've been wearing these daily?" Josh grabbed the box and scanned the label. He tossed it to Tammy. "He's been wearing these daily."

She, too, scanned the label and snorted. "Well, no wonder you can't feel magick for shit. These come pre-treated with antibiotics."

"That is the ointment?" Diego asked.

Tammy nodded. "The brand name is Neosporin, but it's made of Bacitracin, Neomycin, and Polymyxin." Diego and Morgen shared a look. "What? I have a day job."

"She's a chemist," Josh clarified.

"Tamara, schatz, pretend for a moment that neither Master Bimini nor myself need to suffer mortal healthcare."

"And *that* is why working with your local cult is important," Josh said. "You dumb witches would be lost without us." Diego caught the faintest twitch of Morgen's pinky, and a spoon lifted from the counter to whack the cultist in the head. "Ow."

Tammy rolled her eyes and shook the box at Diego. "They're *salts*, dude. No wonder you couldn't feel anything; you've been coating your palms in salt every time you go near Trav."

SEVENTEEN

"SALT?"

Diego looked down at his hands, scrubbed pink and clean. He crooked his fingers, catching them in the strands of magick stemming from Morgen and himself. Without a thought or effort, he felt her illusory Way and the warmth of the rising sun. Felt his Way picking and prodding at the materials of the room. It whispered the age of the wood that made Morgen's table and the poly-cotton blend of Tammy's shirt and told him the beaded necklace Josh wore was strung with synthetic thread.

Around his little finger was an orange-yellow strand leading to the cuckoo clock on the wall. A chronomantic spell ensuring the clock never needed to be wound. On his ring finger, a vermillion strand connected to Josh.

Diego knew without thinking it was the Red Dress hex the cultist had mentioned.

"How..." He looked to Tammy, needing an explanation.

"Did Trav use Neosporin when he cleaned your hands?" She moved to his side, bandage box in hand.

"Sí." Diego nodded. "I did not want to tell him it was futile. My hands healed overnight, my Way, it stitches—"

"You wouldn't have known, Diego." She squeezed his shoulder. "I'm guessing you grabbed these because he used Neosporin?" Another nod. "Well," Tammy addressed Morgen and Josh, "now we know why he couldn't isolate the ouroboros, even with all the time he spent in the store."

"Damn, man, I bet it's really loud in there for you." Josh took her seat at the table, helping himself to her coffee, grimacing, and adding a spoonful of sugar.

Tammy sighed. "So what do we do?"

"Diego is going to bring me the ouroboros," said Morgen. "And if he does not, I will involve C.R.O.W."

Both cultists gave a low whistle, sharing a look. "You sure that's wise?" Josh asked.

"We are beyond the question of wisdom, Joshua. When you noticed the curse on Martin, how much time passed before you again found him in the mangroves?"

Diego's spine snapped straight, Morgen's question combining with Trav's story. "I thought Ward, the sheriff, found him in the mangroves?"

"Ward was called to the scene." Josh's voice went uncharacteristically somber, the jovial light in his eyes dimming. He stared into his coffee, unwilling or unable to look any of them in the eye. "I was working a sunrise paddle. We'd just gotten the tourists in the water; I went ahead to get photos and noticed the body tangled in the mangrove roots."

"Tangled?"

"Best we can figure is his guideline got stuck, or he got turned around underwater. It happens, especially in low light. He'd been missing for two weeks when the body surfaced, so I noticed the curse on him maybe two weeks before that?"

He glanced at Morgen, and her expression softened. She reached across the table, gently touching Josh's arm. It was easy to forget that Morgen cared; easy to forget that beneath the stern exterior was a witch who had taken in a little girl and spared her life, hiding Milla away from C.R.O.W. until she was old enough to keep herself hidden.

This was the Morgenhexe. The singular Morning Witch. A master illusionist who was already a legend when Diego died. She had witnessed the last gasp of the Hundred Years' War and the creation of C.R.O.W. Had sat the Tribunal and established the laws her foster daughter broke by existing.

It was easy to forget that this woman had driven to St. Augustine in the dead of night to bail Diego from jail, calling in favors to create an identity and existence for the Stitch Witch her foster daughter had accidentally resurrected.

Easy to forget that underneath the straight-backed exterior and pressed blouses was a witch with a beating heart.

Josh sent a weak, tight-lipped smile to Morgen. "I told him not to dive in the mangroves without a buddy."

"From what Trav told me," Diego said, "Martin did not seem reckless."

"He wasn't. That's what made it so weird. He kept going back, always at dawn. I get that treasure hunters are superstitious, but every day for weeks? Sure, there's enough wreckage to attract anyone, but even superstitious divers break up their routine."

"I do not understand what is superstitious about diving."

"Not diving, but the location," Tammy said. "They think if they find a little bit of treasure in one location, there's more to be found, but Josh is right—most divers would have moved on after a week."

"We are getting sidetracked," Morgen cut in. "Diego will obtain the ouroboros, I will ensure it is destroyed. Tamara, Joshua"—they straightened, attentive to the Witch of the Demesne—"continue sending those you trust into the store to purchase what they can. If I am correct, the more treasure the pawnbroker has, the stronger the compulsion to collect and hoard."

"I'm not sure sending in more cultists is a good idea," Josh said. "They latched onto him and Diego in Shanna Key. Hell, only Trav's death glare kept me away; the stink of magick is *ripe*."

"Seriously," Tammy agreed. "I had to practically tie myself to Ginger to resist it."

"Once I have the ouroboros in hand to be destroyed, that should no longer be an issue," said Morgen.

"Yeah, but even if you remove the curse, he will still be affected." Josh settled back in the chair, arms crossed over his front. "That amount of magick, there's no way to remove the stain."

"¿Qué quieres decir?"

"He means," Tammy said, "that we take care of our own."

That phrase again. It was not the first time Tammy had said it, but only now did Diego connect the phrase to Trav. "How long have you known this?"

"He's cursed, Diego," Josh said softly as if breaking the news to a toddler. "You can't just escape a curse; the magick gets into your bones and becomes a part of you. Mortals like me and Tammy—we aren't meant to have come across that power, but then we do, and it...it's—"

"Glorious," Tammy said with a sigh.

"Before I was cursed, God, ages ago, opium was a big deal. You know opium?" Josh asked. Diego nodded, sour spit pooling on his tongue. He had been treated with opium in those final days. Francisco de Quesada had visited him in his bunk, administering the pain-relieving drug and muttering nonsense.

"It's just as addicting," Josh continued. "Trav isn't going to walk away from this unchanged. Hell, it's already working on him."

"What do you mean?" Diego was a Stitch Witch. Piecing together a ballgown from panels and pleats came as naturally as breathing. But the only thing worse than hearing what Josh was about to say would be admitting he already suspected the truth.

Josh hit him with an expression stuck between sorrow and sympathy. "You smell really good, dude."

Tammy stepped close and dropped her head on Diego's shoulder, inhaling before she said, "Sweet, like sugar."

⊗

He took the morning to settle his thoughts and come to terms with what he had to do, and after Josh and Tammy's admission, take a long shower to cleanse himself of every uneasy thought. None of which helped. His mind was a jumble of fevered history and terrible implications, and when Diego attempted to follow the strands, he ended up in a muddled mess of his own making.

So he walked back to the very beginning.

The Calusa cursed Ponce de Leon. He filled the holds of his ships with treasure until they sat heavy in the water, hulls scraping over sunken sandbars. He draped himself in gold and, when that was not enough, demanded gold from his crew. The curse had driven him mad and led to Diego's death.

Francisco de Quesada had come to Diego just once, a hippocromantic nobleman making promises to a Stitch Witch. Even now, five hundred years later, the circumstances struck him as odd. The doctor had never sought out Diego's advice or company, but he had knelt beside Diego's bunk, administering opium to a witch on his deathbed.

"Necesito tiempo," he had murmured, more to himself than Diego. A doctor lost in his mind. "Solo necesito tiempo."

I need time. I only need time.

Now, so far removed from that night, Diego's memory was faulty. He had been fevered, coated in sweat and brine, his jaw throbbing and vision hazy, and de Quesada had kept rambling, the same distressed thought over and over again.

"Necesito tiempo. Necesito ayuda, ¿entiendes? No puedo sacarlo...no puedo sacarlo."

I cannot get it out.

And then mutiny had broken out; the storm had hit. The San Cristobal made landfall near St. Augustine, and Diego died.

He could not recall the exact timeline, but he knew with certainty the curse had worked quickly, gripping de Leon in the hours after he donned the ouroboros. If Joshua's assumptions could be trusted, the same had happened to Martin, and now it was preying on Trav.

He claimed Martin had discovered the ouroboros in the mangroves. Morgen and Josh were convinced the magick had always been in the Keys, but how could the curse survive the salt? And why did Martin return to the mangroves day after day?

These questions simmered as he walked down the A1A, and only when he stood in front of Southernmost Pawn did Diego pull himself from his thoughts. Through the window, he made out the silhouettes of customers browsing the shelves and, seated at the register with a scowl on his face, Trav.

Deep shadows clung to his eyes, stubble darkened his jaw, and that lovely mouth was pinched and screwed into a frown. He watched each customer closely, eyes narrowing in shrewd suspicion whenever someone touched an item on the shelves. Without the ointment disrupting his Way, Diego could feel the foule magick through the glass, a prickly, jagged thread pinching his fingers. It was so evident, now, how it wrapped around Trav's ribcage and wormed between the bones to strangle his heart.

Hands shaking, Diego rubbed bandaged palms against his thighs—plain bandages to keep Trav blind to the witchy world. Morgen had demanded it, and even Josh had agreed.

"He's about to have his world turned upside down, man," he had advised. "One thing at a time, right? Let him accept that magick is real before he has to acknowledge his boyfriend is a witch."

Diego could not argue, not when Tammy had repeatedly assured him, "We take care of our own."

Trav would be fine, so long as they could remove the curse. So long as Diego could put aside his morals and steal the ouroboros from his lover's neck. If they could remove the curse, Trav could learn to live in a world where he was drawn to magick. Would that be so terrible? Diego was a creature of magick, and he cared for the man. With the cult to help him acclimate and Diego to guide him, Trav would be fine.

He would be fine.

That thought alone spurred him through the door. Trav looked up as he entered, the sour expression easing for half a heartbeat before his brows dropped, and he frowned.

"Where have you been?" He slid off his stool and rushed around the counter, crowding into Diego's space. "I woke up, and you were gone; where did you go?"

"Home." He raised a hand, showing Trav the bandage. "I needed to replace these."

"I could have done that for you." Trav reached for Diego and stopped when a customer approached the counter.

"Hiya!" The woman was young-ish and fit, her curly hair cropped short and dyed bright electric pink. She dropped a stack of albums on the counter. "I wanted to buy these."

"Sure." Trav tapped the tablet screen a little too hard.

"I work over at Zero Mile Music"—she leaned over the stack, pulling it a hair closer to herself— "I'd love to get a line on whoever pawned these."

"He's dead," Trav stated. He tried to take the topmost album, and the woman's grip tightened, causing a minor tug-of-war before she finally relented. Something about the way she watched Trav was unsettling. Her attention was too keen, her eyes too wide and greedy. Diego edged closer, and the movement turned her attention toward him. It was fleeting, a mere darting of her eyes, but he did not miss the spark of interest or how her nostrils flared.

"That's too bad." Her posture eased. "It's a great collection. Don't suppose you have any more? I'd be happy to put down a deposit and buy whatever becomes available—"

"Anything else?" Trav cut her off, spinning the tablet around. Unbothered, she tapped a credit card and gathered the records into her arms. With one last glance at Diego, she thanked Trav and left. He watched her go, fists clenched on the countertop, and when the door had shut behind her, he pushed away from the counter, grabbing Diego's hand and tugging him into a deserted aisle. "Why did you leave?"

"I—" He could not think of a lie, and the truth stuck in his throat. His eyes dropped to the gold chain visible beneath the collar of Trav's shirt. This close, with his hands clean, the curse twining around the mortal was obvious. It hissed and fizzed, and Diego's fingers twitched, his Way reaching for the taint and longing to pick it apart.

He pulled Trav close instead, silencing his fears by kissing him. He tensed, grunting in surprise before his mouth softened, and he returned the embrace. Diego held him tight, letting the beat of Trav's heart and the warmth of his mouth ground him as he pressed his hands into his back, sliding them up to his shoulders.

Trav would be fine.

Diego fanned his fingers, tugging Trav's collar wider and hooking the gold chain in his pinkies.

With the cultists to guide him and Diego to hold him, he would be fine.

His fingers found the clasp, and he caught the trigger with a nail.

He would be *fine*. He had to be.

Diego twitched his little finger, tugging on the trigger, and Trav ended the kiss, eyes darting over Diego's face. "What was that for?"

"Do I need a reason to kiss you?"

"No." A blush tinged his cheeks, erasing the last echoes of anger. "Just unexpected."

"I am sorry I did not say goodbye this morning." He brushed his lips against Trav's cheek. "You are so peaceful when you sleep, I did not wish to wake you."

His shoulders relaxed, and he snaked an arm around Diego's back, fingers knotting in chambray. "You probably think I'm being ridiculous." His low chuckle puffed against Diego's temple. "I guess I am. After Martin went missing, I, I don't know..."

"Entiendo."

"How can you understand?" Trav leaned back. Goddess, he looked exhausted; his skin stretched too thin over those lovely cheekbones. It had been just over a week, and in that time, the curse had eaten away at this beauty of a man, consuming all that made him shine. Martin had lasted two weeks with the curse, and here was Trav wasting away before Diego's eyes and he had been too blind to notice.

Two weeks. The life cycle of the curse. Two weeks to consume its host, two weeks to sail from Calusa waters to the Keys, how in the nine rings had Ponce de Leon survived *eight years*.

"—couldn't get back to sleep when I realized you were gone, so I went for a dive. I didn't know where you'd gone and thought maybe I'd done something to … God, I sound like an idiot."

"No, you do not. " Diego shoved his thoughts aside, focusing on the man in his arms. "I should have left a note or sent a message."

"I don't like when my things go missing." The fingers in Diego's shirt knotted tighter. "And I know you're not a *thing*, but you are a treasure, Diego." His voice dropped with the statement, the words a declaration. "You're my treasure."

Diego ought to be alarmed by his possessive tone, rejecting or blaming the idea on the curse, but when had anyone ever claimed him as theirs? When had anyone treasured Diego like this man had from the moment they met?

Never.

Never in either of his lives.

"Mm," Trav buried his face in the crook of Diego's neck. "Smell so sweet."

Gooseflesh erupted down Diego's spine in warning. How often had Trav said those words? Already, he had lost count. Heat bloomed in his belly, too hot to be pure affection, too warm to be anything but. He leaned into it, embracing the feeling even as fear sparked to life in the back of his mind.

How often *had* Trav said those words? He did not know the number but knew he had first heard them a little over a week ago when Trav washed his hands and smiled softly at Diego, sitting on his toilet with bleeding palms.

Well, whatever soap you use smells good. Sweet like sugar.

He had not thought much of it then, but now, knowing the truth of what Tammy and Josh had said—even if he or Morgen could remove the curse, the damage had been done by Trav's years in this store surrounded by the dull throb of magick. Without the ointment on his palms, Diego could feel the many mired strands pulsing through Southernmost Pawn, each thread a vibrant frequency as loud as those in the store he ran with Milla.

He wrapped arms around Trav's narrow waist, relishing the heat and solidity of the mortal. Beneath his palms, the prickling magick of the curse poked and pinched, just one thread among the many wrapped around Trav like a spider's web trapping its prey. Consuming and claiming him with the same greedy compulsion as the curse he bore.

He needed to act before he lost his nerve, and, holding Trav close and treasured, Diego finally believed he could do this. He could steal from his lover, a man who trusted him, and take whatever pains awaited him as Trav learned about the witchy world. He would be mad. He would be frightened and confused, and if he would have him, Diego would be there every step of the way.

He cupped the back of Trav's head, speaking around his desires. A lesson learned in his first life. How to lie without lying by asking an innocent question none could hold against him.

"What time do you close?"

EIGHTEEN

Strands of bistro lights illuminated the tiny yard, casting the firepit and Adirondack chair in a fanciful light. A stone path bled from the back door of Southernmost Pawn, disappearing under the long swaying branches of a willow tree and obscuring what Diego now realized was a far larger space than he had first assumed.

Trav led him down the path, sweeping aside the willow to reveal an enclosed garden. A glass mirror ball on a podium reflected the bistro lights nailed to the tree trunk, giving the space a dreamy glow. Solar-powered stained-glass butterflies peppered a row of bushes hugging the fence, and a chicken pecked the grass beside a teak four-poster daybed.

Diego stopped short, gaping at the bed. It was easily king-size, with cream-colored curtains tied to each poster and colorful pillows clustered in a purposeful mound at the head of the bed. A woven cotton blanket in bands of teal, off-white, and black was artfully draped across a corner, the fringed edge just dusting the ground. Trav followed Diego's line of sight and chuckled.

"It's a little much, right?" He placed their food on a wrought iron cafe table, arranging the sushi boxes. Diego set down the glasses and bottle of white wine he had selected from upstairs. "Martin would sleep out here whenever he stayed out too late."

"Instead of going home?"

"His condo was on Stock Island," Trav named the small island east of Key West, "so whenever he drank too much on Duval Street, he'd come here." His gaze went distant, and a faint smile appeared. "I'd wake up to find him cooking pancakes and nursing a Bloody Mary."

"I am glad you had him in your life." Diego poured a glass for Trav and handed it over. Their fingers brushed, and a warm tingle bled up his arm. Trav blushed, dropping his chin to look at Diego through his lashes.

"Me too."

The moment stretched, words poised on the tip of Diego's tongue, a question perched on Trav's lips. They leaned for each other, the magick of the moment drawing Diego closer and closer to a new edge he was dangerously at risk of falling over.

He wanted to. Goddess knew he had wanted to all his first life; his second was no different. If he could remove the curse, if he could be certain Trav was safe, if he could tell him he was a witch.

If...if...if...then maybe—

The chicken clucked and pecked Diego's toes.

"¡Maldito pollo!" he shouted, spilling wine as he jerked back. "What is it with these chickens?"

Trav laughed, his wine glass clinking against wrought iron as he set it down. He ushered the bird out of the private glade, half scooping it in his arms and gently tossing it over the fence. Feathers rustled, the bird squawked, and a light *thump* sounded from the other side. He wiped his hands off on his pants and picked up a pair of chopsticks, breaking them apart. "They like you."

"I wish they did not." Diego downed his wine and refilled the glass. "Why was there a chicken back here?"

"The neighbor has a coop; they get in sometimes." Diego stared at him long enough that Trav huffed. "What?"

"Are you telling me that that *maldito pollo* who tripped me lives *next door?*" His voice rose, sharp and shrill as a chicken squawk, and Trav burst out laughing.

"You really hate those birds, don't you?"

"Did you know they are descended from dinosaurs?"

"Oh my *God*. Come here." Trav flicked the lid off a box and selected a piece of sushi, holding it out for Diego. "Eat."

"And the bed?"

Trav glanced at the four-poster daybed. "What about the bed?"

"Do they not sleep on it?" Diego jabbed his chopsticks at the fence and made a face.

Trav arced out of his relaxed pose, setting his elbows on his knees. Wine glass dangling from one hand, he lowered his glasses with the other to stare at Diego. "Are you seriously still going on about the chickens?"

"I do not like them!" Diego threw his hands up in defense. "And they have been clucking through our dinner." He shuddered as a chicken did just that and drew his feet from the ground. "There are three of them now; it is very distracting."

"And so you're worried about the bed." Trav stood and set his glass on the table. Their bottle of white was long gone, as was the sushi, and they now shared a rosé as soft as their surroundings. Throughout the meal, the conversation remained light, as though both were unwilling to break the easy bubble of safety by delving too deep. Diego lied about his day and rambled about Morgen's wardrobe. Trav recounted an exchange with a customer and told stories from his years in the Keys.

It was almost enough to forget about what he needed to do, but every so often, Trav would angle just so, and the gold chain around his neck would glint in the light. Or he would twist, his shirt pulling tight, and the ouroboros would be visible through the fabric.

So Diego filled his glass and focused on the man.

The man who seemed determined to either punish him or delay the inevitable for his enjoyment. After their kiss in the pawnshop, Trav had kept his distance, letting the air between them charge until Diego feared it would combust.

Oh, there were touches and lingering looks. He had leaned across the small wicker table to feed Diego a piece of sushi and brushed the pad of his thumb across Diego's lower lip, and hovered close to his side while pouring the wine. His eye contact had been intense and direct, gaze heating as the night went on, but he denied Diego the full body touch he desired until he was trembling with need.

And so he had mentioned the bed, now surrounded by three roosting chickens.

"How do you keep them from sleeping on it?"

Trav crossed the meager distance to stand beside Diego's chair. He swept strands of hair behind his ear and lightly trailed a finger along his jaw. Hooking a knuckle under his chin, Trav angled Diego's face up. "I keep the curtains closed."

He tried to swallow, but the angle of his throat and the heat of Trav's touch made it difficult. Instead, he moistened his lower lip with his tongue and lowered his voice. "They are not closed now."

"No." Deftly, he swept the wine glass from Diego's hand, set it on the table, and strode away.

Diego was not a hasty man. He had learned in his first life that there was too much risk in being who he was to act hastily.

But the sway of Trav's hips as he approached the bed, and the smooth, seductive manner in which he sat and stared expectantly at Diego tested his resolve to act with intent in all things.

Then again, desire and intent often went hand in hand.

In a heartbeat, he was out of his chair and standing between Trav's knees, cradling his cheeks and gazing down at him. As Trav had done to him so many days ago, Diego trailed his thumb along the corner of his eye, damn near dying when Trav pressed his cheek into his hand.

"Near or far?" he asked.

"Near," Trav answered.

"Thank the Goddess for small favors." Diego swept his glasses away, immediately drowning in those rich hazel eyes. The bistro lights caught in the gold and copper flecks nestled in among the green, sparkling like fireflies in the depths of his pupils. It was mesmerizing and intoxicating to take his time with this, with him. Diego savored the moment, ignoring what he must do to lightly sweep his thumbs up Trav's cheekbones and run his fingers through his hair.

He leaned into the caress with a soft smile on that tantalizing mouth, letting Diego touch his fill. And touch he did, running knuckles down Trav's throat, lightly scraping his nails along his scalp, and sweeping his thumb across a plush lower lip until Trav's eyes were heavy-lidded and his every breath heavy. Until Diego felt a slight tremble in his lover's body and knew he had returned every teasing touch and heated smile he had been tortured with over dinner.

Until he whispered, "Please."

Diego knelt on the edge of the bed, caging Trav between his legs. With hands bracing his skull, he pulled him into a kiss—soft at first, but soft and sweet—a kiss worth remembering if this all went wrong.

Trav's hands came up, gripping Diego's thighs and sliding to cup his rear, hitching him higher as he gave himself over. His lips parted at a stroke of Diego's tongue, letting him in to claim his mouth. Goddess, he could get lost in the easy way Trav let him lead, how he submitted with enthusiasm evident in every tiny whimper and the pressure of his hands.

Gently, Diego eased him back on the bed, laying that long body out for his pleasure. "The neighbors?"

"Stores on both sides," Trav answered.

"And behind us?"

"Early risers." He palmed the back of Diego's head and pulled him in for a kiss, tongue sweeping his mouth as his hands flew to the front of Diego's shirt, undoing each button. The press of his palms against bare skin earned a groan, and Trav broke away from the kiss to grin drunkenly up at him. "They've got a massive cock."

"*What?*" Diego sputtered.

"A rooster," Trav cackled, "damn thing crows at dawn."

"Por la Diosa." Diego dropped his head against Trav's chest, a giggle bubbling in his chest and shaking his shoulders. "So it is not only the chickens I have to worry about but also the giant cock next door?"

"You've nothing to worry about there." Trav rolled his hips, halting Diego's laughter with the press of his erection against his inner thigh. He raised his head and found Trav staring at him hungrily. He bit his lower lip and slipped a hand around Diego's waist, pressing down on his lower back so their groins brushed. "Nothing to worry about at all."

"You are going to be the end of me, dulzuro."

"I hope so."

The heat in those words, the low growl punctuated by a thrust of his hips, had Diego slinking low. He tore Trav's shirt free from his pants, hitching it high to lick his navel and pepper his waistband with kisses.

"Diego." Trav pawed at his shoulders, trying to bring him back to his mouth.

He shook his head, working Trav's belt free and pausing at the button of his fly. "Is this alright?"

"Yes." He dropped his head back, throat bobbing. "God, yes, let me fuck your mouth."

"Mierda," Diego murmured, earning a shiver of delight from Trav. He leaned into his Way to ease the zipper, not wanting anything to delay the heat and weight of Trav's cock in his mouth. Tiny threads erupted from his fingertips, his magick peeling the garment away. Trav gasped, the startled sound melting into a sensual moan as Diego freed his cock and licked it from base to tip. Salt burst on his tongue, and he moaned at the taste. "You taste so good, dulzuro."

"So sweet, Diego—" His voice had a pleading note, almost a whine, and Diego glanced up, taking Trav's cock again in his mouth as he waited for his lover to continue. "My shirt, tesoro, please." His pupils were blown wide, and a flush splashed across his cheeks. "I want you to touch me."

Diego grinned around him, reaching out with his Way. He trailed a finger down Trav's front and buttons slid free, the shirt peeling away to reveal a lean, tanned torso. The ouroboros sat like a weight on his sternum, absorbing the hazy glow from the bistro lights. It called to Diego, the magick in the totem fizzing and spitting a hideous green. He could all but see it burrowing into Trav and filling the canyon of his bones with its noxious stink, and he wanted nothing more than to tear the cursed thing from his throat.

He could do it; his Way was already pooled, and his lover was helpless beneath him. He could call on the threads in the sheets to bind Trav, rip the ouroboros away, and vanish into the night, destroying the item before it did any more damage. It was not ideal; it was the worst possible means of securing the ouroboros and removing the curse, but Diego could do it, and the cultists would come for Trav; Morgen would ensure his safety, and if Diego were lucky, he would have a chance to explain.

If...if was better than when. Because when the curse ran its course, Trav would be lost, and Diego was not sure he could survive the pain.

Not with his every gasp and moan searing itself in his memory.

He would rather the mortal live, rather he survive, even if it meant never again holding him or kissing him.

With that in mind, Diego splayed his hand over Trav's belly, relishing the roll of his muscles and the rise of gooseflesh as he slid his palm up the length of his body. Magick spooled from his fingers, reaching for the gold chain around Trav's neck as Diego kept him distracted with his mouth and his tongue, working his cock with one hand while he prepared to steal with the other.

His fingertips brushed cool marble and a static shock shot into his bones. He jerked his palm back, a cry of surprise muffled by the cock in his mouth, and watched in horror as Trav blindly groped for the ouroboros, pulling the medallion up over his shoulder and out of reach. The gold chain lay flat against the base of his throat, his chest rising and falling in deep bellows as the man fought to maintain control. With trembling fingers, he guided Diego's hand to a nipple, a needy whimper telling him what he wanted.

He brushed the nub with his thumb, furious for missing the moment.

And then Trav wormed his fingers into Diego's hair, gripping at the roots and tugging with demand.

"Like that, baby," he groaned, body quivering beneath Diego. "Pinch them for me."

Fuck.

How in the nine rings could a man be so submissive and so demanding...

Diego hitched forward on his knees, working Trav's cock with a hand and his mouth, pinching his nipple and moving to the other. Each pant that left the mortal, each moan and whispered cry of Diego's name tempered his rage and rooted him firmly in the moment. A strangled cry of, "¡Tesoro!" sent a rush of blood to Diego's cock, and suddenly this was not enough. He needed Trav's weight, needed the man over him, needed to plunge within him. Needed his mouth and his hands and that plush lower lip between his teeth.

He popped off of Trav, smiling ruefully at his frustrated whimper. A whimper he turned to a sigh when Diego licked up the center of his chest. Trav's hands skated down his shoulders and arms, fingers digging into his wrists when he flicked his tongue over a nipple.

"I want you over me," Diego murmured into his skin, teeth grazing, tongue flicking, lips sucking. "I want your weight on me."

"Baby—"

"Can we?"

"Yes, fuck, yes." Trav released his arms, working onto his side as Diego settled at the head of the bed. He had just gotten into position when Trav's hands were at his waist, loosening his belt and undoing his pants. He sighed as his cock sprang free, and then Trav was there, taking Diego down to the hilt in one slick movement.

The heat of his mouth sent him to the stratosphere. He dropped his head back, blinking at the lights and the tree above as Trav tugged his pants and briefs low, all the while lathing Diego's cock with an unfairly talented tongue.

"Dulzuro," he groaned, pumping into Trav's mouth, "you keep doing that, and I will not last."

He responded by curling his tongue around the head and swirling his fist down the length.

Diego hissed, grabbing Trav by the shoulders and hauling him up, frantically tearing away his shirt and tossing it aside. Their mouths collided, desperate with need. He tasted himself on Trav's tongue, and the wildness of the moment had Diego groaning. The mortal man had bewitched him, utterly and wholly. He had captured Diego and run away with all of his good sense, leaving him splayed on a bed with his half-naked lover above him, wantonly rolling his hips and giving over to a desire that was returned ten-fold.

Goddess, he would be a ruined man after this.

Trav tugged at his pants, urging him to raise his hips so they could be stripped away and discarding his own just as quickly before melting over Diego, knees on either side of his hips and fingers plunging into his hair, holding Diego's mouth to his. "Ready me," he murmured, slipping his tongue in when Diego parted his lips to speak.

He ran his fingers down the curve of Trav's rear, teasing the ring of muscle until the man was again trembling from his touch. Every twitch of his hips had their cocks rubbing together, the friction a mutual tease.

"Oil?"

"Under the pillow," Trav panted in his ear. He reached back, digging under the mound of pillows until his fingers closed around a bottle. Realization struck, and Diego broke into laughter at the audacity of this man. Tying the curtains back, teasing him through dinner, and now this—stashing a bottle of lube in the pillows. Heat crawled from his belly into his cheeks, that peculiar warmth from earlier blooming in his chest. Never had he been so treasured, so desired. Never had any man gone to such an effort for him. It was enough to have him forgetting about the ouroboros, shouldering his worries, and giving over entirely to the moment.

Trav stole the bottle from his hand, pouring a liberal amount on his fingers before reaching behind. He held Diego's startled gaze as he pressed into himself. "I can't wait, baby. I need you."

"Dulzuro," he breathed, heart skipping as Trav straightened. His head fell back on a groan that Diego felt in his toes.

"Touch me," he demanded, and who was Diego to disobey? He took Trav's cock in hand, stroking his length. The scars on his ribcage winked in the low light, calling the Stitch Witch on a level he could not resist. He trailed his fingers over the old wounds, Way bleeding into his skin. Not to heal the mortal, not to erase the scars, but to acknowledge the pain and hurt, the grief of his past, and stitch it into his person, easing the sting by sewing it into the memory of this pleasure.

"Fuck, tesoro." Trav panted. He gripped Diego's shoulder for balance, a sheen of sweat breaking out across his forehead. "I'm so fucking needy for your cock, Diego. Let me have it, please?"

"Always," he promised, kissing the words into Trav's wrist. He stole the bottle back, coating himself with the oil. "Take what you need, dulzuro; it is yours."

"Baby." Trav removed his fingers and adjusted his position. "I need you. I need to feel you." The moment he was notched, Trav lowered down, taking all of Diego in a slow, steady drop that had his belly swooping and scrotum tightening. They cursed in tandem, Trav taking slow breaths to adjust and accommodate Diego. "God damn, you feel so fucking good, baby."

"Sí, sí." He nodded, near frantic, needing to walk back from an immediate edge. Hand still slick, he stroked Trav, drinking in every twitch of muscle and the trembling of his lower lip. "Tú también."

"Have you done this before?" Trav rolled his hips with the question, eyelids fluttering and nostrils flaring. "This position?"

"No."

"Thrust up, match my pace," he advised, rising ever-so-slightly only to slide back down. A rough, rattling groan rolled out of Diego's throat at the texture, the tightness, the *heat*. He gripped Trav's hips, fingers dimpling his skin, and guided him through another roll and slide. They increased their pace, panting each other's names and gasping adulations in both languages. Still, Diego needed more. Trav was too far away, too out of reach, and Diego wanted to feel all of him. He reached up, twining his fingers in Trav's and tugging him low. Every thrust of his hips had Trav's cock rubbing against his belly, a sticky-slick slide that had sharp, cut-off sounds catching in Trav's throat.

"Baby," Trav panted, fluttering kisses along Diego's jaw, his throat. "Mi tesoro."

"Sí, soy todo tuyo," he breathed, his brain lacking the oxygen to guard his words.

I am yours.

The words sparked a kindling fire to flame, increasing Trav's pace with a hungry fervor. He speared himself onto Diego's cock, crying out with each thrust. Beneath him, Diego worked his hips, matching his lover's need and chasing his release. Their bodies collided again and again until stars danced in the corners of his eyes. He arched his back, seeking to strike the place within Trav that had him crying out, finding home again and again until the mortal went taut over him. Cries of pleasure strangled in his throat, Trav's eyes flew wide, and with the barest stroke of Diego's palm, his cock pulsed and released.

"Fuck, baby, fuck." Trav doubled over, hips still rolling as he rode the throes of orgasm, drawing Diego closer and closer to that same edge. In one instant, it was a distant mirage, and in the next, pleasure slammed into Diego without warning. Trav swallowed his groan with a kiss, tongue stroking and driving deep as Diego emptied inside of him. Shivering and trembling, every muscle danced with the ecstasy of release. Slowly, the stars faded, the world sharpening back into focus, and above him was Trav. His lover, his pawnbroker.

His.

NINETEEN

As threatened, the rooster crowed at dawn, hauling Diego from a bone-deep sleep. He blinked at the blurry surroundings, vaguely aware he was outside, naked, and in bed with a man. Mentally, he prepared to leap from the bed and rush into his clothing, charting his exit and ready to walk away as if the night before had never happened.

But the panic never came.

His pulse remained steady, no rush of adrenaline pumping through his limbs, and the man beside him snored lightly, hair tousled, and face softened in sleep. Diego savored the peace. Trav had changed something in him, bringing Diego into this new world in a manner Milla never could. With every kiss, every flirtatious comment, Trav had proven what the last year had not been able to: he was safe.

In his second life, he could be who he was without fear, and he knew with the dawning of the sun he wanted to be that person with Trav.

He rolled onto his side, drinking in the fine bone structure and thick lashes, silently thanking the Goddess for putting a baseball bat into this man's hands. Reaching out, he moved to sweep the flop of hair from Trav's forehead, stopping when he saw the gold chain around his neck.

And just like that, the cozy warmth soured and chilled.

He curled his hands against his chest, letting his magick rise. As cruel as it was, he knew this was his best chance to steal the ouroboros and get it into the hands of a witch who could help. He had been willfully blind to the corruption of the curse after their dinner, turning his attention to the mortal in his arms and away from his distasteful task. Soothing him in the come down with soft words and tender strokes until his heart slowed to a steady, exhausted beat, and he fell asleep with his head on Diego's chest.

But with the rooster's harsh crow came a more brutal reality. If Trav woke, Diego would again be tempted to turn his thoughts aside, ignoring the threat of the curse for one more morning in his lover's arms when he would have weeks instead.

Magick prickled in his palms, and threads wormed between his fingers in search of something to unstitch. Carefully, Diego raised onto an elbow, casting one last glance at Trav, asleep and beautiful in the first light of day, before running a finger along the delicate gold chain.

True metals were tricky, and none of the Ways Diego knew were adept in manipulating them, but jewelry was made. It was manufactured. It was a product of many pieces stitched together to make the whole and *that* he could work with.

Focusing on the seam in a link, Diego exhaled, long and slow, forming the desire in his mind and binding it to his intent.

Every ritual required three things: intent, desire, and sacrifice.

His intent came easy: to steal the ouroboros.

His desire was obvious: free Trav from the curse.

He did not want to think of the sacrifice. Did not want to dwell upon what this would do to Trav or how he would react when he woke and found himself robbed and alone. It was painful enough to know the cost of the ritual he performed, and Diego hoped that pain would suffice without needing to delve deeper for this to be a success.

"*Deshacer*," he whispered, verbalizing his intent. *Undo.*

Trav hummed in his sleep, inhaling deeply, and Diego froze as his fingers brushed the soft skin of his throat, holding his breath as the magick worked on the near-invisible seam in the gold link.

He almost wanted the mortal to wake, to get caught, to have a reason to explain, Morgen and C.R.O.W. be damned. Lying to mortals had been what caused the pyres in the first place, and here he was, repeating history at the command of an ancient witch and making the same Horned God-damned mistakes they always made: not trusting humanity to understand, not giving them the benefit of the doubt and sharing their world with their fellow man.

Not again.

Diego had lost a sister and a lover. He had lost a life to the lies of C.R.O.W. and gained a second through the desperation of a witch they decreed Forbidden and Foule.

And for what?

Her *magick*.

Condemning one of their own out of the same fear humanity had condemned them.

Not. Again.

Let him wake; let Diego have the difficult task of pulling the wool from his eyes and helping Trav see the truth of the world and the witch. There were other ways to rid him of the curse, and they could seek them out. *Together*. With full honesty and, hopefully, a foundation of trust. Ponce de Leon had survived for eight years with a hippocromantic at his side, and the Ways had evolved in the half a millennium since. Diego might not be the one to find a cure or means of dispellation, but he had Morgen. He had Milla. They could navigate this new world, and he could save Trav without stealing from him.

He closed his hand into a fist, snuffing out his magick. Trav frowned in his sleep, a tiny little whine escaping. He rolled onto his side, none-the-wiser, and the gold chain slithered from his neck.

"Mierda."

Diego stared at the ouroboros lying innocently on the bed, weighing the potential of sheer coincidence.

But witches did not believe in coincidences.

Goddess, he missed Milla and her fractured sight. If ever there were a time to weigh the potential of a moment, it was now. But Milla was Horned God knew where, and Diego was here. He eased from the bed, dressing as quietly as he was able, and, at the last possible moment, he reached across his lover and stole the ouroboros.

It was lighter than he thought it would be, a near-weightless bauble in the palm of his hand. Too easy a thing to carry for holding such destructive power. Without looking at Trav, Diego shoved the ouroboros into his pocket and fled the enclosed garden.

The sun was just reaching over the horizon, the gray-blue sky brightening to a cotton-candy pink. He tripped over a chicken on the path, stumbling to the backdoor and releasing a sob when he was safely indoors, a wall between him and the man he had just stolen from.

Sniffling, he retrieved his bicycle from behind the counter and let himself out the front door. He sped around the corner, almost running down a morning jogger.

"Watch it!" The woman leaped out of his way, pink curls bouncing.

"Disculpe." Diego waved his hand in half-an-apology, gripping the handlebars and pedaling away.

Gold chain looped through her fingers, Morgen held the ouroboros up to her eye, the halo of her Way gleaming. She frowned and twisted her wrist, spinning the medallion. Her eyes flicked briefly to Diego, and her lips formed a pout.

"Nothing."

"Qué?" He straightened from where he'd leaned against the counter, gripping a coffee mug in both hands to keep them from trembling. "What do you mean nothing?"

"Just that—there is nothing here. No magick, no echo, no fragment; see for yourself." She tossed the ouroboros across the room, and Diego barely managed to untangle one of his hands from the mug to snatch it out of the air. As in Trav's yard, it was too light, too innocuous. Unlike then, without the distractions of the pawnshop and the man sleeping next to him, Diego noticed what he had overlooked in the garden.

Glancing at Morgen, he gripped it in his palm and teetered head first into his Way. Magick erupted around him. Great swathes of power, like reams of incandescent silk, wound around Morgen and draped throughout the kitchen. He tracked the chronomantic power stemming from the clock, a Kitchen Witch allure cast on the refrigerator, his own Stitch Witchery wafting as threads in a breeze, and a bauble in the palm of his hand.

Empty and devoid of magick.

"How is this possible?"

"It is unusual but not unknown," Morgen said. "The Calusa sought to destroy Ponce de Leon. What better way to ensure the outcome than with a malediction carried in a totem given as a gift? The curse takes hold, and removing the totem does nothing, ensuring his downfall."

"No puedo sacarlo," Diego blurted, half-forgotten words taking on new meaning. He met Morgen's gaze. "He could not remove it. He came to me in the hold saying he could not remove it, that he needed time to—"

The kitchen door slammed open, and Josh barreled in, skidding to a halt. "Oh good, you're both—whoooooaaa." He swayed, eyes rolling and face flushing. "Holy *shit*, that's a lot."

Morgen cursed and darted to his side faster than Diego had ever seen the witch move. She gripped Josh by the arm, easing him into a seat. "Diego, step out of your Way."

"Nah, man." Josh's head lolled. "This's grrreat. Way better'n what's happening out there." He blinked drunkenly and hit Diego with a watery grin. "Way. Heh."

"Now, Diego." Morgen snapped her fingers in front of the cultist's face.

"Qué? Oh, yes." He called the magick back into himself, skin heating at the rush of power.

"Nooo," Josh whined, pawing at the empty air to grab hold of the magick permeating Morgen's home.

"Control yourself, Joshua," Morgen snapped. "And Diego, explain."

"He said he could not remove it."

"Who?"

"The hippocromantic. Ponce de Leon's doctor, de Quesada. He came to me in the hold before I died, rambling about needing time to remove something only I did not understand." He frowned, reliving one of his last days. "I am still not certain I do; what could he have needed my help with? And if the curse is a malediction as you think, how did it survive the salt?"

"Salt?" Josh asked. "What salt?" Diego opened his mouth to explain, and the cultist waved his hand. "Never mind, we have a problem."

"We have *had* a problem," Diego argued. He looped his middle finger through the gold chain and dropped the ouroboros from his palm. It spun in a slow circle, sunlight glinting off the gold and catching in the scales. "The ouroboros has nothing. No magick, no curse, but that is impossible."

"Why?"

"Because of the salt!" he hollered. "How did the curse live in this-this *thing* for so long? If it bound itself to de Leon, it should have died when he did, but it lived, and it caught Martin in the mangroves, and by all the laws of magick, it makes no sense."

"Mangroves." Josh shrugged.

"What about the fucking *mangroves!*" Diego lurched toward him, stopping at a glare from Morgen. "I do not understand the draw to the mangroves and why you keep shrugging whenever we mention them, so *please*, by the Goddess and the Horned God, explain it to me."

"It's just the mangroves, I don't know what you want me to say." He glanced at Morgen, silently pleading with her to intervene. When she did not, he brushed off her hand and rose, approaching Diego with open palms. "Please, man, it's just the mangroves; it's how they are, and seriously? You need to listen to me. We have a *problem*."

"What do you mean 'how they are'?" Morgen filled the space beside Diego, towering over him.

"It's just—ugh," he grunted. "Okay, biology time, I guess. Mangroves can tolerate salt water. They thrive in intertidal zones, like the shoals around Key West which is like, really fucking weird for a tree, right?" He glanced from Morgen to Diego, seeking something from them and rolling his eyes when they both remained silent. "God-damned witches," he muttered, pinching between his eyes. "Alright, look, they do well in saltwater environments because they can obtain freshwater *from* the saltwater. Something about their roots and, like, multiple layers of skin."

"Trees do not have skin," Diego pointed out. Josh sent him a withering look.

"Seriously, man, that's what you're going to argue?" he asked, then shook his head and continued. "The water up near the base isn't as salty as the surrounding water. The mangroves desalinate to survive."

"Oh," Morgen stated. Her hand slipped from Diego's shoulder, and she pressed it to her mouth, crystal clear blue eyes rounding in surprise. "I see."

"What," he demanded. "What am I missing."

"The mangroves predate the Keys," Morgen said in a low voice as though she were trying to keep herself calm. "Before Flagler's rail line, before this was a fishing village, the mangroves thrived in the shoals, their roots catching the bones of the sea."

"Shipwreck and salvage," Josh added.

Diego staggered back, more of de Quesada's mad ramblings coming back. "Los Mártires."

"The Martyrs." Josh nodded. "Old name for the Bone Islands, which became the Keys."

"The Santa Maria." Diego's mind reeled, five hundred years of lost history crashing down all at once. "He spoke of the ship and a martyr, but I misunderstood. I thought he was calling de Leon a martyr, but he martyred the *ship* with the ouroboros aboard, running it aground on the shoals to remove the curse, oh, por la Diosa."

"I told you, man, the mangroves. There's a ton of wreckage down there, some of it as old as the conquistadors. It's why it's a popular diving spot."

"Martin found the ouroboros in the mangroves." Morgen eased into a chair, cheeks pale and face stricken. "He returned time after time seeking more of the treasure until the compulsion killed him." She took one long breath before addressing Diego. "The salt would have been enough to dull the magick and keep it dormant enough that neither Joshua nor myself noticed until it was freed from the roots ..."

"But not enough to kill it entirely," Josh finished.

A heavy silence fell over the kitchen, witch and cultist alike processing what this meant until Diego finally blurted, "How did he survive for *eight fucking years?*"

"I don't think that's what you need to be worried about right now." Josh pulled his lips between his teeth, twisting at the waist to face Morgen. "This is super embarrassing, but ... I lost the pack."

A light flared behind the Morgenhexe, and her back went impossibly straighter. "What do you mean you lost the pack?"

"Just that." He shrank away from the witch, his voice losing its jovial edge. "We met for our morning run. I laid the trail we set up last night, and about half a mile in, the front runner picked up a new scent."

"A new scent?" Morgen angled her head, each word as crisp as a winter morning.

"Well, not new." Josh cupped the back of his neck and ducked his head. "I followed it for a block and came here the minute I realized what it was."

"And?" she pressed.

"It was him." He pointed at Diego.

"Oh ... mierda."

Morgen reeled on him, looming over the witch with a cold fury burning in her eyes. "What did you do?"

"I ..." He shrank back, darting his gaze between Morgen and Josh. "I may have stepped into my Way to steal the ouroboros."

"*Dude.*" Josh gaped at him.

"What else was I supposed to do?"

Morgen raised her hand, cupping her brow in the crook of her palm and sighing. "Did you consider wire cutters?"

"Do you have any?"

She threw her hands up and spun away, muttering in German. Josh took her place, gripping him by the shoulders. "This is bad, man. If that cotton-candy-headed nutjob finds him first, she'll have half the pack screaming for blood."

"Cotton-candy-headed ..." Diego's stomach plummeted. "Do you mean the woman with the pink hair?" He flexed his hand, curling his fingers like he was scrunching his hair. "With the curls?"

"Fucking Fornicata." Josh shook his head. "She's been a problem since she got down here. Wants us to be more aggressive in sourcing magick."

"She seemed nice enough," Diego said. "She was in the store yesterday, buying records." He recalled the woman's pink hair, near neon in the sunrise, certain it was the same person. "And I ran into her a few blocks from the store this morning, almost ran her over with my bicycle."

"Shit." Josh's cheeks blanched, and he began pacing in tight circles. "She wasn't one of the people we sent to the store, which means she went on her own. She's been talking about you two since Shanna Key, and this morning she had half the pack rallied before we even started; oh fuck, this is bad."

"How bad?" Morgen spun around.

"She took off on a new trail a couple blocks in. We were gonna stick to Old Town and finish over in Mallory Square, but Fornicata took them and—aw man." Josh ran a hand down his face, his cheeks paling further with the motion. "She hijacked the trail on Flagler Avenue and headed east. I sent Tammy ahead to cut them off and sprinted right here. Fornicata said the trail was faint but that she could follow it backward."

"Can she?"

Josh nodded emphatically. "I've seen her do it before. She learned it from the cultists in San Francisco."

"San Francisco," Morgen muttered, her face darkening. She summoned a smartphone to hand and began tapping on the screen. "Headed east on Flagler?" Another nod from Josh. "I can have a team of Enforcers on the streets in under five minutes. Did you scent the trail? Do you know where they were headed?"

Josh swallowed, Adam's apple bobbing as he faced Diego. "East on Flagler, toward Southernmost Pawn." His words were like arrows shot directly into Diego's chest. He staggered back, catching himself on the counter. "Tammy and the rest of the pack are trying to disrupt the trail. We have tools we can use, things Morgen has given us to distract from the trail, but whatever you did coupled with whatever is in that store is waaay too powerful, man. We won't be able to keep them off forever."

"And if they find him?"

Diego was still unclear as to what the cultists did to get magick or why their frequent runs were so important, but Milla's fear and Morgen's close relationship with them were telling enough. Foster daughter and mother they may be, but their differences were vast and varied. Milla pushed away what she feared, secluding herself from risk, whereas Morgen held it close and kept a weather eye on what threatened her position and power.

"We're a *cult*," Josh answered. "They'll do what it takes to get what they want."

"When I was last alive, cults were known for their sacrifices," Diego snarked. Josh only stared at him. "Josh."

"The cult will not have a chance at your pawnbroker, Diego," said Morgen.

"What will you do?"

She glanced at him sideways before returning to her phone. "I am the Witch of the Demesne," she snipped. "I will do what I must."

He took in the Morgenhexe tapping on her phone, her mouth pinched. He glanced at Josh, who looked like he would be ill at any moment. Then, Diego swallowed down his fear and ran.

TWENTY

WHISTLES PIERCED THE AIR, echoed by the cries of a pack running wild. Diego pedaled as fast as he could, thighs burning and fingerbones creaking from his white-knuckled grip on the handlebars. Splotches of white powder thrown against the base of mailboxes and light posts blurred in his periphery, and he sped through an intersection marked with the arcane symbols of the cult.

A cloud of mist rose, obscuring the next intersection. Diego charged through, flinching as whispy threads of meteomantic weather magick tickled his cheeks—one of Morgen's summoned Enforcers at work.

He swept a hand to clear his path. Magick snagged in his fingers, the tendons in his arm aching from the strain of unstitching another witch's Way, and he swerved at the last moment to avoid running down yet another Horned God-damned chicken. He backpedaled to brake, bicycle wobbling, and tires nearly skidding out from beneath him. The chicken glanced up, beady eyes black in the heavy fog, and resumed its pecking. Heart pounding in his chest, Diego squinted to read the street name painted in black block letters on a light post.

George Street.

He whipped his head to the right, listening for whistles. A few muffled *peeps* came from blocks away, less frantic than before, and he exhaled for the first time since leaving the tower. Southernmost Pawn was a block away, and the whistles were growing fainter in the opposite direction. Resuming his ride, he pedaled down the road, dismounting as he turned onto the A1A.

The state road was abandoned in the fog. Magick curled around his wrist, tugging him back from the road, and a whispered suggestion rose in his ear, telling him to turn around and walk the other way. He flicked his fingers, dispelling the look-away hex and glancing over his shoulder, half expecting to find an obnubilari mind witch sneaking up behind him. Only fog drifted across the road, growing thicker with each passing second and plunging the world into an unnatural twilight.

Unnerved, Diego all but tossed his bike against the wall and sprinted for the pawnshop. The front door stood wide open, and fog drifted into the aisles, plying him with whispers of elsewhere and anyways. He ignored the clench of fear at that open door and ripped the allures and hexes away, charging up the stairs and into the apartment, only half aware of the ransacked shelves and debris on the floor. His only thoughts were of Trav and getting to him before the cultists did.

"Trav?" Diego twisted to squeeze through a pile of hoarded junk, making note of every overturned box and opened cupboard. Kitchen drawers lay on the tile, their contents strewn across the floor, and try as he might, Diego could not help but catalog what was missing.

Magick.

All that remained, all of the junk littering the apartment, was mortal and mundane. The absence of the occult, of the strands, swathes, and threads of magick Diego had grown so accustomed to in this space, hit him like a baseball bat. It was worse than the muddled cocktail he had endured for a week with the ointment on his palms. This was a negative space utterly devoid of life.

He pressed a hand to his mouth, stifling a cry as he staggered forward, past the bathroom and the brick wall with its quirky paintings and into the partitioned space that served as a bedroom. The comforter and sheets lay in a mass at the foot of the bed, and the entire frame was askew. Dresser drawers were open, the bedside table tossed on its side, and items were missing: the small bronze dish and the jewelry it held, tchotchkes, and the painting hanging on the wall. Trav.

Diego's knees buckled. He hit the floor, barely catching himself on the corner of the bed.

He was too late. The cultists had gotten here first; they had taken everything Trav treasured, emptying the store of all magick, and if he were reading the room and destruction correctly—they had taken Trav.

"I cannot do this again," he sobbed aloud, unable to keep the words inside any longer. It was all too familiar. A man hunted, his home ransacked. The terror was too real, too tangible, and Diego could not do this. Not again. "Goddess, oh, Diosa, please. *Por favor*, I cannot—"

His words came in stilted, halting pants, his lungs unable to breathe enough air. Tears burned in his eyes, and he pulled off his glasses, pressing the heels of his palms to his eyelids in a vain attempt to keep the panic and rage restrained.

If his first life had taught him anything, it was that anger led to haste, haste led to mistakes, and mistakes got you killed. His sister had been hasty, rushing to the bedside of a woman dying in the throes of labor. She had been too late; she had *known* the woman was dying. Her hippocromancy would have been screaming the truth, but she had been hasty. She had been angry with the woman's husband for waiting to call on her, and she had made a mistake.

The woman had died, and Diego's sister had burned on a pyre, screaming that it was not her fault.

Ruben had made a similar mistake. Angry at their weeks of desperation, angry at Diego for wanting to keep his head down when stepping into their Ways would have helped them survive. He had been hasty, assuming the crowd in Santiago de Compostela was too drunk, too revelrous, to recognize real magick when they saw it.

But they were not, and Ruben's anger and haste had seen him torn apart by a rabid crowd.

Acting with intent had kept Diego alive. Refusing to give into his panic and fear, avoiding those same mistakes, had kept him alive until another man's curse had killed him. The same curse that now saw Trav hunted across Key West.

He took a shallow breath. And another until his heart slowed enough for his lungs to fill. The panic was still there, tingling in his fingers, toes, and teeth, but his head was clear enough to *think*.

Sliding his glasses on, he eased onto his knees, staring at the end of the bed as he thought. He had left Trav at dawn and run into Fornicata. Josh had come barreling into Morgen's kitchen an hour later, and they had wasted time arguing over the mangroves while the cultists ransacked Trav's store.

But he had left Trav in the garden, fast asleep.

Diego blinked, the room slipping into focus. His eyes landed on the door on the other side of the bed, accessible now that the frame had been shoved away from the wall.

He lurched to his feet, spinning slowly and viewing the space with fresh eyes. The missing items, the frame that had been shoved *into* the room. He darted over the mattress, hope stuck in his throat, and ripped the door open.

A small landing overlooked the garden, and a rickety set of stairs clung to the rear wall of the pawnshop, leading down to the firepit. Chickens waddled in the patchy grass, and from this vantage, Diego could make out the empty day bed under the willow tree.

"Oh, por la Diosa," he exhaled, a plan forming in his mind as his panic subsided. "Gracias."

He ran for the kitchen, leaping over piles of boxes, clothes, and other mundane junk, tearing through the cupboards and drawers for what he sought.

Trav must have been asleep when the cultists sacked the store. From the angle of the bed and the items missing from his bedroom and apartment, Diego felt certain he had shouldered open the door from outside, grabbing what he needed without the cultists knowing he was there. Which meant Diego had *time*.

"*Trenzar.*" His fingers trembled along the cooking twine, magick bleeding from the tips to braid into the cotton. "*Trenzar.*"

Braid.

The tendons in his casting hand cramped, and he dropped the ball of twine, grunting as he flexed his fingers. A chicken clucked happily beside him, pecking the grass and not at all concerned. Four more chickens wandered nearby, trailing kitchen twine imbued with Diego's magick.

He picked up the string with shaking fingers and tied it into an easy loop. "Ven aquí, gallina," he cooed at the bird, knee-walking closer. "Come to me." The chicken straightened its neck, beak working as it swallowed a mouthful of lentils, and Diego tossed the loop over its head, tugging gently to tighten the knot.

The chicken bawked and fluttered away, glaring at Diego through a beady eye.

"I am sure you will get over it." He rose to his feet and slung a canvas bag over his shoulder, grunting from the weight and snatching the bag of lentils from the edge of the daybed.

Diego strode for the willow curtain, sprinkling lentils in his wake and smiling when he heard the flutter of feathers at his back. He led them through the side gate, pausing to listen to the faint whistles in the fog. They sounded closer, or so he hoped. He had worked enough magick in the yard to call them to the scent, and if the cultists were still running, it meant he had time. Dropping the canvas bag in the front basket of his bicycle, Diego slung his leg over the seat and took off.

He sprinkled lentils as he rode. Two blocks, three, and he finally found their trail. Marked by a circle with an X drawn through it, the symbol lacked the hasty arrows pointing the pack in the direction of the magick they hunted. The fog had thickened to a proper cloud, dropping the daylight even further. As he rode, he had seen the cultists' headlamps bobbing down parallel roads. Erasing the mark would not stop them; it would only slow their progress. Diego could *feel* the trail of magick, and the cultists could smell it. They were quick and clever, and even with Morgen's Enforcers muddling the air with their Ways, he doubted they would lose the trail so easily. Unless...

Gritting his teeth, Diego plunged his left hand into the canvas bag. Flour sifted through his fingers, softer than sand, and filled the fine lines of his palm, muffling the tickle of magick he felt at all times. He exhaled, grabbing a fistful and throwing it on the arcane symbol. Without hesitating, he delved into his Way, reaching out with his right hand, his casting hand, and waving it over the mark.

Nothing.

"Yess," Diego hissed. It had been a weak theory, but it had worked, and he was thankful for the hoarding compulsion of the curse. Without it, Trav would have thrown out the flour he claimed had gone bad, prompting him to cook Arroz con Pollo for their dinner, Goddess, less than a week ago. But he had kept flour. The self-rising flour, treated with baking powder and enough salt to disrupt the magick of a witch and a trail.

Grinning madly, Diego waggled his fingers, catching hold of the prickly curse magick wafting on a phantom breeze, caustic and all too familiar. Pinching it in his fingers, Diego looped the strand around his wrist to keep his heading and followed it to the next pile of flour and the next, disrupting the trail before doubling back to the intersection.

More chickens had joined those from Trav's yard, following his trail of lentils. He wasted no time imbuing more twine and looping it around their throats, then pedaled in the opposite direction of the curse's trail, sprinkling lentils and taking random turns with a trail of chickens clucking behind him. With any luck, and Goddess knew he was in short supply, his nullifying the trail with salt-laced flour and unleashing the chickens to roam Key West with strands of his own Way tied around their throats would buy him enough time to find Trav first.

It was the work of half an hour to empty his flour onto the streets of Key West and another fifteen minutes to double back to that first intersection, following the prickling strand of magick he had tied to his wrist. Moisture beaded on his glasses, the heat of exertion steaming the lenses. His thighs burned from the effort, and each breath sawed through his lungs, but he had bought Trav time, and that was all that mattered.

Morgen's witches continued their work, plunging the visibility in Key West to less than twenty feet. Sharp whistles filled the air, paired with shouts coming from all directions. He tore past the high school and jerked the bicycle onto a residential street, narrowly avoiding half a dozen headlamps bobbing toward him in the gloom. Restraining his Way, Diego coasted down the road, glancing over his shoulder. Headlamps bobbed past, not a one turning down the road, and he dropped his feet, sagging over the handlebars and dragging in desperate breaths.

The magick on his wrist tugged, urging the witch onward with more force than before. With a groan, he set his foot on a pedal and pushed off, cycling in a teetering line down the road. Gravel walkways gave way to shrubs, the houses growing further and further apart until the pot-hole-ridden asphalt vanished altogether, replaced by hard-packed dirt.

He dismounted and propped his bicycle against a signpost. A quick review of the map on his phone told Diego he was on the road running along the northern edge of the airport. Fog rolled over the tops of the trees and shrubs; the only sounds were the distant whistles, shouts, and his every rasping breath. Not a car, barking dog, or airplane running up its jets.

Diego held up his casting hand, fingers splayed to test the air. It was faint, nearly drowned by the power of the meteomantic magick at work, but just beneath the weather Way, he felt the soft lap of other magicks — hexes, allures, and an echo of the occult. Without much thought, he muttered, *"Coser."*

Stitch.

Magick slapped against his palm, whipping around his fingers in response to the Stitch Witch's version of a sticky hex. He closed his hand to a fist, dropped it to his side, and followed the trail into the trees.

TWENTY-ONE

"Trav?" Diego ducked beneath a low branch, feet slipping in the soft sand. The magick stuck to his casting hand wound tighter, guiding him deeper into the trees and, he hoped, to the pawnbroker. "Trav, baby, it is Diego."

He halted at a cry from somewhere to his left, a high-pitched keening, muffled in the fog as though someone held their hand over the mouth of whoever had cried out. He cocked his head and strained to hear more.

"Dulzuro?"

The cry came again, slightly closer, and Diego adjusted his direction. He swept aside shrubs and stepped over roots, chasing the phantom sound deeper into the brush. Branches caught in his shirt and snagged his hair, tangling around the witch. He twisted and kicked to free himself and skidded in a patch of mud. He pinwheeled his arms, grabbing a branch and narrowly avoiding falling face-first onto a wooden platform. Straightening, he tested the strength of the wood and stepped up, cleaning his glasses on his shirt before slipping them back on.

The platform extended in both directions, bending at lazy angles and disappearing into the gloom. Low-lying gnarled trees formed curved walls, snagging the unnatural fog in their branches. He vaguely recalled mention of a nature walk near the airport and assumed this must be it, which meant he was headed straight for the mangroves.

"Of course," Diego grumbled. He held his arm out like a dousing rod, seeking a heading. "Of course, it is the mangroves." Magick prickled to his left, the strand on his wrist pulling taut, and he started in that direction as another muffled cry floated in the heavy air. "What is the deal with these *mangroves.*"

The ground around the walkway gave way to shallow water as the raised path twisted through the trees. Warped planks creaked under Diego's feet, and the skin on his neck prickled. He brushed the feeling away, identifying it as a weak malediction—a fraidy-hex, as his roommate would call it.

That was enough to have him spinning around and scanning the path. A fraidy-hex was an obnubilari special, an illusion of fear deployed by mind witches when a look-away hex failed. That he felt one now meant Morgen's witches were near.

He splayed the fingers of his casting hand, wincing at the tightness, and reached for more magickal strands. A whistle blew in the murk, and again, that quiet cry came from somewhere just ahead, the witches and cultists closing in.

"Mierda," he spat and ran, tearing down the path, around a corner, and directly into a warm body.

"Dude!" Nails pinched his arm as whoever he had collided with steadied him. "Thank all the gods, you're here."

"Tammy?" He startled at her sudden appearance. A headlamp hung from her neck, and her cheeks were flushed. Strands of hair had escaped her ponytail, curling in the sweat on her forehead and neck. The compression tank she wore clung to every curve, and from the thighs down, she was filthy. "What are you doing here? Why do you smell like a swamp?"

"*Rude,* and I'm trying to get to your boy before the pack does." She released his arm and shuffled a bundle to her front. "Was this you?"

Diego stared at the squirming mass in her arms, dumbfounded. Tammy grunted and pulled the fabric away to reveal a chicken.

"You have a chicken."

"Yes, I have a chicken. Was this you?" She tugged on the twine looped around the chicken's neck, gently winding the end around her index finger. Diego nodded and she inhaled before letting a rapid stream of words fly. "Hella clever; half the pack is chicken-hunting in the cemetery. I caught this one and recognized your magick. Well, I thought it was your magick. Hoped it was. Had to catch it with my shirt. Nuts. Didya know there're witches out here?" She hooked her thumb at the trees and the swamp beyond.

"I had an idea," Diego managed, eyeing the cultist closer. Her pupils were blown out, and her cheeks flushed, which could have been from the running, but he suspected it was from the same magick he felt dancing around his fingers and tickling his palms. "Are you okay?"

"I am fucking *great*." She beamed at him, blinking one eye at a time. "Hangover's gonna suck tomorrow, though. You should go, get your boy."

"I do not know where he is."

"Out here, somewhere, I can feel it." She inhaled again, this time swaying back on her heels. "Gods, there's so much magick out tonight." The chicken clucked in agreement. Tammy flinched and held the bird out at arm's length. "Holy fuck, I forgot I had this."

"Tammy, you need to get out of this swamp."

"Nah, man." She ambled past with a lazy smile. "*You* need to get your boy. I'm gonna stay in this swamp forever."

"Tammy..."

"Hold this for a second." She shoved the chicken into his arms. More whistles sounded, closer and less muffled than before. Tammy frowned and crouched on the walkway's edge, lowering into the water. She pulled the headlamp up from where it dangled at her neck, adjusted it on her forehead, and waded a few steps into the swamp before turning around. "Chicken?"

"What are you doing?"

"Keeping your trail alive. Can you"—she circled her hand in the air—"do the thing?"

"The thing."

"The magick thing. I'm gonna keep your trail going." She tapped the headlamp, blinding Diego as she spun around, her light catching on the trees and casting long shadows over the swamp. "Thattaway, I think. Magick?"

"Ah." Diego pinched the twine, murmuring, "*Trenzar.*"

His fingers cramped, a tendon in his palm pinching in protest as he braided more of his Way into the twine. Tammy shivered, humming happily and reaching for the chicken.

"That's the good stuff. Man, I'm gonna eat a whole bag of Skittles after this. The *big* bag and Josh can't say shit."

"I doubt he will comment." Another volley of whistles and shouts pierced the muggy air, and in response, a wave of magick rushed through the shrubs and mangroves from the opposite direction. A sticky magick that grabbed Diego's chin and turned his head away. Tammy gagged and gripped the edge of the walkway.

"Damn mind witches, that's a nasty look-away."

"Morgen's Enforcers are near. Here." He crouched low and handed her the chicken. "Be careful, please."

"You too, amigo." She sent him a bright grin and tipped her head in the direction she'd come from. "Try that way; there's magick for sure. I was trying to lead the pack away."

"Thank you, Tammy."

"Don't thank me just yet." She tucked the bird under her arm and squeezed Diego's knee. "Now go get your boy."

Diego ran, feet thudding against the wooden walkway. Splashes echoed through the trees to his left, punctuated by terse shouts and short, shrill whistle bleets. On his right, wave after wave of magick shot out of the bog. Look-away, fraidy-hexes, a sleep allure, and scattered illusions as the witches fought to secure Morgen's demesne.

He swept his hands in the air, catching what he could and sending it flying wildly out of his path. Ducking under low branches, he grabbed a wobbling metal rail as he skidded around a particularly sharp turn.

The prickling magick he had followed to this Goddess-forsaken corner of Key West grew stronger with his every frantic footfall. Diego clenched his teeth, hissing as a cramp twisted in his side. He had never been particularly fond of the bicycle, but Goddess, he preferred it to running. He had spent too long running in his first life to take it up as a hobby in his second, and this Horned God-damned day was doing nothing to change his mind.

Another twist in the path drowned out the shouts and whistles, leaving only Diego's footfalls and ragged breaths to accompany splashing footsteps from somewhere up ahead.

The fog rolled thick over the wooden path, and without warning, it fell away. Diego came down on his foot at an odd angle, crying in pain. His knee buckled, and he twisted, hitting the ground with a wet squelch. The bulk of his weight landed on his hip and shoulder, and his ankle barked, a sharp twinge running up his leg.

"Maldita sea." He rolled onto his side and rose on an elbow, just able to make out the edge of the walkway and a six-inch drop. "Excelente, just *great*." Carefully, he rose to his knees, attempting to stand and biting off a whimper when he put weight on his ankle.

The splashing footsteps accompanying him as he ran stopped, and leaves rustled somewhere in the brush to his left.

"Diego?"

Prickling magick flared and tugged at his arm, but the sound of that voice, so close, almost in reach, had Diego lurching forward. A white-hot flare of pain shot up his leg, and he fell against a tree, already reaching for the next. "Trav?"

"D, where are you?"

Horned God, he sounded so frightened and so *close*. "Dulzuro, baby, stay where you are—*ow*." Diego gripped a tree branch, hauling himself into the muck. And again, until saltwater lapped at his shins and mud threatened to pull off his shoes. His legs tingled, a thousand pinpricks crawling up his calves as the salt doused his magick. Ahead, barely visible through the trees, a shadow shifted, water sloshing as it moved deeper into the swamp. "Trav, baby, do not move."

"You left," he said, his voice soft and heartbreaking. "You left like Martin left, and I didn't—I don't know what I ... why does everyone leave?"

"Trav, please, stay still," Diego begged. His foot caught on a root, and he tugged, biting his lips as his ankle screamed at the motion. "I am coming."

"Martin said he'd come back. I saw him that morning; he slept in the back-yard, and I woke up when he came in for coffee." Trav sniffled and stepped into a clearing, the fog parting to reveal his silhouette. Odd bulges curved his spine and distorted the shape of his legs. "He said he was going for a dive, that he'd be back for lunch, and he left." Diego squinted, trying to make sense of what he was seeing and slamming a hand over his mouth to stifle his cry when he did. Canvas totes and backpacks were slung on Trav's arms, back, and front, each filled to bursting. Bracelets, watches, and necklaces draped his arms and dripped from pockets bulging with whatever else the man had deemed a treasure. "Everyone leaves me."

"Martin did not leave you," Diego grunted, pulling himself closer. "I did not leave you; I am here."

"You weren't there when I woke up," Trav whispered. "You left like Martin left. Like *they* left."

He was close now; Trav's features were a blur instead of a shadow, but Diego did not need to see his expression to know he was in pain. This close, the caustic magick of the curse snapped and bit like a cornered dog, warning Diego away. He ignored it, rolling his wrist and binding the magick deeper to himself. A few more feet, and he could reach out. Just a little bit closer, and he could haul the mortal out of this fetid swamp. "Who left?"

"They did!" He threw his arms out and teetered off balance. Diego's heart lurched, and he reached for Trav, too far away to help. He righted himself and beat a fist against his chest. "They left me there at that *camp* and took the rest of the family to Disney World. Disney World! Do you know what they did to us?"

Diego could only shake his head, mouth forming the word, "No."

He did not know, but from the research he had done in this second life on men like himself, how they were perceived and accepted, he could imagine that the horrors Trav faced in that camp were not unlike the terrors Diego had endured in the last days of his first life.

"They left me in that camp, and Martin left me, and you left me." Trav backed away from Diego. "Everyone leaves me, *everyone*, so I left." He beat his chest again, and magick crackled from his person. The force of it sent Trav back a step, and he dropped lower, teetering in the silt. "I left, and I took the only things that matter."

Diego lunged for the next tree, catching himself before landing on his injured ankle. This deep in the mangroves, even the trees bore a fine coating of salt, muting his senses beneath the sensation of a fading slap. "Trav, dulzuro, please, come here. Let me take you home, I will not leave, not again."

"Everyone leaves," he whispered, shoulders stooping further under the weight of the over-stuffed bags and years of pain and grief. "Now it's my turn."

"Where will you go?"

"Here," he whispered, so low Diego almost did not hear him. "I need to....I need to be here. I need to bring it all together."

And it clicked.

Trav's morning dives, Martin's return trips to the mangroves, de Leon martyring the ship on these shoals. The Mangroves, Los Mártires.

The Bone Islands.

"Not marble," Diego murmured. "Not marble, *bone.*" It was bone. This whole time, the ouroboros had been bone dredged from the sea, tempered and treated to resemble marble. Because how could it be *marble?* Marble absorbed magick; the Inquisitors had built their prisons from marble and treated the walls with salt. Witch-proof, magick-eating prisons. A marble totem could never house a curse, but *bone...*

Magick was built on intent; intent was tied to desire, and like called to like. The ouroboros wanted to be rejoined to the Bone Islands, and the Calusa were crafty indeed. Their tribe had extended along the western coast of La Florida, and the Spaniards had been allowed to leave so easily. Too easily. With de Leon leading his fleet and the ouroboros around his neck. Goddess, it was a wonder Diego had survived long enough to die in St. Augustine, and a miracle de Leon had lived for eight years after the sinking of the Santa Maria.

But how?

De Quesada was the answer. Coming to Diego's bunk, begging for help from a dying witch, but why? What had he figured out?

A whistle shrieked. Trav twitched, throwing his arms out wide to maintain balance.

"Trav, come to me," Diego demanded, limping deeper into the brackish water and reaching for his lover. The how was a problem for later. Now, he needed to get Trav away from this swamp and the killing compulsion of the curse. "Now, baby, please."

"I can't." He stepped back, unsteady under the weight of his treasures. More whistles joined the first, and beneath their shrill bleats, Diego heard the calls of the cult. "I need to be here; I need to bring it together and keep my treasures safe." He blinked, shook his head, and stretched out an arm. "Diego?"

"Sí, baby, I am here."

"Mi tesoro," he rasped. "I need you, D."

"I am here." He edged forward, reaching for Trav with one arm. "Ven a mí, dulzuro."

Trav stretched his arms forward, grasping for Diego. His balance was tenuous, the silt beneath their feet shifting and uneven. Diego grabbed hold of a branch and reached for Trav, the pads of their fingers brushing.

"On on!" A voice bellowed through the gloom.

Trav flinched, the motion throwing him off-balance. He threw his arms out, waving them in the air and stepping back to regain balance. The fog thinned in that instant, daylight bleeding into the clearing. For a brief moment, a flash, there and gone again, true fear overtook his face. "Help me."

Diego lurched forward, crying out as he landed on his injured ankle. His knee buckled, and he staggered in the water as Trav teetered back and sank into the swamp.

TWENTY-TWO

TRAV'S BACK HIT THE water with a loud splash, sinking under the weight of the bags. The water frothed as he kicked and clawed for the surface, but his head never rose.

Diego waded forward as fast as he could, wincing and clenching his fists, arms swinging wide to maintain balance. He stumbled over roots, cursing as they caught on his legs and tripped his feet. Every step was a struggle, as though the mangrove forest was determined to reclaim the curse it harbored.

The water rose to his chest as he neared where Trav had fallen. He took three quick, short breaths, exhaled, and filled his lungs, diving beneath the brackish surface. Screwing his eyes shut, Diego groped blindly, praying to the Goddess for her aid, her intervention. He could not afford a ritual; there was no time to properly appeal to the Goddess. No time for the focus a ritual required, not when Trav was drowning under the weight of pawned gold and an ancient curse he did not deserve.

His hand hit something hard and covered in cloth. A leg, he hoped. Diego latched on, tugging with all of his strength. It jerked, and something smacked him in the head. He reached up, grabbing Trav's hand and using it to pull himself closer.

Salt burned as he opened his eyes, the world a dark, murky blur, but there was Trav, mouth pinched in a line, eyes wide in fear. He frantically shook his head when Diego tugged his arm, jerking his chin to the side. It took Diego a precious second he did not have to realize what Trav was trying to show him—the straps of the bags and gold chains looped around his neck, and arms were snagged in the roots, pinning him to the silt.

No, no, that was not right. He surged closer, a cry of horror escaping as a mangrove root *moved*, worming along Trav's arm and coiling around a length of gold.

Water rushed into his mouth, raising minor blisters on his tongue and cheeks. The urge to inhale rocketed, and Diego pushed his feet into the mud, launching for the surface and breaking through with a gasp.

How was he supposed to free Trav? How was he supposed to fight a Horned God-damned *sentient* swamp? He tread in a panicked circle, licking his lips and frantically trying to come up with a solution. Diego was a Stitch Witch. He dealt in fabrics and fibers, and a man was *dying*. What use was magick when it could not save the one damn mortal Diego gave a shit about? If this were a wound, he could stitch the skin closed; if this were a pair of Horned God-damned pants, he could hem this with a flick of his finger, but this was a curse that had sewn itself into the very fabric of Trav's being—

No puedo sacarlo.

De Quesada's words blazed across his mind. Those rambling words muttered to a dying witch. He had said it again and again.

I cannot get it out.

Necesito tiempo. Necesito ayuda, ¿entiendes? No puedo sacarlo...no puedo sacarlo.

The hippocromantic had begged for time, for help, and he had tended to Diego's fever, feeding him opium and asking for help.

From a Stitch Witch.

"Mierda." Realization struck like a bolt of lightning. He took in another lungful of air and dove, ignoring the salt burning his eyes and skin. De Quesada had said he needed a little time and, as a hippocromantic, he could buy de Leon time. He could hold the curse at bay but could not unstitch the magick. He could not get it out, and Diego ... Diego was a Stitch Witch, the only one in the Armada. If he could not unstitch the curse, then what good was he?

But Diego had died, and de Leon had lived with a hippocromantic by his side until a poisoned arrow proved to be too much.

Trav lay still, having ceased his struggle to slow the roots. They wound up his arms and legs, crawling up the sides of his face and pulling him into the muck. Cheeks still puffed, his eyes widened slightly when Diego swam up close. He had been under the water for a good ninety seconds, and though he dove regularly, Diego had no idea how long the man could hold his breath.

So he worked quickly, calling on the dregs of his Way and ripping open the front of Trav's shirt, not wanting anything between his hands and Trav's skin. His heart clenched at the rapid pulse, the feel of his lover's panic loud beneath his palms. Diego tried to keep calm, to exude confidence when he was anything but. It was a weak theory founded on the fevered memory of the man he was five hundred years ago.

Still...

"*Desenredar.*" The word left his mouth as bubbles and a faint tingle fizzed down his arms. Trav twitched, nostrils flaring, and precious bubbles slipped from his lips. Diego ignored his reaction, wasting more air to repeat the minor casting, one of the first all Stitch Witches learned.

Unravel.

"*Desenredar,*" he burbled a second time, lungs burning for want of air. Trav twitched beneath him, his heart skipping a beat. Every muscle in his body went taut, his eyes bulging. He opened his mouth in a silent scream, the roots on his cheeks quivering. A prickle of thorns poked Diego's palms, and the roots wriggled away from Trav's face. He thrashed his head from side to side, bucking against Diego to throw off his hands, but he held fast, connected to the mortal by the curse crawling from his bones into Diego's arms.

Emboldened by that sharp sting and the roots' retreat, he curled his fingers, nails digging into Trav's chest. The burning in his lungs rose to a panicked blaze, the muscles in his chest twitching with the desire to inhale. *"Desenredar."*

Like a rope snapping under strain, the curse whipped into Diego, lashing against his hands and arms. Weakened from the brackish water, it wriggled and writhed, slippery like a fish fighting for its life. It slipped from Diego's hands, reaching for a mortal host. He was only half aware of Trav wrestling free from the roots and bags, only half aware of the involuntary gasp he let out, of the risk the curse still posed, and so Diego did the only thing his oxygen-deprived brain could think to do.

He pressed his casting hand against his chest and sacrificed his last breath. *"Coser."*

Stitch.

"No, no, nonono," Trav chanted, his voice distant and tight. "Come on, you fucking idiot, come on."

Something hard came down on Diego's chest. A fist or a rock or a …

A bat. He had a baseball bat.

"Don't you fucking dare leave me." Again, that hard beating against Diego's ribs, forcing a surge of bile and brackish water up his throat. His stomach heaved, every bruised muscle clenched, and he gagged at the foulness on the back of his tongue. The world spun, and the beating resumed on his back. Not a bat, he dazedly realized. The heel of a palm coming down again and again with force just this side of physical assault. "Come on, baby, you've got this. Get it out."

"I—" he choked on something thick. Mud or silt or stomach lining. Who knew? "Cannot. Me lo cosí."

"Diego, baby." Trav whacked his back again, forcing more grime and gross out of his mouth. "I literally cannot translate Spanish right now."

"Me lo cosí," he heaved, reaching blindly and catching damp fabric in his fingers. "No saldrá, me lo cosí." He tightened his grip and yanked on the shirt, tugging Trav to him. The mortal's eyes were wide, his glasses lost to the swamp, but it was no matter. He would be with them soon. All Diego had to do was keep him safe. Keep him treasured. "No sale, lo cosí. Lo cosí y ahora todos mis tesoros estarán a salvo."

"Tesoro, please." Trav gripped his wrist, prying Diego's fingers free. "We need to get out of here, I need to get you to a doctor, you weren't breathing—"

"Debo mantener todos mis tesoros juntos." Diego hooked his arm around Trav's back and scrabbled at the ground—the ground? When did he get to solid ground? No, nono, this was all wrong. His treasures were in the mangroves, sunk beneath the waves and *safe*. Jerking to his feet, he bit off a scream at the eruption of pain warbling from his ankle, struggling with his treasure and dragging him step by aching step toward the mangroves and the water where they would be *safe*. "Ven, tesoro mío. Te mantendré seguro."

"Diego, *please*—"

"*Durmak*," a sharp, feminine voice hollered at their backs, and a hex hit Diego between his shoulder blades. Warmth embraced his ribs and bled down his legs faster than he could dispell the halting hex. Trav was torn from his arms, and he hissed, gripping both thighs to grab hold of the magick and calling his Way to hand.

"No, I don't think so." A woman dressed in a black wooly-pully and tactical pants charged through the trees, her Way a blood-thick tongue lashing around the witch. "*Durmak*," she spat again, directing the hex at Diego's hands. That same sickly warmth rushed up his arms, freezing him in a half-stooped posture, hands firmly stuck to his thighs. "Morgen! I've got them!"

"Let me go," Diego demanded, jerking futilely at his hands. "¡Déjame ir, perra estúpida!"

"Wow." The woman's brows flew up her face as she whipped her head around, ponytail flying out in a black arc. "Pleasant."

"D, what's happening?" Trav called from the shadows at his back, jerking Diego's head around. The trees were a blur without his glasses, Trav one shadow tucked among the rest. A caustic prickle sizzled over his sternum, crawling along the backside of his ribs and igniting a panic so foreign it sent his mind reeling.

"Trav?" His voice did not sound like his own. It held a nasty, cruel note, coarse like a rusted blade. "Where are you? Who has you? Come here, tesoro. Let me see you, please!"

"Don't let that Staid go," the woman barked, pointing over Diego's shoulder. "Not until Morgen gets here."

"She was right behind me," Josh's voice answered from the dark.

"Thank fuck." The woman paced a slow circle around Diego, eyeing him closely. "Damn, that's a nasty one. And he had it?" She jerked her chin toward where Trav and Josh's voices had come from. Diego tried to twist around, but the halting hex held fast.

"What did I have?" Trav asked.

"A curse, man," Josh answered. "A real piece of shit curse."

"A ... curse."

"Oh, Goddess, he's not one of you?" the woman blurted. "We're gonna have to bottle him to keep this quiet."

"¡No lo toques!" At the spoken threat to what was *his*, the acid gathering in Diego's chest exploded. "¡Me cago en tu puta madre!" He let fly a litany of foul language, each word fueling the stinging, caustic anger building inside of him. They could not touch Trav. Trav was his. He belonged to Diego, and he needed to keep him safe. How could they not understand?

"Gott in Himmel, Master Bimini, control yourself." Morgen strode into the glade, haloed in her Way's pale, gleaming yellow light. She nodded to the witch who had flung the halting hex. "Thank you, Sahar. Impeccably handled."

"What about the Staid?" Sahar tipped her head toward Trav, and Diego tensed, his next nasty shouts silenced by the arched brow of the Morgenhexe.

"There will be no bottling. C.R.O.W.'s Light Witch is occupied elsewhere, and even if she were available, no mortal could escape a curse of this magnitude unscathed." She studied Diego as she spoke, eyes dropping to the center of his chest and narrowing. "A nasty piece of magick."

"So what do we do with him?" Sahar pressed.

"He's one of us," Josh stated. "We take care of our own."

Sahar's jaw dropped. She looked to Morgen, who still studied Diego, her expression impassive, and shrugged. "Whatever. It's your demesne."

Morgen's mouth twitched, a ghost of a smile flashing. She stepped close to Diego and withdrew a gold chain from her pocket. Holding it high, she let him see the ouroboros as it spun in a slow circle. "This was clumsy of you, Diego."

At the sight of the medallion, his entire body twitched despite the halting hex. He gnashed his teeth, wanting to reach for the precious bone and cursing when he could not. "Vete a la mierda."

"Rude." Morgen tapped between his eyebrows, causing Diego to blink. "Now unstitch it."

"Unstitch?"

She cocked her head and tapped her lower lip. "A little help, then."

Light gleamed in her eyes, and Morgen tapped between his brows again. An image unfurled from her touch, the vision as clear as a film. His hands released from his thighs, fingers shortening and softening to those of a child's as they curled to form the sigil every Stitch Witch learned as a child. Another pair of hands cupped his finger, correcting the bend of his pinky. Familiar, long-forgotten hands. He blinked, eyes stinging, and his sister swung around to his front.

"Like that," Daniela said. Soft brown eyes flitted up from his hands, meeting Diego's gaze. "*Desenredar.* It is a little different than how I would work with their veins, but our Ways are not so dissimilar. We must learn to use them together, especially when dealing with a cancer or a curse."

"Why?"

"Because I am only a hippocromantic." She grinned at him and cuffed his shoulder. "I can only keep the infection from spreading, but *you* can unstitch it. When you see me do this"—she formed the same sigil with her casting hand, then lengthened her little finger—"then you make this sigil, and it will detach the tendons and the veins simultaneously."

As quickly as the illusion formed, it faded, and Diego was again in the mangroves, stooped and sobbing.

Morgen held the ouroboros before his face, her stern mien softening as she whispered, "*Desenredar.*"

"*Desenredar,*" he repeated. *Unstitch.*

The halting hex bled away, and he slammed a hand over his chest, grabbing hold of the curse. He screamed in agony as each thorned prickle was torn free from the fiber of his being. The wretched magick had burrowed deep in the short time Diego had held it, driving him through his fear and panic to embrace the need to protect Trav. To keep him safe.

A voice cried out somewhere behind him, only to be immediately shushed, but that singular cry was enough.

Desenredar, he thought, grabbing hold with both hands and wrenching with all his might. The curse whipped free, stinging and thrashing, seeking a new host. He shoved it at the ouroboros, taking the bone medallion in both hands and clamping down until the wickedness was again bound to the ancient hollows.

Morgen snatched it away, her eyes blinding bright and focused on the cursed Calusa totem. "*Zerstören.*" The scent of burning flesh rose around them. Nothing happened, and she spoke again. "*Zerstören.*" The warmth of her Way flew from the witch like a desert wind, rustling leaves and blowing sodden hair away from Diego's face. For a breath, he thought the mighty Morgenhexe had failed. That even she could not destroy the wretched item. She huffed, her nostrils flaring as she inhaled to try a third time, and that was when Diego saw it—the blackening of a singular scale.

"Morgen," he croaked, pointing a shaking hand at the ouroboros. Another scale began to blacken, and another, the bone rotting away and taking the curse with it until the ouroboros was nothing but a shriveled ring.

"Oh, Diosa," Diego wept. The last of his strength fled from his body, and he wavered, pain erupting in the absence of adrenaline. The ground rushed to meet him, and someone caught him under his arms, hoisting Diego against a lean, damp body.

"I've got you," Trav murmured, lips hot against his temple. "And I am not letting go until somebody explains what the fuck just happened."

TWENTY-THREE

"A witch."

"Sí." Diego laced and unlaced his fingers, looking at Trav from under his brows when he kept silent.

He sat on the edge of the bed in gray sweats that barely brushed his ankles and a New Orleans Saints t-shirt a size too big, hands clenching the mattress and mouth pressed in a line. Diego shuffled on his sewing chair, fighting the urge to drag Trav to him and soothe the mortal with his hands while making promises he absolutely could not keep. Morgen had had them brought to the tower, barking instructions that they shower and change before stinking up her home with swamp, and they had done that, keeping to their corners until Diego could no longer tolerate the heavy silence. So he sat Trav down and blurted the truth.

"I understand it is a lot to take in."

"Not really," Trav answered. "I mean, I am a little hung up on the gender normativeness of a man being called a witch, but in light of everything, that's the most believable bit."

"The Ways are matrilineal," Diego explained. "Magick flows from the mother to the child, and the word is non-binary, like human."

"Diego," Trav leveled, "I'm kidding."

"Oh."

"All of this is *wildly* unbelievable." He reached out and grabbed Diego's hand, squeezing once. "And if I hadn't seen it with my own eyes, I would call you a liar. To be fair, everything was hazy, and this prescription is at least three years old." He flicked the plastic arm of his glasses, retrieved by one of Morgen's witches. "So who's to say I saw what I saw, but the minute you did whatever it was you *did*, it was like I could think clearly for the first time in weeks."

"Weeks?" He swallowed, pulling his hand away. Trav held tight, refusing him the distance.

"I found that thing on Martin's bedside table wrapped in a cloth and brought it in to process after packing up his condo." So the medallion truly had been a host. Diego had assumed as much. While bearing the curse, he had not felt compelled to seek out the ouroboros. His only drive, his only thoughts, had been to get Trav, his treasure, and return to the mangroves and the bones buried beneath. Without a host, the compulsion to return would have sent the curse straight back to the ouroboros after Martin died. The medallion lying in wait for the next person to come along.

"God, I only put it on because I missed Martin." Trav sniffled, blinking rapidly. "That's what I get for being sentimental, I guess. Put the damn thing on, and then it … and I …" He dropped his gaze to the floor, throat bobbing. "God, he *died* because of that thing, and I almost—"

"I as well." Diego leaned forward and cupped Trav's cheek, lifting his head. "But we did not, you understand? You cannot live in the almost."

"Please don't say something cheesy like, 'live in the now.'"

"Alright, I will not," he said, brushing a tentative kiss to Trav's lips instead. He tensed, a muffled grunt of surprise escaped, and then Trav clamped his arms around Diego, hauling him from the sewing chair and into his lap.

He laughed against Trav's mouth, nipping his lower lip and pulling away to look him in the eye. "I do not frighten you?"

"You almost *drowned* trying to save me, Diego. If anything frightened me, it was that."

"And after?"

Trav frowned and rolled them on the bed, lean body pressed over Diego's and hands on either side of his head. "You mean when you tried to drag me into the mangroves?"

Diego nodded, unable to speak. A lump grew in his throat as he watched Trav work through his thoughts, and his heart flipped when that frown eased.

"I lived under that curse for weeks, tesoro." He bent his elbows and took Diego's lobe between his lips, sending a shiver down his spine. "I know what it feels like, how it makes you react when something important to you is threatened." He tugged Diego's ear with his teeth and kissed his jaw. "Do you know how jealous I was in Shanna Key? How tempting it was to pull you into a booth and beg you to fuck me in front of all those runners?"

"Oh, por la Diosa."

"Never forget, witch," his voice dropped on the word, desire curling in the consonants, and Diego's hips rolled of their own accord. "Curse aside, I treasure you."

"Goddess," Diego panted, grabbing Trav's head and guiding him into a deep kiss. Somehow, he rolled them in the bed. Somehow, he stretched that glorious body out beneath him, savoring the strength in Trav's arms as he held Diego treasured and dear. They were too exhausted to do more, but this was all they needed—the heat of their bodies, the slide of their tongues, and *time*.

"Ahem," Morgen cleared her throat from the hall, rapping knuckles on the doorframe. "I hate to interrupt..."

"That is absolutely untrue," Diego grumbled and dropped his head onto Trav's chest, smiling as the man ran fingers through his hair, toying with the dark, shoulder-length strands.

"Regardless," she sniffed and stepped into the room, "we need to discuss Mr. Bergstrom's future in Key West."

Diego rolled off Trav and stood, favoring his sprained ankle as he ran a hand through tousled hair. He pulled it back into a tail, securing the mass with a tie he summoned to hand. Trav gasped as the casual magick and Diego shot him a saucy wink. "Do we need to discuss this now?"

"Yes," she said. "The sooner our stories are aligned, the sooner I can put C.R.O.W.'s hivemind at ease." She hit him with a stern look. "We deployed a lot of witches in those mangroves, and the trail you laid throughout my demesne sent the cultists on a merry chase." He did not miss how her gaze flicked to Trav at the word "cultist," nor how he hunched his shoulders and dropped his eyes away. "We have much to review, and there is much for Travis to learn about his new role."

"What new role?" He straightened and glanced between the two witches. "Can't I go back to running the pawnshop?"

"Of course you can." Morgen waved her hand, dismissing the question. "How else is my foster daughter going to move your occult items out of harm's way? No, I am more concerned about you acclimating to your new state."

"Diego? What is she talking about?"

"The curse," he began, glaring at Morgen as he limped in front of Trav, shielding him from the witch. "Mortals like yourself are not meant to come into contact with magick, any amount of magick. The curse it—te alteró, it—"

"It *altered* me?" Trav finally balked. "Am I a-a mutant or something? Like an X-man?"

"A what?" Diego asked. Morgen fluttered her lips and waved the question away.

"Absurd," she said. "What use would mutations be if they granted each individual *individual* powers? Ridiculous from both a Darwinian and Lamarckian perspective."

"You will excuse me for not following," Diego deadpanned, "considering I was dead for all that."

"Reincarnation." Trav shook his head, mumbling to himself. "My boyfriend's Shirley Maclaine."

"Lucky for you; it was an ethical disaster as far as the Staid were concerned," she replied.

"Staid?" Trav focused on Morgen.

"Humans," she said. "And what this means is that your body was forced to acclimate to a large amount of magick very quickly. Most humans only come into contact with magick in low doses throughout their very short lives—"

"Rude," Trav interjected.

"Factual," Morgen said. "You, on the other hand, bore a curse of excess strength for weeks without going mad. Your body has been forever altered; you must have noticed by now."

"Noticed what?" He looked from Morgen to Diego, appealing to them with his hands.

"The scent," Diego answered. Trav blinked at him. "Magick has a scent. When I used my Way—"

"Way?"

"It is how we designate the different strands of magick," Morgen explained. "I am a Morgenhexe, and my Way is illusion. Diego is a Stitch Witch, and his Way is fabrics."

"And fibers," Diego added, casting Morgen a wary glance. Trav had been conscious when Diego unstitched the curse and sewed it into himself, and he was damn near fluent in Spanish, so why omit the truth of what a Stitch Witch could do? No, not again, not anymore. So much could have been avoided if he had explained the curse and the occult from the start, and he refused to let Morgen control the narrative in the same irresponsible way C.R.O.W. had done for centuries. "Any fiber, down to muscles and tendons. And anything stitched, including curses. Apparently."

"That sounds ... disgusting." Trav reached for Diego, lacing their fingers together.

"To a cultist, our magick presents as a scent, thus why Joshua and Tamara run their pack through the streets of my demesne," she finished. "They are on the hunt, as it were, for magick to satiate the craving."

"Craving?"

"Josh likened it to an addiction," Diego said.

Trav exhaled with puffed cheeks, sitting with this knowledge momentarily before meeting Morgen's gaze. "So I've joined a cult," he huffed a laugh. "After all these years, my mom was right to be afraid."

"That is your takeaway?" Diego gaped at him.

"Honestly, D, if I can't laugh about this right now, I will probably cry. Can you let me have the moment?"

"Sí, yes, absolutely."

"Joshua has offered to sponsor your membership, with Tamara as his second. I have worked closely with them both for several years and trust them to teach you about the Ways and the means with which you operate within my demesne."

Trav paled further. "Demesne?"

"I will explain," Diego sat beside him on the bed. "And answer any questions I can." Morgen sniffed, and he shot her a glare. "I am not going anywhere."

A synthetic chord punctuated his statement, rising and falling through a quartet of notes. Trav and Diego glanced at each other and Morgen before all three began scanning the room. Guitars joined in, and Trav laughed. "Is that *Time After Time*?"

"Sí, it is Milla's ringtone."

"Oh my God, you still use a ringtone. How old are you?"

"I did not set it; she did. As a joke." Diego dropped to his knees, searching under the bed. "I think. I do not get it."

"Ah," Morgen snapped her fingers. "I do; that is quite clever."

Cyndi Lauper's voice cut in, and Diego straightened, scanning the room for his phone and finding it stashed under a ream of cloth on the sewing table. He dashed over, whipping the device out and smiling at his roommate's name. "Finalmente." Swiping the screen, he grinned at Trav and answered, "Pequeña bruja, I have been trying to get ahold of you for over a week; where in the nine rings have you—"

"Diego?" A hoarse, thickly accented male voice came over the line. "Diego, mate, is that you?"

"Darkly?"

"Oh, Goddess," the witch exhaled into the phone. A muffled sob followed as if he had covered his mouth to keep from crying. Diego glanced at Morgen, her head cocked and intent on his every word. "Diego, I fucked up."

"¿Qué quieres decir?" He gripped the edge of the sewing table. The last time he had spoken with Darkly, he had promised to take care of Milla. Had promised to keep her safe after whatever had gone down in St. Augustine with her apprentice. That he called now, sounding like he had been in a three-day screaming match, sent Diego's stomach plummeting to the floor. "What do you mean?"

"Everything was fine; I had it under control, and then she ... and they came, and I couldnae—"

"Could not what?" He went ramrod straight, an uneasy chill running down his spine. "What happened?"

"They came, Diego," Darkly said. "They came, and I dinnae ken how to run the store or clean any of this up, and, oh, Goddess, I need help."

"Help with *what*?"

"With Milla," Darkly said. "They have her."

EPILOGUE

"Tea?"

"Depends," Jennifer answered. "Was it made by you or one of your vinefica?"

"Neither." Morgen sent her a smile that was more like a baring of teeth. "I had a houseguest until recently, and he proved adept with blends."

"That doesn't answer my question." She set her bag on the table and withdrew a tablet, powering the device on. "His Way?"

"Stitchery."

Jennifer tipped her head at the Morgenhexe and slid into a chair. She ran sweating palms over her thighs, smoothing faint wrinkles in her skirt. The flight down from Houston had been brief, but the three-and-a-half-hour drive from Miami to Key West had left her feeling less put together than she would prefer. "Then I would love a cup of tea, please."

"So formal."

"This is a business arrangement, is it not?" she countered.

Morgen smirked and pinched a doily out of thin air, placing it on the kitchen table beside a small marble box. The teapot and two Bone china teacups with gold foil rims followed.

Jenny picked hers up, eyeing the cluster of daffodils, tulips, and African violets painted on the side. Non-poisonous blooms. Running her finger along the rim, she closed her eyes and opened her senses, divining no ill intent in the witch, the tea, or the china. Satisfied, she opened her eyes and found Morgen regarding her from across the table with a look that ought to make her squirm. She did not. It was a matter of principle, of knowing one's place, and Jennifer knew hers well. "Shall we begin?"

"Your professionalism is a breath of fresh air," said Morgen. She poured a full cup for Jennifer and one for herself, making a show of sipping first. "I am pleased you could attend to this matter so quickly."

"Mr. Holfstaedter was quick to identify your request as an absolute priority, although I must admit we are both somewhat surprised. Typically, you broker sale of occult items through your ... foster daughter, was it?"

"Yes, well." Morgen set her teacup down and steepled her fingers. "This particular item is best left off of the occult boards."

"If it is that powerful, why not keep it yourself?"

"This is the wrong sort of power. A corrupt power." Morgen's eyes dropped to the marble box. She frowned. "Some magicks are best put out of sight."

"Understood." Jennifer tapped on her tablet's screen and spun it to face Morgen. "Mr. Holfstaedter has prepared a bid, and I am sure you will find the details agreeable." Morgen nodded, face impassive. "And beyond the question of price, he has taken pains to attach a detailed summary of security measures for both transit and storage of the item." She waited as the witch read through the file, anticipating her next question.

"It will not be stored in his vault?"

"Mr. Holfstaedter hosts the foremost museum of the occult on the West Coast, if not all of the Americas. He maintains a security team to rival your C.R.O.W. Enforcers and utilizes mortal tactics to ensure the safety of all items under his care."

"Hm." Morgen swept her finger on the screen, returning to the offer Jennifer had first shown. "This is higher than I expected."

"Consider it a suggestion that you bring these items to his attention first rather than sending them along to your foster daughter.'"

"He is not still upset over losing the bid on the seance table?"

"I would never presume to speak to my employer's emotions," she said. Morgen fixed her with a bright stare, and Jennifer allowed herself a smile. "But yes, he's still upset and whines about it weekly."

"Tell him she is using it as a display for hideous leggings," Morgen confided. "That should give him something new to complain about."

Jennifer snorted and sipped her tea. "You find his proposal agreeable?"

"More than," she said. "He has my banking details; I trust you to manage the transfer."

"You don't want to witness?"

"I want this *thing* out of my demesne and in the hands of someone who can keep it safe."

Jennifer straightened, surprised by Morgen's blunt appraisal of her employer. "That is far more trust than I thought you had in Mr. Holfstaedter."

"Yes, it is, but thus far, he is the only one yet to let me down." She set a hand on the marble box, sliding it to the center of the table. "Please convey my sentiments to him, word-for-word."

Jennifer swallowed and nodded, unsettled by the implication and what Morgen was not saying. It was not often a person, or witch, managed to make her feel small, but seated at the Morgenhexe's table, Jennifer felt every year the witch had over her. "Yes, ma'am."

"Sehr gut." With that said, she opened the box and pinched a gold chain in her fingers, lifting a pristine white medallion from the velvet lining. It spun in a slow circle, allowing Jennifer to observe every fine detail, from the intricately carved scales to the pulse of magick humming in the—

"Bone?"

"Good eye," Morgen said. "Carved, tempered, and treated to house a vicious curse. We have had no small amount of trouble with this item in the last few weeks, and I am eager to see it gone."

Holding out her hand, Jennifer again slipped into her senses and quickly withdrew, pushing back from the table in disgust. "Horned God, who would lay such an awful curse?"

"Can Mr. Holfstaedter keep it safe?"

Jennifer regarded the medallion with a wary eye. "The afflicted?"

"Cured. Can he do it?"

"Cured?" she argued. "A curse like that, Morgen, it leaves a stain."

"The most recently afflicted believes the item to be destroyed, and whatever temptation arises in him will be managed by my cultists. The rest are dead. Can he do it?"

"Yes," Jennifer said. Mr. Holfstaedter could. She believed it wholeheartedly, as did Morgen; why else would she contact them directly?

"Good." Morgen nodded and let the chain slip from her fingers. With a quiet thud, the medallion landed in the velvet-lined box, and she slammed the lid. She slid the box closer to Jennifer. "Now get it out of my demesne."

THE WORLD

ST. AUGUSTINE, FL

Bells jangled as the door swung open, shattering Diego's peace. A humid wind tore through the store, rustling clothes on the rack and teasing his hair. He blinked at the tablet in his hands, taking a moment to center himself and smile before dealing with a customer.

Goddess, how had Milla done it day after day? He'd never given her enough credit. Never understood how hard it was for her to feign politeness when grief and guilt weighed her down like iron shackles. He'd been too distracted by all that modernity had to offer even to consider how hard this was for Milla. Televisions, telephones, and cuisines he had never known existed in his first life. Architecture that still amazed him, and the freedom to live in a city where no one cast him a second glance.

But now, the cramped floor and narrow walls of Southern Gothic pressed in against him, making it hard to breathe. His sewing room was too small, too tight, the walls closing around him. He could not bear to look at the scorched and rotted carpet beside his sewing table without getting nauseous and had only lasted an hour before the walls began to pitch and roll, the room reminding him too much of the hold of a ship.

He had relocated to the front counter, lasting another fifteen minutes before the back of his neck began prickling. So he'd taken the store's tablet and shoved his rococo throne up against a wall where he could observe the entirety of Southern Gothic while remaining unseen—just another piece of the eclectic collection.

Everything had happened so quickly after Darkly's phone call. Trav had been ushered out of the Martello Tower by Tammy, and within the hour, Diego and Morgen were on the road to St. Augustine. The Morgenhexe cast illusion after illusion to keep them invisible to highway patrol as they blew through the keys, past towns and cities, driving well over the speed limit. By evening, she was screeching to a halt in front of Southern Gothic, kicking Diego and his duffel bag to the curb and speeding off to Jacksonville to throw her weight around at the Panhandle Coven.

That had been days ago. Days without a word from Morgen and only phone calls from Trav to keep his mind occupied. Julie, Milla's closest friend outside of Diego, had sent him a text asking if he knew where Milla was and what had happened at the Fountain of Youth.

He didn't, so he left the message unanswered.

When Darkly finally showed himself the following morning, Diego wished with all of his second life that the witch had stayed away.

He had slipped through the store's rear door and lingered at the edge of the hallway, calling out softly to Diego. Haggard and drawn, Darkly looked as though he had not slept in weeks. His normally styled auburn hair was disheveled and slightly greasy, as though he'd been constantly running his hands through it. Deep shadows clung to the underside of his eyes, his broad-shouldered posture stooped, and then he started speaking, telling Diego everything that had happened with the leggings, and the Fountain and Youth, and—

No.

He could not dwell on that.

A hand flew to the vial at his neck. Bone chips and dust, matted hair. The remnants of the witch he had been used to summon him to a second life. A gift from Milla, who had never wanted to hold power over anyone or anything. Milla, who was—

"Hey, Brown Eyes," a soft, achingly lovely voice hauled Diego from his thoughts.

Ah, yes, the customer.

He blinked, staring down at a pair of brown leather boat shoes and cuffed olive green khakis revealing tanned ankles.

His heart flipped, and he gripped the vial tighter, not wanting to hope. Better to think this was a dream — the hallucination of a tired mind.

But there those shoes were, and a hand was lightly gripping his upper arm.

"Sorry I couldn't get here earlier," Trav said, crouching to look up into Diego's face. Round glasses, wind-blown, sun-bronzed hair. That distracting mole beside his eye. "Flights were booked solid, and I don't have a car."

Diego blinked again, fully expecting Trav to vanish into the aether. When he didn't, he cast the tablet aside and launched into his arms, wrapping himself around the pawnbroker like a koala in a tree.

"Hey—" Trav rocked back at the collision, his arms clamped around Diego. "Hey, D, it's alright."

"You're here." He could weep. Was he weeping? His eyes hurt, his chest felt like it was locked in a vise, and either Trav was wearing a damp cardigan or Diego *was* weeping, and he did not care. He was here. Trav was here in St. Augustine, in the store, in Diego's arms. "How are you here?"

"Josh." Trav managed to gain his feet, bringing Diego with him. Warm lips pressed against his temple, his hair. "He has some cultist thing in Tallahassee coming up. When I found out he was headed north, I bummed a ride."

"What about the pawnshop?"

"Tammy has a few cultists keeping an eye on things while I'm gone." He slid his hands to Diego's arms, prying him away and pushing him back enough to look him in the eye. "How are you?"

"I am fine."

"Liar." His mouth quirked, hazel eyes soft.

"Sí," Diego whispered. His throat tightened, another wave of tears burning in his eyes. He shook his head, wanting to look away, but Trav held him in place with that warm, welcoming gaze. "Lo siento, I ... I—"

"Shh." Trav pressed his lips to Diego's cheek, hands cupping his face and tilting his head back. "It's alright, D." His words crashed against Diego's lips, teasing him with their warmth and sweetness. "Take your time; I've got you."

He nodded, unable to express how Trav's mere presence had eased the pain of the last few days. He had been drowning in worry and fear, unable to sleep or eat. Yet a minute in Trav's presence had awakened a deep hunger in Diego. A hunger that he clung to like a lifeline, needing it to haul him from the depths of his own despair. To remember what it was to live, if only for a moment.

"I'm realizing I don't actually know you very well," Trav said, worry entering his gaze. "Probably should have called first. If this is too much, if you want me to leave ..."

"No." Diego shook his head, sliding his hands down Trav's back to settle at his hips, tugging them forward. "No, I want you here."

"Then how can I help?" he asked. "Do you need to take a break from the store? Have you eaten?" Diego shook his head again, stunned by the thoughtfulness.

Would he ever stop being stunned by this man? Showing up unannounced, wanting to care for him, to make sure he was alright, even without knowing the full breadth of what had happened in St. Augustine ... to Milla ...

Trav kissed him. A soft peck, enough to steal Diego from his thoughts and capture his attention. Those lovely eyes darted over Diego's face; his lips pouted, and Diego closed the subtle distance.

This is what he needed, what he wanted. Trav in his arms, his thoughts silenced for a few moments. After the last few days, Diego needed this bliss, this moment of connection, more than he had ever needed it before.

Enforcers lurked around every corner, trawling St. Augustine for the Forbidden and Foule. Darkly did what he could to keep them away from Southern Gothic and Diego, but they were still *everywhere*. There had been no word on

Milla, no communication from Morgen. What little Darkly could tell him when he stopped by had been dissatisfying at best. It was Zaragoza again, in those final days before his sister burned. Diego tiptoed around the city, working with his head ducked low, seeking to avoid notice.

And now Trav was here. Trav, who knew him, knew what he was and how he'd come to be in this modern world—Trav, who was kissing him with his pillow-soft mouth, his long, lean body pressed against Diego. Sucking his lower lip and holding him close.

Diego arched into him, teasing the seam of Trav's lips with his tongue. He slid his hands over the curve of his rear, gripping firmly as if he could keep them in the here and now.

"What do you need, Diego?" Trav murmured, a darker tone coloring his words. The sound ribboned along Diego's jaw and into his ear. He grunted low in his throat, dropping his head back as Trav repeated, "What do you need?"

"This," he gasped, rocking his hips into Trav. "I need this; I need to not think for un minuto."

Trav chuckled, the rumbling in his chest vibrating into Diego's ribs. He nipped his lobe, hot breath crashing against fevered skin. "I think I can help you with that."

He kissed along Diego's jaw, fingers worming into his hair, working the bun loose and then free. Nails scored Diego's scalp as his hair tumbled free, sending a web of sensation cresting over his skull. He gasped, and Trav was there, slipping his tongue into his mouth. Sweeping and tasting him the way a foodie savored that first bite.

Their hands were everywhere, gripping and tugging, groping and squeezing, yet it was not enough. Diego needed to feel Trav, needed his rapid pulse beneath his palms and the warmth of his body erasing the chill of the last few days.

He wormed his hands between them, fumbling over the buttons on Trav's cardigan and never breaking their kiss. One button, two ... the third stuck, and he grunted in frustration. Magick shot to his hands, his Way fraying threads until the button fell away and tocked against the floor.

Trav groaned. He gripped Diego's rear, pressing their groins together, and his following moan buzzed into Diego's mouth, matching the frisson of pleasure from the feel of Trav's cock rubbing against his own.

"Trav," he gasped, head too empty of anything but more of this—Trav's tongue, his hands, his cock, *him*—to form a coherent thought.

"I'm here, baby." Trav worked him backward, laying frantic kisses against Diego's cheekbone, his temple. "God, I missed you." He nuzzled Diego's hair, inhaling and moaning out, "Missed you so fucking much."

"Dulzora." He pulled Trav's shirt from his pants and slipped his hands beneath the fabric. Goddess, he was so warm—all smooth skin and heat. Muscles danced under his touch, bunching and flexing as Trav's fingers undid the buckle of Diego's belt, grabbing the ends and jerking Diego's hips forward. He deftly undid his button and fly, slipped his hand into his pants, and cupped him, thumb rubbing the head of his cock. It was all Diego could do not to combust.

How had he lived so long without this? Days, less than a week, the entire year of his second life. How had he not sought out a companion like Trav? Someone who knew who he was and how to touch him in ways that made his mind melt.

"Goddess, I need to touch you," he said between gasps, fingers fumbling with the buttons on Trav's shirt.

His lips curled against Diego's mouth, his answering nod no more than a slight tremor of his head. "Use your Way."

"¿Qué?"

"You're a Stitch Witch." He nipped Diego's ear, pressing down with his thumb as he continued stroking his cock. "Shouldn't be too hard to put the buttons back on."

"Brat."

"Mmhmm," Trav hummed. He pressed Diego's palm flat against his chest with one hand, milking his cock with the other. Goddess, it was all too easy to call on his Way. The magick bubbled beneath his skin, wanting to be used and deployed if only to get Trav's clothes off quicker than any mortal could manage.

"*Cortar.*"

Sever.

Threads split, buttons fell away from fabric, and Trav dropped his head back, moaning as Diego separated the front plackets of his shirt, sliding palms up his smooth chest.

Horned God, he was beautiful. Suntanned skin stretched over lean muscles. The tiny white-flecked scars along his ribcage winked like stars, drawing the eye to perfectly pink nipples. Diego swept his thumbs over both before taking one in his mouth, flicking the nub with his tongue. Trav shivered against him. He cupped the back of Diego's head, keeping him in place with the gentle pressure of a power bottom.

"Baby," he breathed.

Diego flicked his eyes up, warming at Trav's intent, hungry gaze. His pupils were blown out, his breath raspy and uneven. A wicked thought occurred, prompted by the effect of his Way on Trav and the openness with which he could be himself.

Stretching out his right arm, he crooked two fingers on his casting hand, seizing the curtains with his Way. Trav's moans turned wanton as Diego unspooled more of his magick, alluring the threads in the curtains to draw together, shutting them off from the prying eyes of the Colonial Quarter.

"Oh, God, Diego." Trav rutted against his hips, the fingers in his hair pressing harder, guiding Diego lower.

"Need something?" He teased, trailing fingers around Trav's cock, hard beneath his pants. Little bits of Way slipped free, loosening Trav's belt and undoing the button of his Chinos. He whimpered and panted, hips rolling in search of more friction.

"D, please," Trav begged, and it was music to Diego's ears. Gently, he turned them both until Trav's back was to the rococo throne. With a pulse of magick, his fly unzipped, and Diego tugged his pants low, pushing the mortal into the throne at the same time.

Trav landed hard in the chair. Wooden feet scraped across the floor, and Diego dropped to his knees before he could recover, curling fingers around Trav's cock and wrapping his lips around the head.

"Oh, *fuck*." Trav slammed a hand down on Diego's head, pushing as he lifted his hips.

Diego relaxed his jaw, swallowing Trav to the hilt. He wrapped his tongue around rigid flesh, hollowing his cheeks as he sucked and teased. Every moan and curse from Trav's lips was a dream, filling Diego's head with sounds of pleasure and desire, his name uttered as a prayer. It drowned out the stress and worries of the last few days, and if Diego could curl up in Trav's every moan, he would, basking in the warmth and respite of his voice and his body.

And just like that, the hunger that Trav's mere presence had awoken became ravenous.

Diego gripped his knees, spreading him wide, stroking as he sucked, chasing the movement of his mouth with a fervent grip. He cupped Trav's scrotum in his palm, massaging the sensitive bridge of flesh and finally pressing against his tight opening.

Trav twitched and tensed beneath his ministrations. His fingers knotted in Diego's hair, tugging and pinching his scalp. Each sound he made, every whimper and groan, became more desperate, more needy.

"Please, baby," he begged. Diego pressed one finger in, working Trav's hole until the muscle loosened enough for a second finger. "Just there, baby. *Fuck*."

Trav's cock gave a warning twitch in Diego's mouth, his body tensing.

Diego pulled away, halting his strokes and stilling his fingers, leaving them two knuckles deep in Trav.

"Breathe, dulzura," he said, drinking in the sight of Trav panting in the chair. A delicious flush colored his cheeks. His wide eyes were feverish and fixed on Diego, and his mouth worked to protest, to breathe, to settle himself. "I am not done with you."

"Oh, Jesus." He dropped his head back, chest rising and falling. Sweat dotted his brow, and he flexed his fingers, disentangling them from Diego's hair to grip the armrest. "Tease." Diego crooked his fingers. "*Fuck*. God damn, okay. Okay."

He drew in a ragged breath, squirming in the chair and twitching his hips as if he could force Diego to crook his fingers again. The swollen, purple head of his cock waved enticingly, and Diego gave in, flicking his tongue against the tip. A tight whine eked out of Trav's throat, a sound he wanted to swallow. Gently, he eased his fingers away, smirking at Trav's protesting whimper as he rose and stood between his legs.

Horned God, this man was going to be the end of him. Splayed wantonly Diego's rococo throne, cock leaking and plump lips pouting. He was a feast for the senses and the eyes. Supple and lithe, gorgeous beyond belief, and on the verge of being wholly and utterly wrecked.

"On your knees," Diego growled. He hardly recognized his voice or the command in his tone. He jerked Trav's belt buckle, tugging the leather free from the loops and casting it aside. Trav licked his lips, gaze drifting from Diego's face to his rock-hard cock tenting his pants.

Diego palmed himself, pressing fabric tight against his length. "You want this?"

"God, yes, D." Trav gripped the armrests, knuckles blanching as if he fought against the urge to touch Diego. Challenge lit his hazel eyes, a playful smile quirking his mouth. "Where do you want me?"

"I already told you." Diego freed himself, stroking as he advanced on his lover. "On your knees." Trav bit his lip and began to slip from the chair, halting as Diego clenched his casting hand and barked, "*Cincha.*"

Fabric closed at his ankles, binding them together. Trav shivered, gooseflesh rising down his torso and arms. "Baby."

"In the chair," Diego clarified, loosening his Way. Trav wasted no time, kicking a foot free from his pants and twisting around to kneel on the wide seat of the rococo throne. Diego stepped close enough to feel the heat wafting off of him. He ran his hand up Trav's spine, hooking fingers in the collar of his shirt and tugging. Trav dropped his arms, allowing Diego to disrobe him. He did so slowly, savoring every inch of skin and spine revealed. He brought his lips to Trav's back, kissing fevered skin and tossing his shirt aside to sweep fingers over the curve of his rear.

Soft and round, firm and sweet enough to bite. So he did, nipping one perfect peach of a cheek as he reached around, taking Trav in hand. "Grip the frame."

Trav's hands flew to the headrest, fast and desperate. He was trembling beneath Diego's touch, hard and hot and ready for him.

Diego kept his strokes slow and deliberate, teasing Trav along a lovely, razor-thin edge. He bit, nibbled, and finally licked his seam, relishing the shout of surprise it earned.

Trav edged his rear back, urging Diego on. Fingers joined his tongue, and when Trav trembled and moaned, when his every breath was reserved for Diego's name, he pressed his hand at the center of Trav's back, easing him flush against the backrest.

Diego dropped his pants and knelt behind him. Embroidered brocade dimpled beneath their weight, and he brought his thighs flush with the back of Trav's, slipping his cock between his legs.

"Pants," Trav gasped, twisting his head around to catch Diego's mouth with a kiss. "Pocket."

Diego glanced aside, locating Trav's pants. A crook of his finger summoned the garment to his hand. He dug in a pocket, pulling out a tiny bottle of lube. A disbelieving laugh escaped his mouth, and he smacked Trav's rear.

"What on earth made you bring this?"

"Boy Scout," he replied with a heartbreaking grin. His eyes twinkled, and he adjusted his grip on the frame and pressed his ass against Diego. "Always be prepared."

"No se que significa eso." Shaking his head, Diego opened the bottle and coated his palm, edging back and stroking his cock as he dribbled more along the seam of Trav's ass. Goddess, he was aching for this man. For his heat and tightness. Cock throbbing with the need to spill inside him, ears wanting nothing more than to hear his cries as Diego pounded into him.

He notched against Trav's entrance, sweeping the head of his cock through the lube. Teeth dug into his lower lip as he restrained a moan, and grasping Trav's shoulder, Diego pressed into him.

A wild groan left them both. Relief and want wound together in one guttural utterance of bliss.

"Dulzura." Diego snaked an arm around Trav's front, fingers splayed over his heart. He rocked back and plunged into him, eyes rolling at the overwhelming sensation. Horned God, he would never get used to this. To the pleasure of enjoying another man on his own time. With every thrust, every moan, Diego fell further and further under Trav's spell. How his smaller frame curved perfectly around him. How his lover's head draped back, his sweet gasps filling Diego's head with the sounds of his pleasure.

The chair creaked from their movements. Trav's cries of pleasure shot to the ceiling and bounced in stereo off every surface. Diego slid his hand higher, caging Trav's throat, cupping his chin, his fingers seeking that lovely, filthy mouth. Trav knew what he wanted without being told, taking Diego's fingers into his mouth and sucking and—

"Por la diosa." He tightened his grip on Trav's hip, fingers dimpling that lovely flesh, pounding as stars burst at the edges of his vision. "Ay diosa, dulzura, no puedo."

Trav grunted, closing his lips tight around Diego's fingers and sucking hard. His thrusts turned erratic, the hand on Trav's hip flying to his rigid cock, stroking him thrust for thrust for—

"Ungh," Trav groaned around Diego's fingers. He slipped them free, nuzzling Trav's neck to get as close to him as he could. Wanting to feel Trav's pleasure as well as he could hear it. "God, Diego, baby, yes. Tesoro!"

His body twitched and tightened. Trav went utterly still for one lovely heartbeat before he groaned and spilled in Diego's hand. His lithe body sagged against the backrest, firm muscles clenching around Diego's cock. The tightening pressure hauled him over the edge. He buried his face in Trav's neck, biting down as he pulsed his pleasure into tight heat. Goosebumps erupted over his body, the salt and sweat of Trav's skin flooded his mouth, and for the first time in days, Diego thought of nothing at all.

"You sure it'll come out?" Trav's voice carried down the hall from Milla's office, where they kept the cleaning supplies.

"Trust me," Diego called back. "I've removed worse from lesser fabric." He blotted the embroidery, muscles loose and head wonderfully light. After the comedown, when their heart rates had settled and reality trickled back in, he summoned a rag to hand, cleaning Trav before slipping himself free.

There was no shortage of smiles and kisses as they dressed and a spate of embarrassed laughter when Trav spotted the stain he'd left on the rococo throne.

"Still," he called down the hall. "I feel terrible; it's a nice chair."

"Made all the nicer by a wonderful memory." Diego drew a circle around the damp stain with the tip of his finger, stepping into his Way and calling on the threads to release Trav's ... release.

A muffled groan of, "Oh, *Jesus*," echoed down the hall, followed by what sounded like a lanky body toppling against cardboard. Diego bit his lips to stifle laughter. Trav would develop a tolerance to magick over time, just as a witch did with their Way. Until then, Diego was all too happy to enjoy how even the most minor use of the Ways affected him.

Smiling to himself, he pulled his finger away from the upholstery. A spider silk thin stream of opaline liquid followed. He summoned a handkerchief, collecting the release as the bells on the door chimed.

"Hey, Diego!" Julie's Georgia soft voice called over the wind. Dressed in blue scrubs, she hugged a stack of mail and parcels to her chest with one hand, groping for the door handle with the other. A harsh gust of wind tore into the store, blowing a mass of red curls into her face. "Oh, sugarsnaps."

Diego balled up the handkerchief and vanished it to his sewing room to be dealt with later, hurrying across the store to help. She offloaded her mail into his arms and, with two hands on the bar, heaved the door closed against the wind.

"Wow, that storm kicked up out of nowhere; it is *wild* out there." She swept hair out of her face and patted her front, her hips, digging in her pockets. "Could have sworn I had … ah!" She held up an elastic hair tie and smiled at Diego as she gathered her hair into a tail and tied it back. "Never leave home without one."

"Wise." He shuffled the envelopes and parcels, trying and failing to catch a few as they fell.

"Oops, careful." She stooped and picked up a large yellow envelope with *Urgent* stamped on the front. "Some of this looks important."

"Where did you get all of this?" Diego unloaded the mail onto the front counter, flicking through bills addressed to Milla and the store.

"Collected it while you were gone." She set the *Urgent* envelope on top of the stack and tapped it with a finger. "Since you never returned my text, I thought I'd swing by and drop it off." Julie swept her gaze over Southern Gothic, lingering on the ventriloquists' dummies on a shelf. She shivered and turned her back. "I'm glad you're here, wasn't looking forward to being in the store by myself. Any idea when Milla gets back?"

"None." Diego shook his head.

"Dang."

"Hey, D?" Trav called from the hallway, and Julie snapped her head up, blue eyes slowly widening as a grin stretched across her face. "Did you light a candle?"

"Who is that?" she whisper-hissed.

"Nobody." Heat crawled into his cheeks.

"Doesn't sound like 'nobody'." Julie was halfway to the hallway when Trav stepped out. They stared at one another, her grin broadening as Trav took in the nurse from head to toe. "Hi! I'm Julie."

She thrust out her hand, which Trav took immediately, a shy smile curling his mouth. "Travis."

"Nice to meet you, Travis." She tipped her head toward Diego. "And where did you two meet? Because I don't believe for one second that you're 'nobody.'"

"'Nobody?'" Trav pressed a hand over his heart and leaned back, sending Diego a look of mock affront. "Ouch." Before he could muster the words to explain, Trav winked at Diego and hooked his arm around Julie's shoulders. "Since you clearly know Diego well, I need to know *everything*."

"Oh, my Lanta, where to start." Julie giggled and launched into a story. It took all of three words for Diego to realize he was about to be extremely embarrassed, so he tuned her out and filtered through the mail.

Most of it was junk, as he'd assumed, but a few bills and the large envelope stamped *Urgent* needed his attention. The return address belonged to the landlord of Southern Gothic's building and was postmarked a week prior. Diego called on his Way, slipping his finger along the topmost edge of the envelope.

Trav sighed, sneezed, and rubbed the tip of his nose with a knuckle. He scanned the store, frowning slightly. "Is that your lotion that smells so good?" he asked Julie. "It's nice, like honeysuckle."

"Not wearing any." She shook her head. "So anyways, Milla made him wear these adorable gold lamé shorts, but if you ask me, it wasn't very hard to get Diego to agree."

"You're not wearing any lotion?"

Diego whipped his head up at Trav's tone. He was staring at Julie, eyebrows raised over his rounded frames. Slowly, he lifted his gaze to Diego, his lips pressed into a tight line, and *Goddess*, Diego knew that look. It was the same one he'd worn in the mangroves after Morgen destroyed the ouroboros.

It was a look that said, "What the fuck is going on."

Diego shook his head, reaching out with his Way. The store was as loud as the pawnshop had been, but it was a welcome noise. A wanted noise. Allures and hexes tickled over Diego's hands, greeting him like an old friend. Nothing new, nothing alarming.

"Hey, are you alright?" Julie stepped beside him, blue eyes searching Diego's face before dropping to the letter in his hand. "Is this the one from the *Urgent* envelope?" She took it from him before Diego could respond, skimming the pages and pressing a hand to her mouth as she gasped. "Oh. Oh, my stars, what does this mean?"

"No lo sé," he said.

"I thought they had to give more notice." Julie shuffled the papers, reading through the letter and attached contract. It was all above Diego. As good as his English had gotten in the last year, legal contracts were written in a language even his Way could not pick apart. "Do you think you'll get evicted?"

"Evicted?" He twitched his attention back to Julie. "Why would we get evicted?"

"It's a notice of sale from your landlord." She scanned the page, shaking her head. "He's revoking your Right of First Refusal."

"I have no idea what that means," said Diego.

"It *means* you and Milla might want to start looking into commercial leases." She slapped the paper down on the counter between them. "Your landlord is selling the building."

What in the nine rings happened to Milla? Find out in

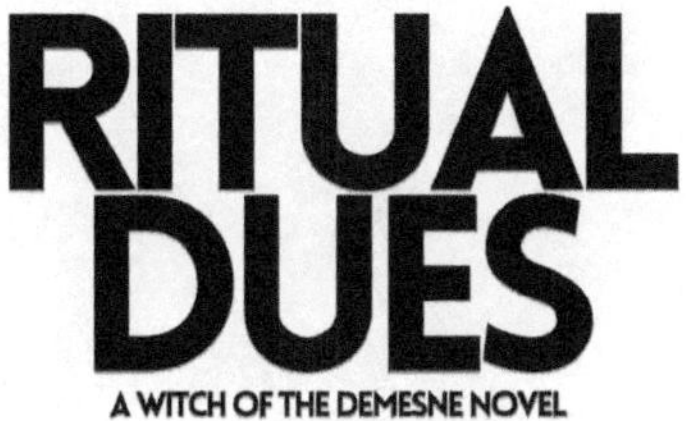

Read the first three chapters now.

RITUAL DUES

A WITCH OF THE DEMESNE NOVEL

B.L. BROWN

THE NEITHERWORLD

He walks in darkness, in a world that is neither here nor there.

Subtle and smooth, toeing a path none can see save for him.

The wind is relentless, harsh, and cold. It bites at his skin, burns his cheeks, and after an hour, a day, a week, he no longer feels it.

The cold has become a part of him, nestled in and among his bones with the Darkness that was always there.

Sometimes, he hears a voice, a wail calling his name, but the wind steals it away in the same gust that drives him deeper and deeper into the expanse.

At some point, his legs give out, so he leaves his body behind to become a passing Shade, and the expanse solidifies with each shadow step he takes. The path becomes cobbled, and the suggestion of brick buildings loom over his head.

Others fall into step behind him, beside him. They bow their heads and bend at the waist for the boy who walks with Darkness.

"Keir!"

The voice wails again. He pauses at the edge of a dead field, looking back down the road to where a pin-point of white light bobs and weaves in the Shade, a will-o-wisp tempting him to leave the Darkness—his Darkness.

"Keir, come back to me! This instant!" the voice calls again. The light bobs closer, and Keir steps into the field.

"She wants you to go home."

He stops at the sound of a small voice at his side. Silk tangles around his ankle and winds up his leg. A small hand slips into his, tugging the boy out of the field and back onto the cobbles.

"Who?"

"The Light," that little voice replies, blunt and brusque. "Obviously."

"And who are you?" he asks, stunned to be addressed, to be touched in a world that is neither here nor there.

"Just a little shadow." The hand in his squeezes again and the boy thinks he sees, for just a moment, a little girl at his side. She vanishes as quickly as she appears, leaving behind a Shade and the whisper of a hand in his. "They want you to come back."

"I don't know how," the boy admits. He left his body behind an eternity ago.

"I can show you," the little voice giggles. "I've done it before; come on!"

They run, the little shadow leading him through his neither-here-nor-there world. She stops beside a fallen form and pulls at his arm before pushing him down down down, and then Keir stands in the body he left behind.

"How did you ..."

"I told you, I've done it before." The little shadow stomps a foot that isn't there and points an arm of empty night to the will-o-wisp, dimmer now. "You don't have much time in here. Not in that body. You should run."

"How far is it?"

"Almost a kilometer." The shadow curls around his wrist, tying itself in a knot. "Come, I'll show you the way."

"What if I fall in again?"

"I'll find you," the little shadow hums, "and I'll drag you back out again."

1

WITCH OF THE DEMENSE

An earned title passed from one witch to another via civil, organized ritual proceedings. In rare instances, the demesne may be stolen through a ritual act performed by a witch of equal, or greater power.

"Come on, you piece-of-shit chain."

Milla focused on the tingle in her fingertips and the warmth pooling in her palm, easing her Way out bit by bit. Too much, and she would pass out again. Too little, and she'd end yet another day screaming her frustrations at the palm trees and startling the birds.

Patience was key. Patience and focusing on the ritual.

All magick was a ritual, from major castings requiring full covens to minor summons any witch could perform without thought, and a ritual required three things: intent, desire, and sacrifice.

Her desire was clear: rust the iron link without tipping headfirst into her Way and waking up with a hangover. But metal was tricky, and her Way worked best with organic matter. She could do it, rust was within her Way, but the purpose of this exercise wasn't to get blackout drunk before noon. It was to control her Way, rust the iron, and reverse the corrosion.

And as for the sacrifice, Horned God, hadn't she sacrificed enough time to this Goddess-forsaken swamp?

So it was the intent she was missing. Intent was tricky—it had to be tied to the desire, but it could not *be* the desire. It was the core of the ritual, the aim, the goal for which a witch stepped into her Way and appealed to the Triple Goddess.

And Milla's intent was to rust the chain.

"Wait." She sat back on her heels and swept lank bangs from her forehead. "I'm sacrificing time, and my *desire* is to rust this iron so I can leave the swamp. Or—no, my desire is to leave to swamp, and the intent is to rust the chain ..." Which she could do. She'd done it before, again and again over the last few days, suffering headaches and nausea and all the other fun after-effects of stepping too deeply into her Way, so was her intent to rust it slowly? To avoid the hangover?

She dragged her hands down her face and glared at the fat chain strung between hefty wooden posts. The unrusted chain.

Heat fizzed in her arms, sizzling and burning into her palms as her frustration rose.

All she intended was to rust that chain and be standing afterward. All she *desired* was to leave this swamp without flinching in fear anytime anybody got too close to her. And Horned *GOD,* hadn't she already sacrificed enough?

"*Koroze.*" Milla flexed her fingers, palms hovering over the iron links, letting her frustration fuel the corrosive hex. Magick coursed through every vein in her body, and as she channeled it into her hands, heat rushed down her arms, flooding her palms. She clenched her teeth, restraining the tide of magick to a fine trickle—slow and steady like Darkly had advised. Too fast, and she'd burn through her Way, but if she kept control, she could rust the iron, reverse the corrosion, and argue her way out of this tick-infested swamp.

She was sick of hiding, sick of day after boring day in the sweltering heat, and the nights weren't any better. The hut had not been that oppressively warm in her memory. It had been cute and quaint and welcoming, hidden from prying mortal eyes by the look-away hexes Ezra had cast on the walls and roof. A witch would have to know the hut was there to find it, making it the perfect hideaway for two witches looking to lay low and get to know one another.

But Darkly wasn't here, and Milla would be stuck here unless she could rust this stupid chain and reverse the damage without passing out.

"*Koroze.*" She released her hold, just a little, just enough, to eke out more of her Way. The tips of her fingers grayed with ash, the skin withering to decayed, blackened points. Magick burned in her veins and still that Horned God-damned iron link remained untouched. "*Koroze.*"

A bird chirped overhead. Palms rustled in a sticky-thick breeze. Sweat trickled down her spine, collecting on the waistband of her shorts, and the damn iron did nothing but remain completely oblivious to the witch trying not to corrode it into a pile of oxidized dust.

"*Koroze!*" Magick filled her palm as Milla's frustration finally won over her patience. The ash crawled down her fingers, bony tips revealed beneath the rot, and finally—*finally*—a speck of flaking brown appeared on the iron, crawling outward like lichen over a stone. She gnashed her teeth as Way bled from her veins. Fast, too fast, heat dripped from her arm, and her head grew light, but she was doing it. It was working. She had control of her Way, she was rusting the iron.

"Hoookay," Milla exhaled, focusing on maintaining the flow. "Nice and easy."

That was the trick and where she'd failed time and time again. Nice and easy. Slow going. Channel the magick to her hands, but don't let it slip through. She could almost hear Darkly whispering in her ear, his rolling accent, and the thick slang she was just beginning to understand.

"Hold on," he would say. "Dinnae get excited, hold your Way, and let it out easy."

But Darkly wasn't here. He was *elsewhere* as he'd been all week, only to show up at the most random times to lecture her on magick.

This was not what she'd had in mind when she told their vampire detective-turned-chauffeur Dies-well to head south, but neither had she anticipated her magick going weird and that weirdness stemming from the Dark Witch. But it had, and it did, and Milla wanted to go home.

"Easy," she repeated. "Easier said than done."

Still, the circle of rust spread, crawling steadily across the surface of the iron. Milla curled her fingers, frowning at the bony tips. Her Way frothed in her palm, pressing against the webbed scars, wanting to burst free and consume the metal, corroding the iron and dragging Milla down with it.

"You control your Way, *leannán*." Darkly's repeated words ran through her mind. "It doesnae control you."

"No, it doesn't," she muttered.

As if needing to prove her wrong, a rush of heat bled down her arm, boiling in her veins and leaving her hand before Milla could form a fist. As fast as it had every damn day since the Loa, and the Fountain of Youth. Since she'd taken hold of Darkly's Shades and hauled them from the Neitherworld, summoning the only thing she could to destroy a revenge-bent Voodoo spirit and spare the women of St. Augustine from untimely death and a multi-level marketing scheme.

The rust surged outward, engulfing the link in flakes of reddish-brown. A divot appeared, deepening to a saddle in the ever-thinning metal. Thin flecks fell to the sandy earth as the iron crumbled beneath her Way.

"No! Nononono." She gripped her wrist, the gesture useless. She needed to reverse the hex. To switch her intent and re-focus her desire before the link rusted through. This was what she had been trained to do. By the Morgenhexe and a revolving cast of would-be Enforcers. It was the groundwork Ezra had worked off of, molding Milla into a witch of his own making. She could do this. She *needed* to do this, needed to *control* her Way, or else what was the freaking point?

The world blurred into swathes of muted browns and greens. Sour spit pooled on her tongue, and her stomach gave one warning swoop.

"*Obnovit*," she grunted. *Restore. Renew. Triple Goddess's tits, reverse!*

The saddle of rust collapsed on itself, a cloud of dusted metal rising as the link tipped to the side, barely balanced on the next link in the thick chain.

Her head spun, the ground tipping off-kilter as Milla's Way took its cost. She grunted, dropping to one knee. Bile rose in her throat as she forced out one last, "Horned God-dammit, *obnovit!*"

Magick rushed into her leg, up her thigh, searing through her belly and torso before surging down her arm into her casting hand as the reversal took hold. It was too much, too fast, and Milla could not catch hold. Like a weighted rope slipping through her palms, the renewal allure ran free, winding around the link and, just as quickly, reversing the damage of the hex. Flecks of rust rose from the dirt, the brownish cloud sank back into the iron. The saddle filled until it was a divot, a dent, and then nothing at all. Not a seam or a speck of rust to be seen on that link, or the one next to it, or the one after that.

Milla staggered to her feet, clenching her fist to cut off the flow of magick. Goddess, it was too much. It was the Shades all over again. Her Way had taken control, using Milla as a vessel to be filled until it overflowed, uncontrolled.

She stumbled back, too Waydrunk to think of a hex, an allure, *anything* to seize control and stop her Way from rotting the world. An impossibly cool breeze licked up her spine, and a hoarse cry tore free—from relief, from fear. She had no idea other than the world tipped to the side, her legs turned to jelly, and the last thing she thought before hitting the ground was, "This's gonna *hurt*."

Milla jolted awake, hurtling upright and caught by strong hands at her shoulders. She gripped the worn blanket, her brain only half-registering that she wasn't lying in the dirt beneath the palms but in a bed, in the ramshackle hut she called a safe house.

Hidden deep in Tomoka State Park, north of Daytona, the one-bedroom fisherman's shack was not much, but it was hers. Restored by bored adolescent witches, it had an artesian well for fresh water and a gasoline-powered generator she had added on a weekend camping trip during college. For all it lacked in luxury, it had been comfortable enough for Milla and Ezra and now secretive enough for her and Darkly.

"Easy," Darkly soothed. "Hasnae been near long enough to sleep off the effects."

"Darkly?" His name was thick on her tongue, and a troubling roil in her stomach followed. Soft flannel crumpled in her palm, disintegrating to nothing until her nails pinched the scars on her palms. She groaned and dropped her head, leaning into his comforting grip. "Didn't think you'd be back today."

"Got here just in time," he answered, his voice tight. His right hand slid along her shoulder to cup her neck, thumb and forefinger gently massaging the tendons. "Hate to think how long you'd be laying in the dirt if I hadnae."

"I had it," she mumbled.

"As well as a slotted spoon holds water."

Milla snorted and raised her head, sending Darkly a bleary smile. Dim light bled through narrow cracks in the western wall and cheap curtains, but not so dim she didn't notice the strain on his face and firm set of his mouth. His eyes were trained on her, the green obscured by wafting shadows, and his normally styled hair hung in lank waves as though the witch had been repeatedly running his hand through the ginger mop.

His eyes darted over her face, lingering on her eyes. He frowned at whatever he saw there, and tipped his head forward.

"Alright, *leannán?*" he asked, voice dropping into a low rumble.

Milla's belly flipped and she nodded. "Better," she answered, turning her head to press a kiss to the back of the hand still at her shoulder. "Now that you're here."

Darkly hissed, a sharp, pained sound. His fingers flexed against her arm, and the motion snapped Milla out of her drunken haze, awareness rushing in all at once and far too late.

"Horned God, Darkly!" She scurried away from him, legs tangling in what was left of the flannel blanket. "Do you have a death wish?"

"There's a joke there." He straightened and flexed his hands, unable to hide his wince or the rising blisters. "Ken it's something like, 'nae, but I've got a death *witch*'."

"This isn't funny," she snapped. "You can't keep doing that."

"Doing what?" He dropped his arms, eyes darkening. "Helping you? Keeping you from passing out drunk in the dirt?"

"*Touching me.*" She threw a hand in his direction, and this time, Darkly couldn't hide his flinch. It hurt, but nowhere near as much as the hurt she'd caused him. He wore the same black v-neck she'd last seen him in but had traded his Enforcer blacks—tactical pants fitted with an absurd amount of zippers and pockets—for a pair of grey joggers. His shirt was rotted through, a diagonal swathe of moldered cotton from the top of one shoulder down across his chest and torso, and the skin she could see through the desecration was raw and red, rotted everywhere her body must have pressed because, of *course,* the idiot witch wouldn't leave her lying in the dirt.

Her eyes dropped to his palms and the inside of his arms, the skin there a puffy, swollen violet speckled in pale blisters. Evidence that he had hoisted Milla into his arms and brought her back to the hut. "Look at you."

"I'd rather not," he said.

"Goddess, what were you thinking?"

"I was thinking that my Death Witch pushed herself too far, *again*, and that she might prefer waking up in a bed rather than a festering crater."

"Yeah, well, what did you expect me to do?"

He stared at her. A long, hard stare silently implying all of the things he had expected her to do, like not overexert herself while stranded in a swamp at the ass-end of Daytona while he was off in St. Augustine doing Horned God knew what. "Milla..."

"I'm fine, Darkly."

"You're nae fine, *leannán*. It's been days, and I cannae touch you without risking my hand rotting off."

"It's not my fault your Way is a freaking battery for mine." And who in the nine rings could have predicted that? Like, what were the odds? "Which," she raised her voice, "one hundred percent, would have been nice to know before I summoned those Shades!"

"And how was I supposed to know?" he hollered back. "Even if you had warned me what you were gonnae do, which, one hundred percent, you didnae, how was I to know how our Ways worked together?"

"And you think I knew? Neither of us is supposed to exist!" She threw her arms wide, swaying slightly. Darkly darted forward, reaching out, ready to catch her, and Milla pulled away. "I don't understand why it's so *hard*."

"It's only been a week, Milla. Seven days, and you're attempting to master what takes a witchling months to get ahold of. This is normal, so normal that C.R.O.W. has legislation protecting witches in your circumstance." He sent her a soft smile, and she scowled in reply. "It will come, Milla. You just need to be patient." Her scowl deepened. Darkly put up his hands in surrender. "Though it is surprising the Morgenhexe never taught you how to do it."

"Morgen taught me how to hide my Way beneath hand-to-hex, not how to maintain a delicate balance of self and magick to keep from rotting a fencepost." She curled over her knees and buried her face in her hands. "This would be easier if I had my tea."

"No." He stepped close, looming over her. She splayed her fingers, watching his shadow extend beyond his person, wrapping around her ankles and crawling up her legs to hold her in the only way he could. "That shite's poison, Milla. I cannae watch you do that to yourself again."

Again.

"There's no need to keep drowning your Way." A wisp of cold traced her chin, urging her to look up. She did, her anger washing away under his gaze. Absent the smoke, jade green gleamed brightly at her, and a faint smile curled the corner of his mouth. "It will get better."

"When?" It was unfair of her to expect him to have an answer, but she'd been gone from her demesne for a week. She needed to get home and run the streets, tending the Ancient City as only she could. She had sacrificed her anonymity to protect St. Augustine, calling every Enforcer in the region to her city when she'd dropped headfirst into the furthest reaches of her Way. But she'd done it to save Darkly and countless women from a vengeful Loa running a pyramid scheme. The idea of losing her demesne now, after giving so much to keep St. Augustine safe and *hers*, was unfathomable.

"Cannae say." The shade at her chin wafted lower and curled around her throat, tracing a lazy path along her collarbones. "From what I saw, you rusted that chain thoroughly."

"How long were you there?"

"Long enough to see you fight against your Way." More shadows stretched across the floor, crawling up Milla's legs, soft as moth wings fluttering against her skin. A sigh escaped, and she edged back onto the mattress, meeting Darkly's heated gaze.

It was a distraction and a welcome one. The few moments they spent together in this hut had been filled with bickering, sleep, and distraction. Then the sun rose, and Darkly was called away by his Enforcer sister, leaving Milla alone to fight with her Way. So she'd take the distraction, embracing a few moments of ill-advised peace before it all started over again.

He stepped closer, green eyes bleeding black. "Long enough to see you call it back faster than you did yesterday."

"Not fast enough."

"Still an improvement, Ludmilla." He rolled her name over his tongue. A shiver that had nothing to do with the Shades pawing at her knees and tracing her thighs ran down her spine. "You cannae push this too quickly. Endurance is earned over time; move too fast, and you'll continue to burn out."

"How am I supposed to gain endurance if I don't push myself?" she argued. His Shades gathered at her waist, prodding gently until she lay back and stretched out on the bed. The edge of the mattress dipped under Darkly's weight as he knelt, a knee on either side of her leg, careful not to touch her skin.

"A drained aquifer refills all the more quickly, *leannán*."

"Oh, my Goddess." She rolled her eyes. "Do not start with that Mister Miyagi bullshit."

"Isnae bullshit." His eyes dropped to her chest, and his Shades followed, rolling over the curve of her breast. She gasped as they slipped beneath the low neck of her tanktop, teasing her nipples until they tightened into buds. A whisper of pleasure, the suggestion of a pinch. Enough to have a low throbbing build between her hips, but not enough.

It was never enough.

These ghostly touches, his intense, hungry gaze, only left her wanting more.

He inched further onto the bed and Milla widened her legs, easily falling into the motions they had discovered days ago. The only way to sate the need to touch, to feel, to *be* together when she couldn't hold him close. Couldn't feel his strong hands on her hips and her waist or those clever fingers driving deep into her, for fear of losing control of her Way.

His knee pressed against her groin, and Milla gasped at the delicious friction—tangible and real when the Shades were a cruel tease. She rolled her hips, a whimper building in her throat and escaping when he asked, "This alright?"

"Yes," she hissed. They would have to strip the bed. Her tank top was going to be a wreck. Already she could feel the heat building in her veins, but Goddess, she wanted more. She wanted him to throw her further into the bed. Wanted his fingers digging into her hips, her arms, her wrists, but this would have to do. The blanket and her clothes would rot, and the mattress would decay, but she wanted this too badly to care.

Shades trailed her jaw and traced her lips, engulfing Milla in Darkly's phantom touch. Over her, he bit his lip, flexing a hand at his side. Every muscle taut, as though he employed all of his restraint to keep from reaching out and touching her.

"*Leannán*." His voice deepened to a growl, rolling over the walls of the hut and vibrating through her bones. A demand that Milla was all too happy to obey. She cupped her breast, rolling the nipple between her thumb and forefinger as she slid her other hand down her front. Shades followed, teasing Milla's exposed midriff and swirling between her thighs. A muscle twitched in his jaw, those black eyes trained on her every move and gasp as she drove her hand beneath the waistband of her shorts, circling her clit as Darkly watched on. "Good witch."

Milla shivered at his praise and the caress of his Shades rolling against her. She moaned, and Darkly tipped his head back, cupping himself as he cursed. He spat into his palm, nudging Milla's legs further apart as he thrust his hand into his joggers. Color rose in his cheeks. More Shades wafted from his body, writhing over her thighs and into her shorts, joining her fingers and the Shades already lapping against her center.

"Darkly," she pleaded, knowing he couldn't give her what she wanted and asking all the same. "More."

"Demanding," he half groaned, working his cock in slow, steady strokes. Milla reached for him, her fingertips barely dusting his thigh and leaving streaks of decayed cotton in their wake. "Touch yourself, Milla."

"Controlling little witch." She half-heartedly glared at him, slipping her hand beneath the waist of her underwear and swallowing a cry at the zing of pleasure.

His Shades kept their steady pulse and roll. She circled her clit, hips twitching, seeking out more touch, more pressure, and Darkly answered her silent need. Shadows shot from his person, blanketing the hut in midnight and driving against her pussy, their cold chill pressing against Milla's fingers. Urging them to dive deeper and seek out the wicked spot that had her crying out his name.

On and on, they drove against her, throbbing and pulsing, imitating the flick of a tongue against her clit as Milla's fingers crooked and bent until the heat in her arms puddled in her belly. Her core tightened, the tidal wave of sensation too much to contain, and she burst, pleasure tipping her over the edge right as Darkly grunted and gasped, "Milla."

He tipped forward, catching himself with a hand at the last moment. They held there gasping and staring at each other, the comedown bittersweet without his arms wrapping around her. Without his touch.

Slowly, the Shades retreated, bringing the room back into early twilight. Slowly, the green reclaimed his eyes. Darkly gazed down at her, his hand curled into a fist beside her head.

"Too much?"

Milla pressed her lips together and shook her head, willing her heart rate to settle and slow before she answered, "Not enough."

2

Enforcer

A.I.I. Aural Insurance Investigator; a law enforcement professional under the jurisdiction of the Coven Aural Review Board (C.A.R.B.). A.I.I.'s investigate and prevent Forbidden and Foule threats to both the magical and mundane worlds.

"When will you be home?" Diego's voice crackled over the line, sounding far more distant than he actually was.

"I don't know," said Milla. "Darkly says they're almost done at the Fountain of Youth, but even if C.R.O.W. left tomorrow, my Way is still being weird."

"That ha—ot gotten—er?"

Milla pulled the phone from her ear, squinting through the cracked screen at the bars—or rather, the lack thereof. "Diego, can you hear me? You're cutting out."

"It is th—ower," he answered. "The serv—rrible."

"Same here." Milla kicked off her checkered slip-ons and scanned the tiny beach, perched on a narrow peninsula at the furthest edge of Tomoka State Park. Once the site of a Timucuan village, the land now hosted several miles of multi-use trails, campgrounds, a complex of ten ancient shell mounds and a web of smaller middens, the remains of a plantation, and two witches in self-imposed exile. None of which had the makings of decent cell service. "Hop on the wifi."

"She turned it off," Diego answered, voice still faint, but no longer cutting out. "When you left for college."

"Of course she did," she grumbled. Setting her phone on the warped armrest, she shoved someone's damp towel to the ground and unrolled her own, gritting her teeth as the cotton loops brittled beneath her hand. "Try heading up A1A toward New Town. The service on Duval can be tricky, but there's an Irish Pub on Flagler. Shanna something, they'll have wifi you can use."

"Bruja, you realize everything you just said to me was nonsense, ¿sí?"

"Just borrow a bike and head north." She eased into the beach chair. One of the back slats bowed and Milla glanced back, frowning at the rotting wood.

"If it is so easy, why do you not do it?"

"I told you, St. Augustine is crawling with Enforcers. I've barely even seen Darkly. When he *is* here, he looks like he's about to keel over from exhaustion, and then he's gone again before dawn."

"And where is *here*, ¿exactamente?"

"In my own private Idaho," Milla stated.

Diego chuckled, and in that warm, comforting sound she felt every mile of the distance between them. He should be here, with her, instead of stuck down in Key West with her foster mother. Not that Milla begrudged Morgen for whisking him away to the Keys. The Morgenhexe had heard the rumblings of a witch Forbidden and Foule in the Panhandle, and her first thought had been to grab Diego and get him to the safety of her demesne in Key West while Milla was chasing down rumors in New Orleans.

"One of these days, pequena bruja, I will understand these references. But today, we have just discovered Annie Lennox."

"Into the Ls!" Milla pumped her fist, even though he could not see her. "Nice. You're going to love her early 90s stuff."

"Whatever you say," Diego laughed, and Goddess, did she wish he was here. "Are you alright, Milla?"

"As good as I can be," she admitted. Though they had only known each other for a little over a year, having Diego was a balm. Even on her worst days, she accepted his disapproval and adhered to his guidance, knowing what he had endured, both in his first life and accidental resurrection, were ten-fold her troubles. If any witch could understand her desire to hide and heal, it would be him. "I just need to accept that this is going to take more time than I anticipated, as much as that sucks."

"I can see how that would be frustrating." Goddess bless this witch and his patience. "The key is in control; you own your Way, bruja, it does not own you."

"Oh my *Goddess*, you sound just like Darkly."

"Good," he said. "That means two of us are talking sense."

"Okay, sure, fine." Milla adjusted her seat, careful of the rotted slat. "I'll just forget years of highly specialized training in hiding my Way and master absolute control overnight." She snapped her fingers. "Easy peasy."

"That is not what I meant, Milla."

"I know, tío." She dropped her head back and sighed. "I just want to go home."

"Entiendo," he said. "I want to come home as well but it is up to Morgen. She says we must wait until, and I stress this is quote, 'the crooked noses of C.R.O.W. stop sniffing around your demesne'."

"She sounds like Darkly," Milla said, "but with ten times the anti-semitism." That earned a half-hearted chuckle, so she doubled down, more to convince herself than Diego. "It'll all blow over." She had to believe that, because the alternative was too depressing to consider—that she might never get back to St. Augustine. That she might have to live her life in hiding avoiding mortals and witches alike. Becoming a Baba Yaga bog witch of legend hiding in the swamp. A thing of local folklore and fairy tales.

"I hope so, sobrina." Her heart warmed at his calling her niece as easily as she called him uncle. "Keep working at it, it will come," he added. "I recall the lessons with my sister. I was so afraid, working so carefully to remove infection for fear of causing further damage. Have faith in your Way, it will come."

"Thanks, D," she said, doing her best to pack away the panic and shove it down, down, down to focus on what she could do in the here and now.

Which was abso-fucking-lutely nothing.

So she did just that, ending their call with a stilted goodbye and a promise to chat once he got somewhere with better service. Diego was safe in Key West. Morgen was looking out for him and, by extension, her, which freed Milla to worry about herself.

She slathered on sunscreen, adjusted her sunglasses and floppy black sunhat, and tried desperately not to think about the mess she'd made of things. Darkly promised it was only a matter of time, Diego swore she'd acclimate to the new bounds of her Way. She had to believe them, with their years of experience both within and without C.R.O.W., or else she'd burn herself out trying to bludgeon her Way into submission.

Humid, midday warmth blanketed her skin, and the easy, slow waves of the Halifax River lapped at the pebbled shore, lulling Milla into a not-quite sleep. That space of soft awareness where dreams crept along the fringes of consciousness, teasing her with whispers of a voice she left in the dark.

Millapet.

Birds called from the trees, and a rabbit or a lizard rustled the undergrowth. Out on the river, a boat motored by as kayakers called to each other.

Millapet.

A cool shadow fell over her legs and Milla smiled. "You're back early." Eyes still closed, she rolled her head along the creaking chair back to face the source of the shadow. "Sun's still up."

"Excuse me?" The voice that replied was deep and crisply accented. With the wrong accent. She opened her eyes, heart racing as she fought to keep her body still, relaxed, and took in the stranger.

Tall, tanned, and trim, he was close to Darkly's height, though where the Dark Witch boasted muscled shoulders and defined arms, this stranger wore the long-armed build of a rower or swimmer, trimmer all around but no less athletic. Water beaded down his chest and stomach, dripping toward a pair of deep red swim trunks that clung to his thighs. Sun-bleached blonde hair was swept away from his forehead, and he stared down at Milla with glacier blue eyes and a faintly amused expression.

"Can I help you?"

"Ja," he said. "You are sitting in my chair."

Milla blinked, startled anew by his accent and how he formed the words. Clipped and brusque, clean like a mountain spring. Like Morgen.

She scrounged her brain for any German she knew, coming up with 'gesundheit', 'wo ist der Hauptbahnhof?', and "'ein Bier, bitte', so she settled on, "And?"

"My chair." He crossed his arms, glaring down at her with all the clinical cool of a man who thinks he's in the right. "You have taken it."

Milla curled her lip, glancing around with over-exaggerated awareness. "I didn't know this abandoned beach took reservations."

"Was it not obvious from the towel?"

"The towel." She glanced around genuinely this time, stilling when she spotted the damp towel she had shoved off of the chair. "Ah," she shrugged and sat back, watching him out of the corner of her eye. "Sorry."

"Tch." A muscle in his cheek twitched in annoyance. "I placed my towel there earlier to reserve my place, and now I find that you have stolen my chair and ruined my towel."

"In what world does abandoning your towel on a chair mean you've staked a claim?" Milla scoffed. "And even if it did, how do I even know that is your towel?"

"I assure you it is my towel, and by right of property, you are sitting on my chair."

Milla stared at him, awed. Just awed by the presumption. A needle-like headache pinched the side of her head, and her palms tingled, her Way itching to rot the chair and see how this audacious German liked that turn of events.

Instead, she grabbed the sodden towel, stood—"Here, fine, take your stupid towel."—and tossed it at him.

It smacked him in the face with a damp squelch. The stranger backed up, grunting in surprise as he pulled it away. She dropped heavily in the chair, tugging on the rim of her sunhat and crossing her arms over her bare stomach.

"And the chair?" he prompted with a whisper.

"Are you for real?" Milla glared at him. "I'm not giving up my chair."

"But ... I reserved it."

She dropped her gaze to the towel in his hand and scoffed. "What are you going to do, Baywatch? Arrest me?"

The stranger's mouth twitched upwards, bright eyes flaring with interest.

No, not with interest.

An icy chill raced down Milla's spine, and she sat up, transfixed by the twists of blue flame in his eyes, recognizing the tell-tale burn of a spalování fire witch and realizing that she may have made a very, very huge mistake.

"Funny you should say that." He grinned, his hands burst into flame, and Milla lurched from the chair and ran.

~

RITUAL DUES is available **now** on Kindle, KU, and paperback

Every witch has her Way

Milla is a witch who wants to hide. Grieving the loss of her mentor, she retreats to St. Augustine, where her only goals are to run her antique store and tend her demesne into obscurity.

But C.R.O.W. has other plans for the formerly wicked witch.

As if being saddled with a new apprentice and trying to get rid of the Aural Insurance Adjuster sent to observe her isn't enough to deal with, a pack of multi-level marketing huns sets their sights on Milla, intent on burning her store to the ground. When a threat to the demesne and the witches and mortals under Milla's care raises its ugly head, it is up to her to decide:

Is living out her days as a nothing witch in a nowhere demesne what she truly wants, or is the formerly wicked witch ready to rejoin the witchy world of C.R.O.W.?

<u>AVAILABLE NOW</u>

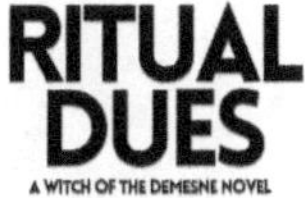

Urban fantasy romance and magick Forbidden and Foule

Milla is a witch who deserves a *break*.

After saving the women of St. Augustine from a soul-sucking Loa, she and the *not* an Aural Insurance Adjuster Darkly head south in search of some peace of mind and a chance to navigate their budding relationship.

But once again, C.R.O.W. has other plans for the formerly wicked witch.

Her Way has gone weird, and she's stuck hiding in a swamp while Darkly tends to the aftermath of their battle at the Fountain of Youth.

When a spate of mysterious rituals backed by a power suspiciously similar to hers wreaks havoc across the southeast, Milla must team up with a coven of Enforcers, the witches she despises, to clear her name and stand once again for the Forbidden and Foule.

<u>AVAILABLE NOW</u>

Camp Cryptid

Faun Over Me

Shifting Hearts- May 2025

Beerhall Brides

Ravished by the Rasselbock

THANK YOU

With every manuscript that makes it to a published work, the list of people I have to thank grows. This is exactly the sort of problem I love to have. Writing is sometimes solitary, but bringing a world and characters to life takes a village. This is my village:

Oliver — You told me to "shut up and write" without truly understanding what you were unleashing. I love you for that and so many other things.

Ana — The World's Best Hype Woman™. Thank you for listening to me ramble over uncountable glasses of wine and charcuterie boards. I am the luckiest person to have you in my corner.

Molly — Thirty+ years of friendship, and all you got was this witch smut.

Kel — MA'AM. You're the best thing TikTok has ever put on my fyp. I am so sad our paths did not cross when we lived in the same city, and so grateful fate saw fit to throw us together on the internet.

Kourtney — for agreeing to edit these witches time and time again. Your insight and expertise make this world the rich, chaotic place it is. Forever grateful.

Lianne — for interpreting my word salad and delivering dreamy, swoony art that captures these witches better than I could have imagined. Thank you for never batting an eye when I drop into your DMs asking for more.

The Ladies of Fort Smut — I could not ask for better company on this writing, retreating, and charcuterie-eating life. Over the years, we have added four tiny humans, survived a pandemic, group-read numerous terrible and not-so-terrible books, and crafted the most rewarding and routinely hilarious group chat. Sorry for all the TikToks. I love you all. Where are we going next?

My Beta Team, Amazing ARC Readers, and the divinely talented authors of *Blood and Pulp, NC Indies,* and *FaRo.*

You — you lovely, lovely human being who read this book. We frequent the same corners of the internet. I feel like we could almost be friends. I hope you stick around for more.

About the Author

Britta is the worst. She doesn't even publish under her real name and responds to things like, "Mom", "B", and "Brown".

As B. L. Brown, she publishes urban fantasy and paranormal romance. Her debut novella, *Shady Depths*, was released in April 2023, and her short fiction can be found in *Tails, Trysts, and Tentacles: One Monstrous Summer*, *Fireside: Modern Legends and Lore*, and *The Future of Us, A Moms Who Write Anthology*.

As Britta, she is a human-wrangling, word-wielding, musical theatre and beer-loving runner with a passion for fairy tales and folklore. She can be found under a pile of digital literature or begging her academic friends for their JSTOR logins.

You can follow her on Amazon, Goodreads, Twitter, Instagram, and TikTok. For less obnoxious updates, join her newsletter at www.brittawritesthings.com